AVOIDANCE

KRISTEN GRANATA

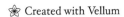

MORE FROM KRISTEN

The Collision Series Box Set with Bonus Epilogue
Collision: Book 1
Avoidance: Book 2, Sequel
The Other Brother: Book 3, Standalone
Fighting the Odds: Book 4, Standalone
Hating the Boss: Book 1, Standalone
Inevitable: Contemporary standalone
What's Left of Me: Contemporary standalone
Dear Santa: Holiday novella
Someone You Love: Contemporary standalone

Want to gain access to exclusive news & giveaways?
Sign up for my monthly newsletter!

Visit my website: https://kristengranata.com/
Instagram: https://www.instagram.com/kristen_granata/
Facebook: https://www.facebook.com/kristen.granata.16
Twitter: https://twitter.com/kristen_granata

Want to be part of my KREW?

Join Kristen's Reading Emotional Warriors
A Facebook group where we can discuss my books, books you're
reading, and where friends will remind you what a badass warrior
you are.

Love bookish shirts, mugs, & accessories?
Shop my book merch shop!

To my parents,
for teaching me to strive towards being the best version of myself, and for always correcting my grammar.

PROLOGUE: 2010

"Can you do my makeup next?" I asked.

"Not tonight, babe. Another time."

"Where are you going?"

"Out to dinner for Roseanne's birthday."

I sat on the lid of the toilet bowl in the bathroom while my mother fixed herself up in the mirror. I watched as she flawlessly swooped her eyeliner across her lid without making a mistake. Her brown hair was the same color as mine, but fell in loose waves around her shoulders. I often wished my hair looked more like hers, instead of the thick frizzy spirals I was cursed with. I didn't think that I looked anything like her. People said I did, but I think that's just the sort of thing people say when meeting someone's child.

"Did you finish all of your homework?"

I nodded. "Yup. Sixth grade is a piece of cake."

She smiled at me in the mirror. "What are you and Dad watching tonight?"

"My Cousin Vinny."

"Oh, good. Something new for a change." She rolled her eyes for dramatic effect.

I giggled. "It's just as funny every time. I never get sick of it."

She spritzed herself with perfume from a blue glass bottle. "I don't know about this top. What do you think? I don't like the way it makes my stomach look from the side."

"I think it looks great. You always look great." I laughed at the way she fussed over her appearance so much before going out. Everyone that met her would make a big deal about how pretty she was – strangers that passed us on the street felt compelled to tell her about her beauty wherever we went. My friends even made comments about how lucky I was to have such a young-looking mom. It got annoying but my best friend, Shelly, would tell me to look on the bright side: "When you grow up, you'll probably look just as hot as she does." I doubted it.

She kissed the top of my head. "I love you. Have fun tonight."

I jumped to my feet and wrapped my arms around her. "I love you. See you when you get home."

"I might be home after you fall asleep, but I'll check on you before I go to bed."

"Okay. Have a nice time."

I followed my mother out of the bathroom, shutting the light behind me. In the living room, I watched my father take in her appearance.

"You look nice," he said as he stood from the couch.

She swung her leather jacket over her shoulders. "Thanks. Have fun."

I stood by the entryway table, watching as she rummaged through her purse. My father and I exchanged matching grins as she became more frantic in her daily search for her keys.

"You two could be helping me, instead of laughing at me," she muttered.

"Where would the fun be in that?" I asked.

"I don't understand how they disappear all the time." She stormed into the kitchen, yanking open a drawer to rummage through.

"They won't be in there," I called.

"Merritt, if you know where they are – just tell me, please! I can't be late."

I held up her purse as she came back into the living room. Her keys were hanging out of the front zipper pocket.

She rolled her eyes. "Sometimes, I really think I'm losing my mind."

"Only sometimes?" I asked.

My father chuckled.

"Don't encourage her," she warned, as she leaned in to give him a peck on the lips.

"Don't act like you have no idea where she gets that sarcasm from."

She wore a smirk as she quickly grabbed her purse. She waved one last time to me. Then, she was out the door. I often compared her to a tornado, blowing around the house looking for her misplaced belongings whenever she was running late for something.

I pretended not to notice my father's expression as he slumped back down onto the couch. "I'll get the snacks!"

It was a usual Thursday night hanging out with Dad, while Mom went out with her friends. She had been a stay-at-home mom for the first eleven years of my life. This past year, she began working as a receptionist for a law firm in Manhattan. She even joined a gym, and bought a new wardrobe to match her new physique. I couldn't blame her for wanting to feel good about herself, or for wanting to pursue her own interests. If my dad could work and pay for things, why couldn't she? He didn't say it, but I think my father took it personally, as if her newfound independence meant she no longer wanted to stay home to be with him. Things seemed different between her and my father lately. Then again, I couldn't tell if they were always this way, or if I was just old enough to finally take notice.

Together on the couch, my father and I laughed throughout the movie. I loved the sound of his laugh; it was a hearty chortle that was contagious to anyone who was in earshot. My mother and I were close, but I was a daddy's girl through and through. Whether we were watching movies, or restoring the old Chevelle in our garage, we were an inseparable duo. Hard-working, loving, and smart, I looked up to him in so many ways.

"Alright, kiddo," he said when the movie ended. "Go wash up for bed, and I'll tuck you in."

Once I was under my covers, I opened my favorite book to the dog-eared page where I had left off the night before.

"Again?" my father asked with a smile, as he sat down on the edge of my bed.

"Again," I replied, running my fingers over the cover of *Romeo and Juliet*.

"You're a sucker for a love story, like your old man."

"I'm just fascinated with how they could love each other so much, that they were willing to die without one another. That's just crazy to me."

"Love can make you crazy, sometimes."

"What was your love story with mom?"

"Tenth grade Biology class. She walked in the room, and sat in the seat right in front me. She was so beautiful. I tried for days to get up the nerve to talk to her, but I couldn't figure out what to say. So one day, I tapped her on her shoulder and asked her for the time."

"What did she do?"

"She turned around, looked down at the watch that was around my wrist, and said, "I don't know. Why don't you check your watch?" Then she smiled, and turned back around. That was it for me."

"What do you mean, that was it?"

"I fell in love with her."

"You didn't know anything about her! How could you be in love with her already?"

"Love isn't logical." He shrugged. "Some things you just know."

"I hope I have a romantic love story to tell one day."

He touched my cheek. "You will, my girl. Just make sure he's worthy. Don't let anyone near your heart unless he deserves to hold it."

"Will you help me, and tell me if he's worth it? In case I can't tell?"

"Of course," he replied with a smile. "I'll always be here to help you."

Chapter One

THE BITCH IS BACK

I gripped the doorknob to steady myself as I felt my knees threatening to buckle from underneath me. My throat felt dry. Staring into her eyes – the same golden brown color as mine – I remembered how much damage the soul behind those eyes could do. It was no wonder that fear was the first emotion I felt upon seeing my mother for the first time in over eight years. Standing before me was the human equivalent of Pandora's Box. Just like that, all of the demons I had fought so hard to lock away were suddenly set free. They came rushing towards me, tightening their claws around my lungs so that I could barely breathe. I took one step back, and swung the door shut with all of my might. I prayed that the powerful slam would send her back to wherever it was that she came from.

"What are you doing?" Chase reached for the doorknob, but hesitated, thinking twice.

I stared at the door, afraid it would magically open against my will.

He gently cupped both of my shoulders, and looked into my eyes. He was resisting the urge to shake me, I was sure.

"Merr, don't you want to know what she wants?"

That question snapped me out of paralysis. "What she wants? I don't care what she wants!"

"It's just me. You don't have to pretend that you don't care."

"Oh, I'm not pretending."

A soft knock came from behind the door.

I looked at Chase, incredulous that she had the nerve to knock a second time. A familiar feeling began creeping its way through my body. It slowly pooled out over my chest, like hot lava, continuing down my arms into my fingertips. Rage and I were old friends, the kind who could pick right back up where we left off despite all the time we spent apart. What was constricting my airways before could no longer stop me as I ripped open the door.

"Get the fuck out of here!" I shouted. "Get away from this house, get off this island! I want you to get as far away from me as you possibly can!"

"Merritt, I–" she began.

"No! You don't get to say anything!" I stepped towards her, with my index finger less than an inch from her nose. "You don't get to say a single word to me. You don't deserve to stand here in front of me and look me in the eyes!"

She leaned against the railing behind her as she took a step backwards. "I know you're angry–"

"You *know*? What is it that you know, exactly? Because if you knew anything about what I went through, you wouldn't have the audacity to come here and knock on my door!"

"What is all the yelling about?" Tanner was now standing at the bottom of the stairs.

Chase popped his head out from the doorway. "Everything is okay, Tan. Go back inside."

"It doesn't sound like it's okay." He remained where he stood, eyeing the woman standing in front of me.

"Everything will be fine once she gets the hell away from me!" I shouted into her face.

She put her hands up in surrender. "Okay, okay. I'll go."

Chase stepped outside onto the landing. "Hold on."

"No, Chase. Don't," I warned. "Let her go."

He stood tall, with his muscular arms crossed over his chest. To anyone else, his stance would have looked aggressive; but I knew him better than that. Chase was not a hothead, like his brother below us. His dark green eyes were calm and focused.

"I just need to know. Why now?" he asked. "You ran out on your family so long ago. You left your husband to die, and you left your child to fend for herself. After all this time, why come back now?"

She cleared her throat, her eyes nervously darting from me, to Chase, then back to me again. "I heard about what happened... to your father, to you. I feel terrible that you had to experience all of that."

"She had to experience all of that alone," Chase interrupted. "Because of you."

Hot tears stung my eyes, as I listened to Chase defend me.

She lowered her head. "I know. Merritt, I am so–"

I put my hand up to stop her before she could get the rest of the words out. "No. I don't want to hear it. You don't get to be sorry for a choice that you made. If you feel guilty, then good. I hope the guilt eats away at you. I hope it kills you, and rots your insides. Nothing you say will ever make this better. I will never forgive you for what you did to Dad." The tears threatened to spill out over my eyelids. I could not allow them to come out. I would not give my mother the satisfaction. Quickly, I turned around, and walked back inside.

Chase remained outside. Their voices sounded muffled, and I was grateful. I did not want to hear another word uttered from her mouth. I felt embarrassed that Tanner had heard me screaming from inside his house. I wished that I did not let her get to me the way she did. I sat on the couch, hugging my knees to my chest, willing myself to stop crying in the silence of the apartment.

Several minutes passed, and finally Chase returned, closing the door behind him. He walked into the living room, running his fingers through his hair, and collapsed on the couch beside me with a sigh.

"Whatever she said, it doesn't matter."

"I know." He shook his head. "I always hoped she had a good reason for leaving... like maybe she witnessed a terrible crime, and had to go into witness protection in order to save you and your father from being murdered; or she was abducted by aliens."

"But now you realize that she is just a narcissistic asshole who abandoned her family for her own selfish reasons." I wiped a stray tear from my cheek.

"Are you okay?"

"Right now, no; but I will be, once the shock wears off." I looked up into his concerned eyes. "Thank you for defending me."

He kissed my forehead, then tilted my chin to bring my lips to his. "I will always stand behind you. No matter what."

"Ditto." I grabbed the back of his head and pulled him in for another kiss. "I have to call Shelly. Do you think you could go explain this to Tanner? And make sure she's not still lurking around out there."

"Of course. I'll be back in a little bit."

After he left, I locked the door behind him. I paced the apartment, listening to each ring of the phone until Shelly picked up.

"I'm still mad at you," she answered.

"Fine, then I guess I can't tell you what just happened after you left."

"You told Chase you didn't want to go to California?"

"Claire paid me a visit."

It was silent on the other side for a moment. "Claire? Your mother, Claire?"

"Yup. The bitch is back."

"Why? How did she find you? What did she want? What did she say?"

"I didn't let her say much. I told her to leave. I yelled. I thought about pushing her down the flight of cement stairs."

"You yelled at her? I wish I could have witnessed that. What did she say?"

"She tried to say she was sorry, and that she felt bad when she heard about what happened." I laughed. "As if that would fix everything she wrecked."

"Are you okay? Is she still there?"

"I'll be fine. I don't know where she went."

"I wonder if she's living here now."

I shuddered at the thought. "I'm more shocked than anything. It feels like I saw a ghost."

"I can imagine. I don't know what I would have done if I was there.

Why now, though? Why would she come back so randomly out of the blue?"

"I don't know. Why did she leave when she did? That was out of the blue, too. There's no rhyme or reason. She does what she wants, when she wants it. She doesn't care about anyone but herself."

"What did she expect you to do when you saw her? Hug and braid each other's hair? She's got balls coming back here. Everyone knows what she did. How did she even find out about what happened to you and your dad, anyway?"

"Again, I don't know and I don't care. None of it matters."

Shelly sighed. "Well, I can't be mad at you now. Claire really does ruin everything."

I chuckled. "Good. Then you'll hang out with me tomorrow?"

"Yes. What time are you working until?"

"We close at five. I'll have to come home and shower the smell of engine oil off of me. Figure by six-thirty?"

"Okay. Merr?"

"Yeah?"

"Don't let this ruin all of your progress. She's not worth it."

"I know."

"Okay. Bye."

I peered out the window from my couch in the living room, looking around for any unfamiliar cars parked nearby. Mounds of snow were piled high along the curb. The usual vehicles were parked in their usual spots. Everything looked as it did before my mother showed up at my doorstep. Still, I felt uneasy.

Claire was a tornado. She came out of nowhere, and destroyed everything in her path before disappearing into thin air. If all the storm trackers in the world still couldn't predict a tornado, there was no way anybody would be able to understand Claire. I didn't want to waste my time trying.

Shelly's reminder about all of the progress I had made echoed in my mind as I sat. Just six months ago, I was waking up in the hospital after a head-on collision with a tree; my father had ended his life, and I was left in a deep pit of despair. A golden-haired boy changed all of that. With his loving heart, and the most gentle of hands, he brought down all of my walls and showed me how to smile again. After the passing of his own father, the man who pulled me from the fiery car wreck to give me a second chance at life, our turbulent times were behind us. Life finally felt normal – I was happy. It was typical that Claire would come back and challenge all of that.

My eyelids felt heavy as I watched cars pass by on the slushy street below. It felt like I had only closed my eyes for a second, but when I opened them again, the streetlights were on outside. I picked my head up and noticed Chase stretched out on the opposing couch watching a muted television.

"What time is it?" I asked, rubbing my eyes.

"Just after six." He reached his arm out for me, and I stood, taking his hand. He pulled me down on top of him, wrapping his arms around me.

"Why didn't you wake me?"

"You were totally knocked out. I figured you needed to rest." He kissed the top of my head. "That was a lot to take in. Are you okay?"

"I'll be fine. I don't want to waste any more time discussing it." I lifted my head off of his chest and pressed my lips against his. Warm and inviting, they were exactly what I wanted to lose myself in. When I kissed Chase, the entire world faded away. The thoughts in my head were overpowered by the warm feeling that swept throughout my entire body. I positioned myself on top of him and lost my fingers in his soft hair, kissing him over and over.

"Don't try to avoid the subject," he said against my mouth. "Your powers of persuasion won't work on me."

I slipped my hand inside of his boxers. "I beg to differ."

He exhaled as I kissed him again. "No fair."

"Looks like my powers might work on you after all."

"You play dirty." In one swoop, he stood with me in his arms and carried me into the bedroom.

We spent the duration of the night in my bed. Neither Chase nor I brought up going to California. We did not speak about Claire's visit. He knew from experience that it was best to let me stew in my own thoughts until I was ready to discuss them. He understood what I needed, and did not make me feel guilty about it. It was one of the things I loved most about him.

Long after Chase had fallen asleep, I remained awake, staring up at the ceiling. My mind kept replaying the scene outside my front door. I had always been level-headed. I learned early on to internalize my emotions, reacting in my head instead of lashing out. Today, I acted like someone I did not recognize. I took all the years of built up anger and resentment towards my mother, and hurled them at her on my doorstep.

I was baffled by the same questions everyone else had: Why is she back? What does she want? Why did she leave eight years ago? Admittedly, I was too afraid to listen to the answer. I knew that hearing Claire's explanation would be anticlimactic, regardless of what the reason was; hearing her explanation would not undo the years of torment she caused my father, and it would not give me back my childhood that she had taken with her when she left. Claire's side of the story would only make me feel worse, like rubbing salt in an open wound. It was safer for me to bury my head in the sand, and pretend like nothing ever happened.

———

SHELLY, UNLIKE CHASE, ALWAYS TOOK A MORE AGGRESSIVE APPROACH when dealing with my avoidant behaviors. When we met up for dinner the next day, I knew I was going to have to face her firing squad of questions. I went home to shower after work, and met her at the campus cafeteria after her class let out.

"Have you started packing?" she asked.

"I would pack if I was going somewhere."

"Aren't you?"

I shrugged.

"Just say it, and put me out of my misery. You have already made up your mind. You know it, and I know it."

I pushed the fried rice around my plate. I scanned the cafeteria, remembering the last time I had been here – the fateful day when

Chase first approached me. Looking back on all that had happened, it seemed like a lifetime ago.

"What are you smiling about?"

"This is where Chase and I met."

"After you flung the soda bottle across the room."

"Because you made me drop it."

She smiled. "You're welcome."

I rolled my eyes, but could not fight the grin on my face.

"Where do you think Claire went?"

"Don't know. Don't care." I shoved a forkful of rice into my mouth, my smile vanishing.

"Your whole I don't care thing is so old."

"It's not a thing. I truly don't care where she is, or why she left, or how she feels. She could drop dead and I wouldn't bat an eye. Why should I waste my time caring about her when she clearly doesn't give a crap about me?"

Shelly sighed. "You always care, Merr. You say you don't care, but you do. You would be cold-hearted if you didn't, and I know you. You're not cold-hearted. Your mother, your flesh and blood, the woman who gave you life, abandoned you. She created a superstorm of horrible events in your life. Then, when you're finally happy and everything is calm, BAM! She comes back."

"Thanks for the recap, Shell. You should be a narrator in a movie."

"Come on. It's the most epic slap in the face of all time. There's no way you're fine and okay with all of this, no matter how much sarcasm you slather on top of it."

I placed my hand on my chest for dramatic effect. "Me? Using sarcasm to cover up my real emotions? I'm offended you would imply such a thing!"

She tossed a fried noodle at me. "You're impossible, you know that?"

I grinned triumphantly. "Thank you."

"That wasn't a compliment, you freak. So, when are you going to tell Chase that you're going to California?"

"If I'm impossible, then you're relentless!" I tossed the fried noodle back at her. "I'm still considering my options."

"Look. I know I've been giving you a hard time, and I know I'm selfish because I don't want you to leave me... but accompanying the love of your life so he can fulfill his dreams is the right thing to do. We both know he would follow you to the ends of the earth if the situation was reversed. This is the one and only time you're going to hear me say this, so take it for what it's worth."

I exhaled as I looked into her light blue eyes. "Thanks, Shell. I appreciate it. I guess I'm just scared to be out there on the other side of the country all alone."

"You won't be alone. You'll have Chase."

"I know, but he'll be busy. What will I be doing?"

"You could get a job. Maybe there will be a car shop nearby that's hiring."

"Chase Brooks, the famous rock star, and his mechanic girlfriend." I grimaced. "Sounds like a match made in heaven."

"You are my match made in heaven," said a deep voice from behind me. Chase pulled a chair next to mine and sat. He leaned in for a lingering kiss. "And don't you ever forget it."

Brody took the seat next to Shelly and gave me a wink.

Shelly let out an exaggerated breath and hung her head. "We've been together since kindergarten. What am I going to do without my best friend?"

"You two can FaceTime whenever you want," Brody suggested. "I'm sure they will come back and visit, and we can take a vacation out there. I've always wanted to go to California."

"Does this mean we're going to California?" Chase carefully asked.

Looking into his expectant eyes, I knew in my heart there was only one answer to his question. "I guess we should start packing."

Shelly groaned and thumped her head down onto the table.

Chapter Two

GOODBYE

"Hey, midget. Pass me the bread." Tanner gestured to the bread basket sitting in front of Khloe.

Khloe's face scrunched up in anger. "Don't call me that."

Tanner sighed, well aware that he would not get any bread until he said it politely. "Can you please pass the bread?"

Her face returned to her usual sunny expression as she placed the bread basket in front of her brother.

"Merritt, you've barely eaten anything," Beverly noticed. "Are you feeling okay?"

I fidgeted in my chair. "Chase and I have something we want to tell you."

"Oh, shit. She's pregnant," Tanner exclaimed.

"Language!" Beverly and Khloe shouted in unison.

"We're not pregnant." Chase took my hand under the table. "I got a call from Donnie out in California the other night."

Everyone at the table put their forks down at the same time, and the metaphorical record jerked to a stop. I gripped Chase's hand harder as he continued.

"A guy from a record label heard my old demo, and wants to meet with me and the band." His leg bounced nervously under the table. "Merritt and I are going to be moving to California for a while."

"Are you kidding me? You think this is a good time to leave?" Tanner began.

Beverly put her hand up. "Do not start fighting right now. We are eating dinner, and we are having a discussion." She exhaled. "How long would you be living out there for?"

"I'm not sure," Chase replied. "It depends on how it all goes."

"How what all goes? You think you're going to be the next Bon Jovi?"

"Tanner!" Beverly raised her voice.

Tears immediately welled up in my eyes, as I remembered how Tim used to come to her aide during times like these.

"There's a lot I don't know right now." Chase was trying desperately to ignore Tanner's provoking comments. "That's why I'm going there – to find out what my possibilities are."

"How do you feel about this, Merritt?" Beverly turned her attention to me.

I gulped, my throat suddenly dry. "I feel that Chase is incredibly talented, and he deserves a chance to see how far this could go."

"But," Tanner prompted, sensing more behind my rehearsed answer.

"But nothing," Chase snapped. "Stop trying to make an issue here!"

"You're the one making the issue!" Tanner stood, pushing his chair back from the table. "Dad just died! We don't even know if we can make ends meet or if we're selling the shop, and you decide you're going to run off to California and leave us high and dry?"

Chase released my hand, and stood. He leaned his knuckles onto the table, his voice lower and more menacing than before. "I am aware that Dad is gone. I already told Mom – you can make ends meet if you sell the shop. It's not my responsibility to take care of everything for you!"

Beverly covered her face with her hands.

I stood, and walked behind the battling boys. I took her arm, leading her away from the table, and took Khloe's hand, too. They both followed willingly, and we sat in the living room.

"I don't know what to do with them," she said.

"Honestly, they just need to duke it out. It's the only way. This has been brewing for quite a while now."

Khloe stared into the dining room from her seat next to me as the boys' shouting got louder.

"I can't be the one to carry this family just because I'm the oldest! You need to step up, now! It's your turn!" I heard Chase yell.

"I can't carry the shop all on my own! The three of us worked our asses off when Dad got sick. How am I supposed to do that alone?" Tanner shouted back.

"I can't blame him for wanting to go," Beverly confessed. "I never want to be remembered as the mother who held her son back from greatness. I just wish the timing was different."

I nodded in agreement. "I know how torn he is between wanting to go, and wanting to stay to help his family. I feel the same."

"This call might be his one and only shot." Beverly looked down at her lap.

I turned to Khloe, who was quietly taking everything in. "What are you thinking?"

Her big, round hazel eyes peered up at me, her eyebrows furrowed. I could not read her expression, until I saw her bottom lip tremble as she tried to hold it in. It was no use; the giant teardrops began to roll down her puffy cheeks.

I wrapped my arms around her, and she sprang into my lap, burying her face in my chest.

"Merry, please don't leave me," she wailed. "I don't want you and Chase to leave me!"

The tears I had been keeping at bay now spilled over my eyelids. I squeezed my eyes shut as I held her tiny body in my arms, rocking her back and forth. She lost her father, and now she would be losing me and her brother. I wanted to tell her that we wouldn't go anywhere – that we would stay here with her – but I knew that would be a lie. There was nothing I could say to console her.

Tanner and Chase's shouting match came to a stop when they heard Khloe's cries.

Chase came into the room and sat beside me on the couch, stroking his sister's golden locks.

Tanner remained standing, his arms crossed over his chest. He finally sat when Beverly wiped her eyes. He put his arm around his mother, and hugged her to him, kissing the top of her head.

"Tanner is right," I opened. "This is the worst possible time to leave. If we are going to keep the shop up and running, we need time to interview new hires."

"What are you saying?" Chase asked, a hint of worry in his voice.

"Why don't you go without me, and– "

"No, no," he interrupted. "I'm not going without you."

"I could stay here to help until everybody got back on their feet. Then I could meet you out there."

"We just won't go then," he stated. "I'm not going without you."

"Why not?" I searched his eyes for a reason for his stubbornness.

"Because he doesn't think you'll actually go," Tanner answered.

Chase's eyes tightened, but he said nothing to deny it.

My mouth opened, but no words came out.

"Enough," Beverly said. "Family is about working together as a team, and we can't do that if we're fighting against each other." She looked at Chase. "You are not responsible for saving this family. You need to live your own life – truly live it – chasing after your own dreams." Then she looked at Tanner. "This business was mine and your father's. It is up to me to think long and hard about what should happen next. This shop is not the end all be all of your life."

"I don't want you to hate me for leaving," Chase said. He was looking at his mother, but I knew his statement was directed at Tanner.

Khloe popped her head out from under my arm. "We don't hate you, Chasey. We love you. That's why we're so sad that you're leaving."

He held his arms out for her, and she curled up in his lap.

"So, you're leaving." Tanner stood.

"Yes. He's leaving. Now sit down so I can tell you all something." Beverly waited for Tanner to reluctantly sit. "All four of you need to hear this, so listen good."

Khloe straightened up, excited to be included in this grownup discussion.

"Your father was a firm believer in following his heart. I will not stand in your way whenever your heart is pulling you in a direction. I will be here to guide you, support you, and love you. Always. You need to go out and live your lives for yourselves – for the things that make you happy. But if you don't call home every week, I promise you: I will hunt you down and I will drag you back here."

Khloe giggled. Chase and I smiled, exchanging glances. Tanner smirked for one millisecond before standing up and walking out of the room.

Beverly held out her hands. I took one and Chase took the other. "I would never hate you. Never a day in my life. I appreciate your suggestion, Merritt, wanting to stay behind and help out. The size of your heart never ceases to amaze me. But you two should go together. I know you will take care of each other out there. Please be smart, and be careful. That's all I ask."

"We will." Chase squeezed my knee.

I took a deep breath as I let Beverly's words sink in.

Khloe jumped onto my back. "Can you give me a bath tonight, Merry?"

I stood up and spun her around. "Are you ready?"

She squealed in delight. "Let's go!"

Upstairs, Khloe and I talked about California, and how far away it is from New York. Khloe always had intelligent questions, and she was my favorite person to have conversations with. In the time Chase and I had spent together, I grew close with his family. It would be heart wrenching to leave them behind. There had been so much loss in my life – my mom, my dad, Tim – and now the rest of the Brooks family, just when I was getting used to having a family of my own. I knew I had to leave, though. I knew I had to do it for Chase. I was following my heart – and he was my heart.

After Khloe was bathed and tucked into bed, Tanner was waiting for me in the hallway. "I just wanted to say that I appreciate you offering to stay behind."

"I tried. I thought it was a good plan."

"Not if you're just looking for an excuse not to go." His dark eyes held my gaze for a moment; he was able to call my bluff because we had the same tells. "Can I ask you something?"

I laughed. "You're asking permission first?"

"I have manners when I want to," he said smugly. "That was your mom yesterday?"

I leaned against the wall in the hallway. "Unfortunately, yes."

"You were yelling pretty aggressively. I didn't think you had it in you."

"Oh, it's in there. I just keep it buried inside." I gestured with my hand. "It's deep, deep in there."

Tanner laughed. "That's a healthy coping mechanism."

"That's what I hear."

"It's going to come out, you know. One day, you're going to stuff too much inside and it's going to overflow. You need an outlet for all that anger."

I raised my eyebrow at him. "You're a shrink now?"

He put his head down sheepishly as he heard his own familiar words thrown back at him. "I know I can be a bit of an asshole some-times... but I've learned a lot. I mean it, Merr. You can't bury your feel-ings forever."

"Did Charlotte teach you that?" I asked with a smile.

"She taught me a lot of things."

"She's good for you, Tan. You deserve someone like her."

He nodded. "Dad would have loved her."

"He would have."

Tanner put his big arm around my shoulders. "I kinda like having a big sister."

I jabbed him in his side. "Good. I like having an asshole little brother."

I walked downstairs with a smile still on my face, though it dimin-ished when I saw Beverly and Chase's red eyes as they sat across from each other at the dining room table.

"Should I give you guys some more time?" I asked, wearily stepping towards the table.

"No," Chase replied. "I'm going to take a shower and let you guys talk."

I took the chair Chase had already warmed, looking across the table at a tired and worn out Beverly.

"Chase told me your mother paid you a visit."

I shifted my gaze. "She's gone now. I made her leave."

"I'm worried that you'll regret that decision one day."

"I won't. It's better with her out of my life."

"I know you don't want her in your life, and that's fine. I completely understand. I wouldn't want somebody like that in my life either... but I feel like a small part of you will always wonder. If you sat down with her and gave her a chance to explain, maybe you could find it in your heart to forgive her over time."

I raised my eyebrows. "You want me to forgive her? How on earth could I do that after what happened?"

She reached across the table and covered my hand with hers. "It's not easy. I don't want you going throughout your life holding this burden of hatred inside. Maybe you would feel better if you heard her side of things. Then, you could let her hear yours."

"Oh, I think she heard me loud and clear yesterday."

"Didn't you forgive your father for what he did?" she asked gently.

"That was different. He was suffering, because of her."

"Maybe she was suffering, too."

I shook my head. "I can't do that. I can't forgive her for what she did to us."

"Do you feel that if you forgive her, you're not doing right by your father? Do you feel like he would be mad about it?"

"He would have forgiven her. He loved her more than anything. He would have taken her back in a heartbeat."

"Didn't you love her, too?"

I looked down at my lap. "I did."

"Aren't you supposed to forgive the people you love? The ones who are closest to you are often the ones who hurt you the most. People make mistakes in life – huge mistakes. Do you think I would stop loving any one of my children just because they made a mistake, no matter how big the mistake might be?"

"I don't know, Beverly. I don't know if I have it in me to do something like that. I can't even think about her without burning up with rage."

"When I look at you, I see a beautiful, smart, fierce young woman with so much love in her heart to give. You have been hurt so badly, and you lock that love away because you're too afraid to give anyone the power to do that to you again. It's self-preservation, and I get it; but life is too short to pack your feelings into a box and ship it out to sea. You think that hating her and shutting your emotions off makes you strong, but there is no greater strength than forgiveness. If you can find a way to forgive her, you will release all of that anger. You will finally be able to let go of all the pain. That's what this is all about. Learning how to forgive."

"So you're the one Chase gets his insightfulness from." I swiped a tear off my cheek.

Beverly smiled. "I'd like to think so."

"I'm going to miss you when we leave," I admitted. "You're an amazing mother."

"You will be the same with your own kids someday."

"Are you going to be alright here? You can tell me the truth. I won't tell Chase."

She sighed. "I know we will be fine. I've got one hell of an angel on my side."

I smiled as more tears poured out. "I miss Tim."

She walked around the table, taking the seat next to me, and hugged me tightly. "I do, too."

Chase soon appeared in the doorway. "Every time I leave you two alone, I find you crying."

Beverly held one of her arms out, motioning for Chase to join our embrace. He put his arms around both of us, and held us there.

"Don't forget about your old mom when you're playing at sold out concerts, okay?"

Chase chuckled. "I would hope you'd be sitting in the front row."

She pulled away from us, wiping her eyes. "So when do you leave?"

"Tuesday."

She nodded. "Alright."

That night, every word Beverly had said to me swam around my mind like piranhas chomping at my brain. I stared up at the ceiling in bed, again, listening to Chase's steady breathing. I had come far since meeting him, yet it felt like I still had so much further to go. I had been so hurt by my mother's abandonment, and so focused on my father's mental health thereafter, that I never once thought about what she could have been going through to make her want to leave her family in the first place. I always thought it was me – that I wasn't loveable enough to make her want to stay. What if that wasn't the reason for her leaving? What if I never gave her the chance to explain? Would it haunt me for the rest of my life?

Chapter Three

WE'RE NOT IN KANSAS ANYMORE

The warm Los Angeles sun felt good on my face. It was a welcomed change from the freezing February temperatures in New York. I looked over at Chase, who was sitting beside me in the back seat of the cab. His eyes sparkled like I had only seen once before, when he told me about his first experience in California. In that moment, I felt confident in my decision to travel to the other side of the country with him. If he would not come here without me, then I had to ensure that he did. He deserved to be happy and make all of his dreams come true.

"Wait until you see the hotel I booked us." Chase turned to me, one corner of his mouth turning up.

"I hope you didn't spend too much."

"It's only for one night. Donnie said the apartment would be ready by tomorrow. I can't believe the apartment is still available."

"It's like it was meant to be."

"Thank you for doing this for me. I know it sucks to leave Shelly and Brody. I feel immense guilt leaving my mom."

"I didn't think I would stop crying after we said goodbye to Khloe." I inhaled deeply, remembering her big, red eyes as she cried watching us walk into the airport. "But we can't spend our whole lives doing things to appease everybody else. Like your mom said: we have to live our lives for us."

He stroked my cheek with his thumb. "You are my whole world, you know that?"

"Good. Remember that when girls are throwing their bras and panties at you while you're on stage."

He shook his head as he leaned in. "Your bra and panties are the only ones I want." He touched his lips to mine. Between the warmth of his lips and the passion behind them, his kiss sent electric shock waves throughout my entire body.

The cab driver cleared his throat from the front seat. "Sorry to interrupt you, but we're here."

Chase reached into the front seat to hand the driver his cash. While he hoisted our luggage out of the trunk, I stepped out of the cab and took a look around.

Los Angeles looked exactly the same as Manhattan – tall buildings, endless stores to shop in, and picturesque outdoor cafes – with the exception of the tall palm trees lining both sides of the busy main road. I craned my neck to look up at the hotel before us. Dance music was pumping from the rooftop, and incredibly fit people in bathing suits could be seen with cocktail glasses in their hands.

"A rooftop pool?" I raised an eyebrow at Chase. "How much did you spend for one night at this place?"

"Don't worry. Look," Chase pointed over the tops of the trees. "There's the Hollywood sign."

I held my hand up as a visor over my eyes, looking into the distance. "Wow. This is so surreal. We're literally on the other side of the country."

He sported his excited grin as we rolled our luggage into the lobby. From his perfectly tousled blonde hair down to his jeans that looked like they were made precisely for him, Chase fit into our new environment effortlessly. I, on the other hand, was used to looking different everywhere I went due to my curly mane, but there were far more brunettes in Staten Island than what I could see here. The women here were definitely taller, too. I wondered if any of them were models. After we received our room keys, I swiped several brochures off of the counter and shoved them into my back pocket as we stepped into the elevator.

"Is everyone tall and blonde here? I stick out like a sore thumb. I want to blend in with all the other fingers!"

"You stand out no matter what color your hair is." Chase hooked his finger into my belt loop and drew me closer to him. "I am so happy to be here with you."

"Me, too."

The elevator dinged, signaling we had arrived at our floor. We rolled our suitcases down the hallway until we reached our room. Inside, the floor-to-ceiling windows displayed a gorgeous view of the city. Chase immediately flopped onto the plush white comforter that was atop the king-sized bed. I laid my suitcase down next to the closet. When I looked at Chase, he was grinning from ear to ear, wearing a devilish expression on his face.

I scrunched my nose up in confusion. "What?"

He pointed to the nearby wall.

My eyes followed in the direction of his finger, and I saw that the wall next to the bed was actually made out of glass – allowing for a complete view into the shower.

I smirked. "How voyeuristic of you."

He chuckled. "I'm going to enjoy myself if we only have one night in this room."

I kicked my sneakers off, and unzipped my pants. "So, your plan is to watch me in the shower?" I shimmied my hips to pull my jeans down over my curves. "That's it? That doesn't sound like much fun."

Chase raised his eyebrows while he watched me step out of my pants. "Do you have a better idea?" He sat up on his elbows as I tugged my shirt up and over my head.

I reached behind my back to unhook my bra, sliding it down my arms, and letting it fall to the floor. "An idea comes to mind." I turned and made my way to the bathroom. "Unless you'd rather stay out there and watch," I called.

Within seconds, he appeared in the doorway, all of his clothes left on the floor in the other room.

I pretended to be surprised while I turned the water on in the shower. "Oh, will you be joining me?"

He followed me into the shower, and pressed me up against the glass wall. "I like your idea better."

———

THE NEXT MORNING, I WAS AWOKEN BY A KNOCK AT THE DOOR. I quickly sat up in bed, forgetting where I was for a second. My memory was refreshed as soon as I saw the room service being wheeled in on a cart.

Chase smiled when he saw I was awake. "Good morning, sunshine."

"Did you get pancakes?"

He chuckled. "Of course I did."

"I can't believe we didn't eat dinner last night." I looked around at all of our clothes strewn about the room while I reminisced.

"You wouldn't exactly let me get dressed to go anywhere," he said with a wink.

"What a good night it was, though. It's worth the starvation I'm feeling right now."

"Here. Don't starve." He placed a heaping plate of pancakes in front of me on the comforter. "I even got you fresh fruit to put on top."

I tugged on his arm until his lips came down to mine. "Thank you. You're the best boyfriend ever."

"Remember that when you're mad about the girls throwing their bras and panties at me."

I smiled. "I'll try."

We ate, took showers, and straightened up the room in time for checkout. I was anxious to meet Donnie, and to see the apartment we would be living in for an unknown amount of time.

"You're quiet," Chase said once we were in the cab. "You don't have to be nervous. Donnie is super nice. You'll love the apartment."

I leaned my head on his shoulder. "I'm not nervous. I'm just tired from our sexcapades last night."

He kissed the top of my head. "You can't fool me. I know you, remember?"

I yawned. "Yeah, yeah."

He gently pulled my chin up so that he could look me in the eyes. "Give it some time. If you're not happy here, all you have to do is say the word and we will leave. None of this matters to me if you're not happy."

"I'll be happy as long as I'm with you."

"Promise me." He wasn't letting me off easy.

I held up my pinky, awaiting his. "I promise I'll tell you if I'm not happy here."

Several minutes later, the cab rolled to a stop. I looked out the window to find we had pulled up to a storefront made mostly of tinted glass. It was surrounded by a building made of beige bricks that traveled up at least a couple of stories high, with a giant red neon sign displaying the words "The Underground" in script letters. A red-haired man with a fuzzy unkempt beard approached the cab. He wore black-rimmed glasses, and was smoking a cigarette. I resisted the urge to make fun of his skinny jeans when I realized that Chase was smiling at him.

The man leaned into the passenger window to give the cab driver money.

"Thanks, Don," Chase said, stepping out of the cab. "You didn't have to do that."

Donnie flicked his cigarette into the street, smoke streaming out of his nostrils. "It's the least I can do. I'm sorry the apartment wasn't ready in time for you." He looked at me and smiled his toothy grin. "You must be Merritt."

I met his outstretched hand with mine. "You must be Donnie."

"It's a pleasure to meet you. Are you ready to make this kid famous?"

"I'm ready," I replied, not sure what exactly I was ready for.

"Come inside. I'll show you around, and then we can get your bags upstairs."

I looked up at the windows above. "The apartment is up there?"

"Don't worry." Chase hugged me to his side. "We're at the top, so you won't hear too much noise."

Donnie held the door open for us as we walked inside. The unfinished wood floor, exposed ceiling, and red string lights gave off a vibe that matched the bar's name precisely. Pinball machines lined the walls along the perimeter of the room. A shiny disco ball hung from the cement ceiling over a bare floor space, creating the illusion of a dance floor.

"What do you think?" Donnie asked, both he and Chase looking at me for approval.

"It's perfect."

"Hell yeah, it is!" Donnie rubbed his hands together. "You have your first show tonight."

Chase raised his eyebrows. "Tonight? Already?"

"Yes, sir. No time to waste. The guys will be over here around five o'clock. You'll rehearse, catch up, and get ready to knock the socks off of everyone in here."

"When will the people from the record label be here to see them?" I asked.

"Tonight. You'll be here to support your man, I hope?"

"Of course." I looked at Chase, who was nervously running his fingers through his hair for the third time. "I wouldn't miss it."

Donnie reached into his pocket and pulled out a set of keys on a ring, dangling it in front of Chase's nose. "The keys to your new digs."

"Thanks, man. I really appreciate you doing this for us."

"When is rent due?" I asked. "Wait... how much is rent?"

Donnie laughed. "Don't worry about the rent just yet. These boys packed this place out last year. If they can do that again, rent won't be necessary."

I raised a skeptical eyebrow.

He laughed again. "All business. I like her. Show her around upstairs. I'll see you guys later."

"Thanks again." Chase held his hand out for me. "Ready to see your new home?"

I straightened my shoulders. "I'm ready."

He led me through a door to the left of the bar. We walked up two flights in a dimly lit stairwell. At the top, Chase twisted the key into the doorknob, and gave the door a push.

"Wow," I breathed. Three large windows allowed the sunlight to come flooding into the spacious one-bedroom apartment. Two red velvet couches were pushed against exposed brick walls, facing a large flat screen television that was mounted to the wall. Nearby, a pool table stood in the open space to the right of the kitchen. At the kitchen island sat three red stools. All of the appliances were stainless steel, and looked unused.

"Bedroom's right through here." Chase motioned to the door that was half-opened just past the kitchen. "I really hope you like red," he called as he carried our suitcases inside.

I stood at the window, in awe of the magnificent view. The sky was blue, the sun was shining, and the Hollywood sign could be seen far off into the distance over the tops of the palm trees. It looked like a dreamland – Chase's dreamland. Though I felt lucky that he wanted me to be a part of his new life, I wondered how everyone was doing back home.

It was difficult leaving my best friend, and all that I knew behind; it was difficult leaving Chase's family, who had welcomed me in with open arms; it was difficult leaving after suffering through the death of my loved one, followed by the death of their loved one; but the thought that was currently stuck on repeat was the look on my mother's face as I screamed at her to get away from me.

People say that a mother's love is unconditional; they say that the connection between a mother and her child is the strongest bond there is; but what about the people who know of no such love? If a mother, who is supposed to be the epitome of selflessness, is only a wolf dressed up in her clothing... what becomes of her child?

I had no time to entertain such thoughts, though. Chase could not know. We arrived in California, and he had to prepare for his big break. I did not want him to feel an ounce of guilt, or second-guess his decision. He couldn't be bogged down with my issues. It was up to me to help keep him focused. I would do anything and everything I could to make this the happiest time for him, even if it meant suffering alone.

Chase walked up behind me, wrapping his arms around my waist. "What do you think?"

"It's really nice."

"It's our first place together," he whispered into my ear.

I smiled, closing my eyes as he planted little kisses along my neck. "It's a big step."

"I'm ready for it." He turned me around and took my face into his hands. "I've been ready since the moment we met."

"We were five when we met. You really knew I was the one back then?"

He jabbed my side playfully. "You know what I mean, smartass."

I giggled, and pressed my mouth against his. Slipping my hands under his shirt, I ran my fingertips along his muscular stomach. "Want to go christen the bedroom?"

"You're not worn out from last night?"

"No, but if you are I understand." I backed away from him, pretending to pout.

Before I knew what was happening, Chase picked me up and threw me over his shoulder. I squealed as he carried me to the bedroom.

Chase and I spent the better part of the afternoon tangled up in our new red sheets. Then, we took a walk to the nearby market for some food to stock our refrigerator with. Before I knew it, it was five o'clock and he was kissing me goodbye.

I reached for my phone on the coffee table and decided to call Shelly. It would be weird going out tonight without her, and I missed having her by my side.

"Can you lie to me and tell me you hate it?" Shelly begged from the other side of the phone.

"So far, it all seems really nice. I won't have an opinion until I've been here for a while."

She sighed. "You sound so far away."

"I know. I wish you were with me. It would make things much easier."

"Yeah. The hours of endless sex with the man of your dreams sounds so difficult. You poor thing."

I laughed.

"Does he know you're avoiding your feelings by having sex?"

"Shut up and just let me tell you that I miss you."

"Fine. I miss you, too. What time does Chase go on tonight?"

"He's downstairs practicing with the guys now." I held my phone away from my ear to check the time. "I'll head down there in an hour or so. It's going to feel so weird sitting at the bar by myself all night."

"Have a drink. It will take the edge off."

"The last time I had a drink to take the edge off, I ended up in a coma for two weeks."

"You need to forget about that. Nobody there knows a thing about you. You don't have to be the girl whose mother left her, or the girl whose father killed himself, or even the girl who crashed into a tree. You can be your new and improved self, fully equipped with a clean slate. Besides, you're not driving tonight. The most damage you could do is stumble up the stairs back to your apartment."

"I guess so."

"I'm sure you'll make friends in no time. Just don't make any new best friends, okay?"

I smiled. "No one could ever take your place."

"Good. Brody and I are already trying to figure out when we can come visit."

"Great." I took a deep breath before asking my next question. "So, have you seen or heard anything about Claire being in town?"

"Nope. I've had my eyes peeled, but it doesn't look like she's here."

"Good."

"Don't worry about her, alright? You're a million miles away. Go have a blast tonight."

I swallowed the lump that had formed in my throat, realizing that I had to hang up with her now. "I will. Love you, Toad."

"Love you, Frog."

Alone again in the apartment, I stood from the couch and made a beeline for my closet. I was not sure how dressy the LA girls would be at the bar tonight. I was equally worried about being over or under-dressed. I decided on a pair of my tight, ripped jeans, a black low-cut tank top, and black strappy wedges. The humidity here was much lower than the usual humidity in New York, so my curls were actually working with me for a change. I shook them out, dabbed some clear gloss on my lips, and headed out the door.

As nervous as I was about being alone in a new environment, Shelly was right. I could be whoever I wanted to be. I didn't have to be the responsible, careful little girl I once was. There was no sense crying over the past, when no one here knew what my past was. I could enjoy myself, and be excited for Chase to take the stage in front of important record label bigwigs. It was the moment he had always dreamed about, and I was lucky enough to be here to witness it.

The muffled beat of the DJ got louder as I descended down the stairs. I peeked out from behind the door and scanned the crowded room for Chase. He was already on stage, while his bandmates tuned up their instruments.

"Are you planning on hiding behind the door all night?"

The voice startled me, and I jumped.

"I'm Dave," he said chuckling. "You must be Merritt."

"You work here?"

"I'm the full-time bartender. I'm here every night. You'll be seeing a lot of this face." He held his hands up around his face, and awaited my response.

I raised my eyebrows, trying to smile. "Lucky me... I think?"

He grinned. "Chase said you were sarcastic. I dig it." He gestured to the stool next to me, at the head of the bar. "Best seat in the house."

I sat with my wristlet in my lap.

"So, Merritt. What's your drink of choice?"

I shrugged. "Surprise me."

His eyebrows raised above his black-rimmed glasses. "Do you like sweet things?"

"Usually."

"How about I'll make you a few different drinks, and you can see which one you like best?"

"Will I have to pay for all of those drinks?"

He laughed. "It's on the house. You and Chase don't pay for drinks here."

"Okay. Thanks."

Dave mixed while I patiently waited for Chase to notice me

from the other side of the room. The bar was crowded, but I was perched in perfect view of the stage. I was also in perfect view of the scantily clad blonde, tanned, and toned girls who were excessively flipping their hair and laughing obnoxiously loud to catch his attention.

"Why does every girl's modus operandi to get attention always involve ear-piercing pitch, and hair primping? It's like watching birds on Animal Planet."

"Don't pay them any mind," Dave advised. He sat two glasses in front of me, one pink and one yellow, along with one martini glass filled with another pink liquid. "Okay, so, these are your basic girly drinks: this one's a Malibu Bay Breeze; this is an Amaretto Sour; and this is your classic Cosmo. If you don't like any of these, I'll go back to the drawing board."

I took a sip of the Bay Breeze, and bobbed my head in approval. I tried the Amaretto Sour, and tipped my hand from side to side, unsure if I liked it enough to drink an entire glass. I took a sip of the Cosmopolitan, and my left eye involuntarily closed. "I definitely don't like this one."

Dave looked surprised. "You don't like vodka. You're from New York. Doesn't everybody there drink Cosmos?"

"Does everyone in California drink kale juice and say, "Surf's up, dude,"?"

He laughed. "Okay. That's fair."

Chase finally spotted me. A wide grin spread across his face as he jumped down from the stage. He walked past the group of blondes without so much as a look in their direction. His eyes were too busy surveying my body as I stood to give him a hug.

"Hey, man. You're girl's a pisser." Dave motioned to me with his thumb. "I'm going to like having her around to keep me company."

"Don't get any ideas. She's mine," Chase joked. He wrapped his arms around me. "You look incredible."

"I wasn't sure what people wore here." I motioned to the half-naked blondes, who were now watching us in dismay. "But I guess sluts dress like sluts, no matter what state you're in."

"It's true," Dave chimed in.

Chase shook his head. "My eyes are going to be glued to you and only you tonight."

"Should I throw my bra at you? Oh, maybe you can sign my boob! It will make you look like a real rock star in front of the guys from the record label."

He scanned the bar until his eyes settled on a man in a suit sitting at the opposite end of the bar. He tilted his head in his direction. "That's the guy we're looking to impress tonight."

"You already impressed him, otherwise he wouldn't be here. Remember that."

Chase turned back to me, his hazel eyes sparkling with excitement. "Did I tell you how happy I am that you're here with me?"

I pulled him in for a lingering kiss. "Knock 'em dead, baby."

He winked, and vanished into the crowd.

The flock of blondes standing by the stage were now staring at me, and talking into each other's ears. I laughed to myself, as I thought about how at home that actually made me feel. I sat back down on my stool, sipping my pink drink, and starting to feel more at ease in my surroundings. I had already made friends with Dave the bartender. Maybe tonight wouldn't be as bad as my anxiety swore it would be.

Dave came by with another Malibu Bay Breeze to replace the almost-empty glass in front of me. "This one is compliments of Mr. Suit and Tie down at the other end of the bar."

I met eyes with the man, and flashed my best smile as I raised my glass to thank him. He raised his glass, and nodded slightly. That had to be a good sign. I couldn't wait to tell Chase.

"Do me a favor," Dave said, leaning in. "Don't take drinks from anybody except for me. Got it?"

"I'm from New York, remember? You don't have to worry about me."

He grinned. "I know, I know. I just had to say it."

The strum of the guitar signaled that it was show time. The crowd cheered as the lights dimmed.

Chase's voice came on the microphone. "Underground, we're back!"

The cheers got louder.

"Are you ready?"

The room erupted even louder than before. I noticed Mr. Suit and Tie smirking as he looked around. His attention quickly settled back on Chase once he opened his mouth to start singing.

Chase looked like he had been doing this his whole life. If he was nervous, even I could not tell. He belted out one eighties hit after another, throwing in several favorites from the nineties after the crowd's response to the first. Everyone was either jumping or dancing to the beat, and singing along with Chase as he worked the crowd. His arm muscles glistened from the sweat that was dripping down his body. His voice sounded amazing over the sound system. I was incredibly proud of him, and proud to witness this moment. I snapped a few pictures with my phone, along with a video. I wanted to document the night Chase was signed to his first record label.

Dave was busy, but continued to check on me to see if I needed anything throughout the night. He was kind, and I was grateful to feel like I knew someone. Tall and thin, his dark hair was perfectly parted to one side, and doused with so much product that it didn't budge all night. His dark almond-shaped eyes were softened by his warm smile. Though he was not my type, he definitely seemed to be a hit with the ladies, considering how they ogled him while he served their drinks. He entertained them, but under the surface, looked uninterested.

"You're new here."

I looked at the stranger who was suddenly standing to my right.

"Where are you from?" he asked.

"New York."

He raised his eyebrows. "Wow. What brings you to the other side of the continent?"

I pointed at the stage. "That man holding the microphone."

He sneered. "You came all the way here because of some wannabe rock star?"

I placed my drink down, and swiveled in my seat to face him. "No. I came all the way here because my boyfriend is being signed to a record label."

"How come you're not off chasing your own dreams? What are you going to do while he's busy becoming a star?"

"Definitely not talk to you." I turned back to face the bar.

Dave handed his customer a beer, and made his way over to me. "Everything okay here?" he asked, giving the stranger a skeptical eye.

"Oh, we're fine here," he responded with a smile. "I was just getting rejected by this beautiful young woman."

"Take the hint," Dave suggested.

"I'd rather take my chances."

I rolled my eyes, and then returned them back to the stage.

When Chase's final set had ended, no sooner did he appear at my side. "Who's your friend?"

"I'm Jake." The stranger extended his hand.

"Jake, this is my – how did you put it – wannabe rock star boyfriend, Chase." I smiled.

Chase shook his hand a bit harder than he normally shook hands. "Nice to meet ya, Jake."

"Have a nice night," he said to us with a nod. "Nice meeting you, New York."

Chase shook his head. "I can't leave you for two minutes."

I laughed. "I had it handled."

"Come on. I want to introduce you to the guys."

I stood and snuck a five-dollar bill under my glass, and made my way to the stage.

"This is Bobby, Philip, and Chad." Chase pointed to the guitarist, bassist, and drummer respectively. They waved.

I returned the wave. "It's nice to meet you. You guys sounded great."

"Thank you," replied Chad. "The suit seemed pleased."

I leaned in eagerly. "He was smiling and tapping along to every song. So what happens now?"

"Now, I make our boys famous." Donnie appeared from behind me. "How did you enjoy the show, Merritt?"

"They were awesome."

"Good. Okay, boys. Let's go make a deal."

Chase leaned in for a kiss. "If this takes a while, you can head upstairs. I'll meet you up there."

"I'm actually going to head up now. My feet are killing me. Good luck."

As I turned, a thin blonde stopped in front of me. "Excuse me. Are you Chase's girlfriend?"

I arched an eyebrow, instantly in defense mode. "I am."

"I'm Brooke. I'm Philip's girlfriend."

My expression immediately softened. "Oh, Philip the bassist?"

She smiled, revealing her dazzlingly white teeth. "Yes. I just wanted to introduce myself."

"I'm glad you did. It's nice to know someone who's going through the same thing."

"We should exchange numbers. I can show you around."

"Sure." I took out my phone, and we inputted each other's information.

"Your hair is gorgeous." A slightly shorter blonde outstretched her hand.

"This is my friend Michelle," Brooke said.

"Thank you." I smiled as I shook Michelle's hand.

"How do you get it to curl like that?" she asked.

"It just grows out of my head this way."

They both laughed identical high-pitched laughs. I did everything in my power to stop myself from holding my ear and closing one eye, as I often did when Shelly squealed.

"Well, it was nice meeting you guys. I'm going to call it a night."

"The time change can take a while to get used to," Brooke offered, making it apparent that one o'clock in the morning was too early to be heading to bed.

"Night."

I waved to Dave as I walked towards the door, but he jogged over. Still, his hair did not move out of place. "You didn't have to leave me a tip. I told you, your money is no good here."

"I really appreciate your hospitality tonight."

"You are very welcome. I'm glad we found a drink for you."

"Me, too."

Chapter Four

CHASING MERRITT

The next day, my phone buzzed incessantly for almost an hour. I tried to ignore it, but I knew the girl calling was quite persistent.

"Why are you calling so early?" I groaned.

"Early?" Shelly screeched into my ear. "It's the afternoon! Are you still in bed?"

"I got in late last night."

"There's a three hour time difference," Chase mumbled. He pulled me over to his side of the bed, and I rested my head on his bare chest.

"Yes, I know," Shelly replied. "I've been up for hours, patiently waiting for a reasonable hour to call!"

I rubbed the sleepiness from my eyes. "What's up?"

"I wanted to hear about your night. How did it go with the record label guys?"

"It went great. They have a meeting today."

"And how did you do?"

"She got hit on by Jake the douchebag," Chase said, chuckling with his eyes closed.

"Jake? Who's Jake?"

"Nobody important," I yawned. "Dave was nice, though."

"Who are all these guys? Anybody cute?"

"Hey!" both Chase and Brody exclaimed in unison.

I giggled. "Aww Brody! I miss you!"

"Him? What about me?" Shelly asked.

"You know I miss you."

"How many times have you had sex this morning?"

"We just woke up, Shell."

"We're about to get started, though." Chase rolled me onto my back and began kissing my stomach.

"Have fun, you two!" Shelly called.

I tossed my phone onto the floor while he took his kisses lower.

Chase's phone began to buzz on the nightstand.

"Ignore it," he ordered, sliding off my thong with my pajama shorts in one swift pull. "I've been wanting to do this since I saw you sitting at the bar last night."

I leaned over to see who was calling him. "Chase, it's your mom. We can't ignore it."

"Sure we can." His kisses made a trail starting from my ankle, and continued to my knee.

I swiped his phone and answered. "Hello?"

"Merry!" the tiny human voice squealed into my ear.

Chase's shoulders slumped as he exhaled in defeat. He knew he was no match for his sister on the other side of the phone.

"Hi, my angel girl! How are you?"

"I'm good. I miss you and Chase. When are you coming back?"

Chase and I exchanged smiles. "Not for a while, but we miss you so much!"

"Mommy, it's Merry!" she shouted.

Beverly took the phone. "Hi Merritt. How's everything going? Did we wake you?"

"No, we were up. Chase was just about to call you to tell you about last night."

He took the phone from me, shooting me a dirty look. "Hi, mom."

I went to get off the bed, but was stopped by a large hand. He gently but firmly pushed me back down, smirking at me while he continued his phone conversation. Holding the phone in between his ear and his shoulder, he tugged on my tank top until it was over my head. His hands began traveling over every inch of my bare skin.

"It went great. I have a meeting with him later."

I took his hand and placed it between my legs, slipping my other hand inside of his boxers. I watched him close his eyes and let out a silent breath.

"Okay, mom. I'll call you after." He was breathing harder as I worked my hand in his boxers. "I promise, I won't sign anything without reading it. Okay, okay. I love you, too. Okay, mom. Bye."

I giggled as he set his phone onto his nightstand.

"No more phone calls," he ordered.

Hours later, Chase finally crawled out of bed to leave for his meeting. We had been spending a lot of time under the covers together, and I was more than enjoying it. Once his new California life officially started, I knew I would be spending much of my time alone. I would miss our physical closeness, and wondered if our emotional bond would be affected by it. I did not yet know what exactly I was in for.

Brooke texted to see if I was interested in going shopping with her. Thankful for a distraction from my thoughts, I agreed to meet her. I knew it was important to make the effort, and to make new friends. I rolled out of bed, took a quick shower, and threw on a pair of shorts and a t-shirt.

I waved to Brooke as I approached her at the storefront. She was dressed to the nines, which I was not prepared for.

"How do you think it's going for the boys?" she asked, sliding her expensive looking sunglasses to the top of her head.

"Hopefully, they're hearing good news. I'm just nervous about what the paperwork might say."

She swung open the door for me. "I know. It's like selling your soul to the industry."

I walked into the boutique, and was greeted by yet another slender blonde. "Hi, welcome to Teal. Would you like a wheatgrass shot, or a glass of our hibiscus water?"

I bit my bottom lip to keep from laughing. "No, thanks."

"We'll take two wheatgrass shots," Brooke answered. "You have to try it. It's hella fresh."

"Thanks," I said, reluctantly taking the bright green glass. I took a sip, and my face immediately contorted into disgust. I turned around and dribbled that sip back into the glass. I tried to play it cool, but began coughing. "This tastes like lawn clippings!" I whispered to Brooke.

She giggled. "But it's healthy for you!"

"I'm healthy enough." I set the glass down on a jewelry display table.

"Thanks for meeting me here." She thumbed through the rack of dresses next to us. "If our boys are getting a record deal, we need to step up our wardrobes!"

I tried to envision what a step up from her already chic wardrobe would look like. Discreetly, I checked the price tag dangling from the sleeve of the nearest blouse. "My wallet is telling me to step down."

Brooke giggled again. "You're funny. So, what's your story?"

"My story?" I pretended to scan the next rack of clothes. "It's not a very interesting one."

"What's it like in New York?"

"You've never been?" I asked.

"No. I've never seen snow before!"

"You're not missing much, trust me. It's cold, the mounds take forever to melt, people fight over parking spots, and it's a pain in the ass to shovel."

"Don't you have, like, people to shovel for you?"

I raised an eyebrow at her. "Like who?"

"I don't know, like, your parents? Did you live with your mom and dad?"

I shook my head. "Both of my parents are dead."

Her blue eyes widened. "Oh my God. I am so sorry, Merritt. I had no idea."

"Don't be." I picked up a yellow satin tank top. "You should try this on. It will really make your eyes stand out."

"You think?" She held the hanger up to her chest and looked in the mirror. "Excuse me," she called to the worker. I cringed as she snapped her fingers.

"How may I help you?"

"Can you start a room for us?" Brooke asked, handing her the yellow shirt without looking up from the rack of clothes.

"Of course."

"Thank you," I called after her.

"You should try this one. You have an awesome body." Brooke handed me something red on a hanger.

I held it up. "What is this supposed to be?"

"It's a skirt, silly."

"I have scrunchies bigger than this."

She laughed. "You are seriously hella funny."

I placed it back on the rack. "I can't wear this."

"Dude, you have a great ass. Show it off!"

I looked around the store to see who else heard Brooke's exclamation about my rear end. "Well, I can show it off in something else."

We spent the rest of the hour trying on different outfits. I actually didn't mind Brooke's company. It was better than sitting in the apartment by myself, and she slightly reminded me of Shelly with her bubbly personality. I checked my phone for the tenth time, and heaved a sigh.

"Nothing on my end, either," Brooke confirmed.

"I think I've shopped until I'm about to drop."

"Are you going to buy anything?"

I sorted through the clothes hanging in my dressing room, most of which Brooke insisted I try on, and did the mental math. I picked up a pale pink dress, and an army green tank top. "Ready."

"You have to wear that dress on Valentine's Day. Chase will just die."

"We don't have any plans for Valentine's Day. I don't think Chase even realizes it is in two days."

Brooke wore a telling smirk as we walked towards the registers. "That's not what I heard."

"What do you mean? What did you hear?"

"Oh, nothing." She dumped all of her clothes onto the counter. "Hers, too," she said to the cashier.

"No," I warned. "You are not going to pay for my clothes."

"Consider it my welcoming present to you."

"Really, you don't have to do that."

She pried my fingers off of the hangers, and set them down on top of her pile, winking at the cashier. "Okay, so, you have to act surprised when Chase tells you where he's taking you on Thursday."

I raised my eyebrows. "How do you know this?"

"He and Phil were talking during their million hour jam sesh yesterday. It's, like, the nicest restaurant in LA. Phil took me there for our one-year anniversary."

I chewed my lip, wondering where he was getting all this money from. First the expensive hotel, now an expensive restaurant.

"Let him do something special for you." She handed the cashier her credit card. "Nothing wrong with that."

My phone began to buzz in my back pocket, and I almost dropped it as I rushed to answer. "Hey, how did it go?"

"Where are you? I just walked in." Chase was out of breath from the stairs.

"I'll be home in five. Brooke and I are leaving Teal now."

"Teal?" he asked, sounding amused.

"Oh, I'll tell you all about it when I see you."

He chuckled. "Okay. Hurry up."

"Phil just texted me." Brooke excitedly held up her phone as I hung up. "Here, this bag is yours."

"Thanks so much, Brooke." I gave her arm a squeeze. "I really appreciate it."

"Any time. I had fun today."

"Me, too."

I walked down the busy block as quickly as I could, and went up the stairs by twos when I got to the apartment. I burst through the door at the top, panting and searching for Chase.

"Where have you been all my life?" He waltzed out of the bedroom and picked me up, twirling me around in the middle of the living room.

"Spill! I want to hear everything."

He landed on the couch, pulling me on top of him. "Mr. Suit and Tie's name is George. He got straight to business as soon as we sat down in his office. He told us that we're good, but we need to build a name for ourselves."

"The place was packed out last night. What more does he want?"

"He wants to start promoting the nights we play. He said there should be a line to get in – that's how packed he wants it."

"Okay. That's reasonable. What else?"

"He said our band needs a name."

"Oh, that's hard. I always wondered how musicians settled on a band name. It could be anything!"

"Want to hear what we came up with?"

"You came up with it already?"

"It's called: Saving Merritt."

My jaw dropped. "Are you joking?"

He smiled. "I'm serious. George liked the play on words with your name."

"And the rest of the guys were okay with this?"

"They loved it. They said it's unique." He touched my face. "Like you."

"How did you come up with something like that on the spot?"

"It wasn't on the spot, actually. I've had that name in my head for quite some time."

I raised my eyebrows, still in disbelief. "How long?"

"Before your mom left, I remember you as this happy-go-lucky girl, always smiling and laughing with Shelly. You were smart, and kind; you stuck up for any of the kids who got teased. I was always in awe of you. You were this force, drawing me in. Then your mom left... and you looked so sad. I would see you in the halls, or at lunch, and my heart broke for you. That vibrant girl's eyes turned dark; it was like your mom took your light with her when she left. I wanted to talk to you; I wanted to make you smile again – to stop your pain – but what could I have said? Everything I thought of just sounded dumb, at the time.

When you left the night of your dad's funeral, I felt like something was pulling me after you. Everything suddenly made sense as I raced after you in my car. That was the moment... that's when I knew why I had to leave California – why my dad had to get cancer – because I had to be there to save you. You were the one for me, and I was the one who could pull you out of your nightmare." He lowered his head. "I have always wanted to save you. My only regret is that I couldn't get you out of the car that night. When it finally came time for me to save you, I couldn't actually do it."

I took his face into my hands to make sure he looked directly into my eyes as I spoke. "You are the reason that I was pulled out of that car. If you didn't follow me, I would have died. Chase, you did save me – and not only from that accident. From the moment our heads collided in the cafeteria that day, you brought the light back into my life. I was lost in the darkness, and I didn't know how to get out. You smiled at me, and the light came back."

He tucked a curl behind my ear. "I feel like you have crept back towards that darkness ever since your mom came back. Sometimes, I lose you in that mind of yours. I can't tell what you're thinking, or how you are truly feeling."

Looking into his eyes, I could not deny it. I felt ashamed that I had somehow allowed him to see what was really going on inside my head. "I just want to forget that she even exists, and I'll be fine."

"You can't keep things bottled up inside, pretending that everything is fine."

"I'm not pretending. Did my mother throw me for a loop? Yes. Is it going to ruin my whole life? No. I really am okay."

Chase held his pinky up. "Promise me that you'll talk to me if and when you need to."

I locked my pinky around his. "Promise."

The rest of daylight was spent in bed together. We only agreed to get out when our stomachs began to growl for dinner. We trialed one of the many food trucks outside of the apartment, and freshened up for our night at the bar. At nine o'clock, we perched ourselves on stools in front of Dave.

"You have the night off?" he asked Chase.

"Yes, sir."

"He's playing tomorrow night," I explained. "And probably every night after that."

"Looks like you'll be my Valentine then," Dave said.

"I'll only share her with you while I'm on that stage, buddy." Chase winked.

"He's taking me out for dinner," I bragged. "Then, I'll be all yours after that."

"Where are you taking your lovely lady?"

"The Spanish restaurant down the road." Chase motioned to the right with his thumb.

Dave's eyebrows shot up. "Whoa, big spender. The food's fantastic. You're going to love it." He placed a Malibu Bay Breeze in front of me, and handed Chase his beer.

"Thanks. Cheers, babe."

I clinked my glass against Chase's bottle.

He took a swig, and wiggled his eyebrows at me. "I hope you put your dancing shoes on."

"He dances, too?" Dave asked. "Is there anything this man cannot do?"

"If I find anything, I'll let you know." I kissed Chase's cheek proudly. "So, you don't have anybody special to spend Valentine's Day with?"

Dave shook his head. "Nope. I'm done with dating."

"Who broke your heart?" Chase asked.

"Oh, look. I have customers." Dave grinned while he waltzed away.

I laughed. "Looks like I'm not the only one who avoids talking about things."

"You're a real pair," Chase smirked. "Come on, let's go."

I took hold of my cocktail as he pulled me onto the dance floor. The DJ was playing a mixture of new and old dance songs. The bar was crowded, but not packed like it was when Chase had performed. By the second round of drinks, we were goofing off and pulling out all the moves between the Sprinkler and the Running Man, until we were doubled over with laughter.

We remained on the dance floor throughout the night, only stopping when we needed refills. I lost count of how many glasses I had downed.

"Do you remember the last time we danced together?" I shouted over the music.

"Yeah. You were about to kiss me when that girl spilled her drink on you and ruined everything."

I giggled, remembering how drunk he was the night of the Halloween party last year. "And now, you can kiss me whenever you want."

He drew me closer, his left hand sinking into the back pocket of my shorts, as his right hand held my chin. "I want to kiss you for the rest of my life."

"Promise?"

"I promise."

I stretched up onto my toes to meet his lips with mine. I had to grip the back of his neck with both hands to steady myself. The room was starting to spin, and it wasn't solely due to Chase's kiss. My face felt numb, and my legs felt wobbly. For the first time since arriving in California, I did not care who was looking at me, or what anyone was thinking. I was enjoying the moment, feeling carefree. More importantly, thoughts of my mom, my dad, Chase's dad, and Khloe's sad face seemed so far away.

It was an exhilarating feeling, and I wanted it to stay.

Chapter Five

THE TREMOR

"Is it too much?" I asked, pulling at the hemline of the pale pink dress that Brooke insisted on buying me.

An open-mouthed Chase stood in the living room, staring at me as I exited the bathroom. His wide eyes traveled down the plunging halter neckline of the form-fitting velvet dress, down my bare legs to the silver strappy heels, and back up again. I took this time to appreciate his attire: a navy button-down tucked into grey slacks, with a matching grey tie. His rolled up sleeves accentuated the muscles in his forearms. I noted the small pink gift bag that was dangling from his right hand; I had a similarly sized red bag dangling from mine.

"Wow. You look... stunningly beautiful. I don't have the right words to do you justice."

"I'll take stunningly beautiful any day of the week." I looked around the room. "I feel like I'm forgetting something."

"You don't need a jacket. It's warm outside, remember?"

"The weather really is perfect here. I'm used to being wrapped up in jackets and scarves."

He gestured dramatically to the staircase. "After you, my lady."

We held hands as we walked down Broadway to the restaurant. The sun was setting, leaving the sky a beautiful mixture of pink and orange swirls. I was happy to be spending this time with Chase. Once he became property of the record label, I did not know how often we would see each other. It would give me a lot of free time to figure out where I was going with my life. I could not get Jake's words out of my head from the bar the other night: "How come you're not off chasing your own dreams?" Jake the douchebag may have been brazen, but he was right.

"What are you thinking about?" Chase asked, sitting across from me inside the restaurant. The flame from the small tealight candle that danced between us illuminated his face.

"What I will do with myself once you're off becoming a superstar."

He reached for my hand. "What do you think you'd be interested in doing?"

"I'm stuck between school and job. I don't know what I would major in if I went back, though."

He thought for a moment. "You really could do anything. What about an automotive school? You know so much already."

"What would I do with that once I graduated? Open my own shop?"

"Maybe. It couldn't hurt to sit down with someone to see what your possibilities are."

I perked up as the waiter set our drinks down on the table. "Thank you."

"You are welcome, my lady. Your appetizers should be out shortly."

Chase raised his glass, prompting me to raise mine. "To the most beautiful girl in the room no matter where we go. I never imagined I would be spending Valentine's Day with Merritt Adams. You have such a special soul, and I am so lucky to have you in my life. I love you more than you will ever know."

We clinked glasses, and I took a sip of my drink. Then I raised my glass again. "To the one who brought the light back into my life – my golden boy. You will always have my heart. You have been there through my worst and best times. I am the lucky one, to have someone as perfect as you by my side."

He squeezed my hand, and reached for the gift bag under his seat.

Taking out the white tissue paper, I reached into the small bag and pulled out an equally small box. I raised an eyebrow at him.

He only smiled.

I flipped open the top of the box. Inside sat a white-gold necklace heart; a sparkling diamond sat where the two rounded tops met. I gasped at its beauty and iridescence. "Chase! This is beautiful."

"I had the diamond taken out of your mother's ring that we found while going through her box last year. I knew you'd never wear the same ring that she wore, but your dad picked it out and I thought it was meaningful."

"This is the same diamond?" I raised the necklace to get a closer look. "Wow. I can't believe you did this."

"My mom also gave me my dad's wedding band before I left. She told me he would want me to have it. I had the metal melted down, and the jeweler made it into that heart for your necklace. So now, you have a piece of both of our fathers with you whenever you wear it."

"Why would you destroy your father's ring? You could have worn it."

"I have plenty of my father's things. I wanted you to have something to remember him by. I know how much he meant to you."

I now had something invaluable to remember two of the most important men in my life – my own father, and Chase's father who saved me from near death. I was stunned.

"Do you like it?" Chase asked nervously. "I know you don't wear a lot of jewelry, but... I hope you like this one."

My watery eyes raised up to meet his. "Chase, I love it." I laughed as tears spilled down my cheeks. "Here, I never thought you'd outdo yourself after restoring my car for Christmas."

He grinned. "Put it on. Let's see how it looks."

I carefully fastened the clasp behind my neck. "I'm almost too afraid to wear it. It's irreplaceable."

"It looks perfect on you."

I swiped my tears quickly, and handed him the gift bag I had waiting under the table. "It's not nearly as special as what you got me."

"It's special because it's from you."

"I knew you'd say that."

He took out the rectangular box from inside the bag. Taking the cover off, he set it down on the table and looked inside. It was a black leather cuff; the silver plate in the middle of the bracelet read, "C & M Forever."

"I looked for something you could wear to every show. Even if I'm not there with you, I'll still be there... in a way. It's dumb, I guess."

His eyes looked glassy as they gazed back at me. "It's not dumb. Not even close. I love it. I love the inscription." He held his arm out to me. "Put it on for me."

I reached across the table to fasten the cuff onto his wrist. "A leather cuff in true rock star fashion."

He held my hand up to his lips for a kiss. "Thank you so much, baby."

As we sat there, staring into each other's eyes and enjoying the moment, I heard a rattling sound nearby. I looked around the dimly lit room, and noticed several couples doing the same thing. The silverware clanked together, and I could see the pink liquid rippling ever so gently inside of my glass. The floor beneath us began to rumble, and when I looked up again at Chase, he was pushing his chair back from the table.

"Babe..." he warned as he stood, reaching his hand out for me.

I sat frozen in my chair, my brain a few steps behind my already aware senses. The one thing I did not remember to worry about in my move to California was potentially the most scary – earthquakes.

Just when everyone in the entire restaurant had risen up out of their chairs, the shaking stopped. We all looked around at each other, searching for a sign that it was safe to resume our dinners.

"It's okay," an older man next to us said. "These tremors happen from time to time. After a while, you just get used to it." His wife smiled reassuringly.

"I don't think I could ever get used to that," I replied, taking my seat.

"There was only one the last time I was out here." Chase sat down, placing his napkin back in his lap. "I completely forgot about it."

All of the couples around us looked as if nothing had happened. They went back to eating and talking, while the waiters bustled around the room. An unnerving feeling began to make its way into my stomach. When our food came, I did not feel that hungry anymore. I made it through one of my tacos before calling it quits.

"Do you like it?" Chase asked, looking down at two of my three remaining tacos.

"It's delicious. No wonder this place is so expensive."

"Would you stop worrying about money so much?" he said gently. "When you are with me, you don't have to worry about money. I will take care of it."

"I don't want you to take care of it, though. I want it to be a joint effort. I don't want to rely on you for everything. I want us to rely on each other."

"I get it. I agree – I want us to be a team... but let me treat the love of my life to a few special things, okay?"

I softened. "Okay."

We had our food wrapped to go, and made our way back over to the bar for Chase's show. He had to help the band set up, and I wanted to secure my seat at the end of the bar.

"Whoa, mama!" Dave exclaimed when we walked through the door of The Underground.

"Are you changing before tonight?" Chase asked, trying to sound nonchalant as he noticed several pairs of eyes gawking at my dress.

"Do you want me to change before tonight?"

"No. I just hope I don't forget all the lyrics when I'm staring at you."

Dave chuckled. He set down a Malibu Bay Breeze in front of me, and a beer in front of Chase. "Did you guys feel the tremor?"

"Don't remind me," I groaned.

"It's totally normal for everyone here. You New Yorkers will get used to it."

"I'd be fine if that never happened again." I took my seat, allowing my mind to run away with all of the what-if scenarios.

"You don't have to worry. I'll be here to protect you if anything should happen. A few shakes and rattles here and there won't amount to anything anyway." Chase kissed the top of my head. "I'm going to help the guys set up."

I hugged him tightly, wishing he did not have to perform tonight.

"Are you alright, babe? I promise, everything will be okay. I'm here, and nothing bad is going to happen."

I wrung my hands. "I just feel weirded out by it. I'm sure it will pass."

He looked into my eyes. "I love you."

"I love you. Thank you for my necklace." I held it in between my index finger and my thumb.

"You are very welcome." He touched his lips to mine tenderly, and then he was gone.

I sighed, taking a big gulp of my drink.

Dave poured two shot glasses full of Fireball, taking one in his hand and sliding the other to me. "To all the good guys out there like Chase. May we find them, may we love them, and may they never break our hearts." He threw the shot back like a natural. "Your turn."

I slowly raised the shot into the air between us. "To figuring out what the hell I'm going to do with my new life." I tilted my head back and let the liquid slosh down into my throat. I coughed a few times. "Oh, God! That burns!"

He smiled, his cheeks pushing up so much that his eyes almost closed. "It is called Fireball."

I took two long swigs of my drink to soothe the burning in my throat. "Okay, Dave. If we're going to be spending Valentine's Day night together, I think we need to discuss your broken heart situation."

He leaned his elbows onto the bar, squaring his eyes with mine. "Fine, but we will have to discuss your situation then, too."

I held my hand out. "Deal."

Dave shook my hand firmly. "Let me get these customers settled." He smiled at each patron, making light conversation as he mixed and poured.

There was a mixture of singles and couples throughout the busy bar. The singles were mostly packs of girls on the hunt. I noticed Donnie sitting at a small table next to the stage with a woman I presumed to be his wife. She was one of the tall blonde clones, sporting a huge diamond ring on her left hand. Though she was smiling, I wondered if she was happy with her life here.

Looking around, I did not see Brooke anywhere. I took out my phone to text her while I waited for Dave to finish making his round of drinks. When I unlocked my phone, I had a text from Shelly. It was a selfie of her and Brody in the car, making silly faces. I smiled, but felt a twinge in my heart. I took three more long swigs of my drink, and tapped out a text to Brooke.

"Okay, so," Dave began when he returned to my side of the bar. "I've got about five minutes before those ladies finish their drinks."

"You seem to be a hit with the ladies. I'll bet you do alright after last call."

He scrunched his face. "They're not really my type."

"Which one?"

"Pretty much all of them."

"I meant ladies in general."

He looked at me over the top of his glasses. "So did I."

"Ah, I see. So who's the guy that broke your heart? Need me to break his face?"

He chuckled. "Calm down, Tony Soprano. He lives in Colorado. That's where I'm originally from."

"Is that why you're not together? Because of the distance?"

"In a nutshell, yes."

"And out of the nutshell?"

"Out of the nutshell, he keeps putting off moving out here, and I can't figure out why. He says he wants to, but when I try to make a plan, he beats around the bush. Last month I told him that I couldn't take the limbo game we were in. He told me we should break up because he doesn't feel ready to move out here. Honestly, I don't think he will ever be ready."

"It's a scary decision to make, leaving everything you know behind. But when you think about never seeing the person you love, the decision should become clear."

He shrugged. "You moved across the country for your man. People do it all the time. I just wish he would man up and tell me the truth about why he really doesn't want to come."

"Yeah, that's really frustrating. How long were you together?"

"Four years. We were friends for a long time before that. It took him a long time to come out to his family. I thought we had made so much progress, but I guess it wasn't enough."

"Maybe he just takes a long time with these kinds of things. It sounds like he might come around after some time."

"I wish I had a crystal ball to look into."

"You and me both." I finished off the remainder of my drink, and felt the wonderful warming sensation in my face and legs begin to set in. "Can I have some water? It's hot in here."

He laughed as he filled a tall glass with water from the fountain hose. "You're cute when you're drunk."

"I am not drunk," I scoffed.

"I can fix that." He began mixing another cocktail for me.

The alcohol was coursing through my veins after the third drink. I was enjoying Chase's show, and the conversation with Dave. I had forgotten all about the tremor earlier, as well as the picture of Shelly and Brody. It felt good to allow the wave of alcohol wash over me, and carry my thoughts out to sea.

"So, you're telling me that your dad was so distraught over your mom leaving, that he killed himself?" Dave's eyes were wide. "That's some Romeo and Juliet shit, right there."

"I used to love reading Romeo and Juliet when I was younger. I was fascinated with how you could love someone so much that you were willing to die without him." I shook my head slowly. "If only I had known that I would actually live through it."

Dave handed me another shot. "To asshole mothers, and their bastard children."

"I'll drink to that one." This one went down easier than the first.

"Did you ever hear from your mother again?"

I laughed. "Funny you should ask. She showed up at my apartment last week." I laughed again, this time finding it harder to stop. "I hadn't seen her in eight years, and she just knocked on my door like it was the most normal thing in the world."

"What did you say to her?"

"I told her to leave, in a nutshell."

"Out of the nutshell?"

"I screamed in her face, told her that I would never forgive her for what she did, and told her to stay away from me."

"Weren't you the least bit curious as to what she had to say?"

I shrugged one of my shoulders. "What could she have said that would have made a difference?"

He whistled, shaking his head. "And you seem so normal. You should be a mental case after everything you went through. I don't know how you could be so strong. You're like..." He stopped to think of the words.

"Xena, the Warrior Princess, as my best friend calls me." I raised my glass and finished the last of my fourth drink.

He slapped the bar as he laughed. "Yes! That is perfect." He turned towards the group of people holding cash in their hands awaiting his service.

I held my phone up in front of me and took a selfie, with Chase on stage in the background. I sent it to Shelly, and told her that I missed her. Though my cheeks were flushed and my eyes were glassy, I was smiling. The Fireball and rum combination churning in my stomach had loosened me up, and I felt much more relaxed.

Dave was swamped for a while before he made it back to me. I noticed one couple in particular growing impatient. The bar was small, but it brought in just as many customers as any regular sized bar. Dave needed help.

"Hey!" The man shouted to Dave, who was out of earshot. "We've been waiting for ten minutes!"

I hopped off my stool and crouched down to get under the bar, popping up on the other side. I did not want Dave to get any complaints from disgruntled customers. I flashed my best smile at the couple. "I'm sorry for the wait. What can I get you?"

They exchanged confused looks, unsure if they should give me their order. "I'll have a Blue Moon, and she wants a rum and Coke."

"I can do that," I said to myself. I searched for a clean glass and pulled on the lever for the Blue Moon. I forgot to ask if he wanted bottle or tap, but I hoped for the best. I also forgot to ask what kind of rum the woman wanted. "What kind of rum would you like?" I shouted over the music.

She pointed to the bottle with the pirate on it, and I poured until I thought I should stop. I had no idea what I was doing. I prayed the couple would be happy enough with their drinks to turn around and enjoy the music.

"How much?" The man asked, clutching two twenty-dollar bills in his hand.

Luckily, Dave had returned. "It's on the house. I'm sorry for the wait."

The man threw a twenty onto the bar before walking away.

Dave handed the bill to me. "Your first tip!"

I giggled as he twirled me around, singing along to the song Chase was belting out on stage.

"Hey, New York!"

The smile left my face when I saw who was calling me. "Oh, look! It's Jake the Douchebag!"

Jake grinned. "You remembered my name. I'm touched."

I gave him my signature eye roll. "What do you want?"

"A Heineken."

Dave was already reaching into the cooler for the bottle.

"You work here now?" Jake asked.

"No."

Dave popped the cap off the bottle and slid it onto the bar. "You should. We would have so much fun."

"I don't know how to bartend." One of my eyebrows arched. "Is Donnie even hiring?"

"He always says that he wants to hire someone, but he never does."

"This tip is for you," Jake shouted, placing a folded up bill onto the bar. "Love the dress, by the way." He winked, and headed back into the crowd.

I scrunched my face up in disgust. "Do I have to deal with guys like him a lot?"

"All the time," Dave said matter-of-factly.

I unfolded the bill and my mouth dropped open. "It's a hundred!"

"The perks of being a female bartender. I'd get double what I make if I had tits like yours."

I held the hundred out to Dave. "Here. You have it."

He shook his head. "That's yours. You just made one hundred and twenty dollars in five minutes."

I started to laugh. Dave laughed with me, which only made me laugh harder. Before we could stop ourselves, we were doubled over with laughter, and had no idea why.

Donnie appeared in front of us, an amused expression on his face as he watched us laughing hysterically. "What's so funny?"

I wiped my eye, and tried to breathe. "I just got tipped over a hundred dollars, and I didn't even do anything."

"You should hire her," Dave shouted. "Look at her." He gestured to my dress.

"Stop that," I said, swatting his hand away.

Donnie raised his eyebrows. "Do you know how to mix?"

"I have not one single clue."

"I'd train her, obviously," offered Dave.

"What if I didn't pay you, and you just worked for the tips you made?"

I looked to Dave. "What if we pooled our tips, and split them at the end of the night?"

Dave looked to Donnie. "Deal."

Donnie looked to me. "You're hired. You can start training tomorrow."

His wife appeared beside him. "Hi, I'm Rachel. Your boyfriend is doing great up there."

"Hi, thanks. He's great." I gestured to her empty glass. "What are you drinking?"

Donnie placed his arm around her. "Strictly water, for the next nine months."

"Wow, congratulations!" I exclaimed. "That's so exciting!"

"Thanks," she said, patting her non-existent stomach. "I'm calling it a night. I've been so exhausted lately."

"Why don't you finish out the night behind the bar?" Donnie suggested to me. "Have a good night." With his arm still around his pregnant wife, they left the bar.

"Good luck with that," Dave shouted into my ear.

I giggled. "You don't want kids?"

He shook his head. "Nope. Not my scene."

"Does your Colorado boyfriend know that?"

"Ex-boyfriend, and yes."

I looked at him expectantly.

He wrinkled his nose. "What?"

"Maybe he wants kids, and he doesn't want to be with someone who doesn't want them."

His face fell as he realized what I said. "Do you think? But we never discussed it..."

I took his phone from the counter behind us, and handed it to him. "Text him. Now."

He quickly typed out a text while I watched over his shoulder. "Now, I need another shot."

I grimaced. "Fireball again?"

"Don't be a wimp." He poured for us, and we gulped them back.

When Chase's set ended, Dave turned to me with a grin. "Want to ring the bell for last call?"

I nodded excitedly.

He pointed to a rope hanging from the ceiling. Midway up the rope was a brass bell. "Shake it, sister."

I swung the rope back and forth, watching a sea of patrons scramble to the bar to place their last orders for the night. Dave quickly began popping caps off of beer bottles, and exchanging money at lightning speed. If I wasn't filled with liquor, I would have felt overwhelmed and nervous. Alcohol had put my nerves to sleep for the night.

Chase waltzed over to me with a grin spread across his sweaty face. "What are you doing back there?"

Dave put his arm around my shoulders. "She's our new bartender."

"Dave was swamped, so I tried helping him. Donnie said he would hire me." I watched his face for his reaction.

His eyebrows lifted. "Is that what you want to do?"

"I made one-hundred and twenty dollars in five minutes tonight. It's better than sitting here while you're on stage."

"You'll take care of her?" he asked Dave, though it was more a statement than a question.

"Of course," Dave replied. "She's pretty tough, though. You don't have to worry about her."

I held up my arm and tried my best to make a muscle. "See, babe? Tough."

Chase laughed, and shook his head. "Let's go, tough girl. I hear the bed calling our names."

I hugged Dave. "See you for training tomorrow!"

He squeezed me back. "I'll let you know what Colorado says."

Chase held on to me as I tried to climb the stairs. Frustrated that my legs weren't working the way my brain was telling them to, I kicked off my heels. "Why do there have to be so many?"

"That's the downfall of living on the top floor. How many drinks did you have tonight?"

"A few. Dave poured us shots of Fireball. It literally tastes like a ball of fire. Hey, did you know Dave is gay?"

"No, I did not."

"Well, he is. He's heartbroken over his ex who lives in Colorado. I don't know how people do long distance relationships."

Chase let me ramble while he helped my feet get up each step. "Last step and we're home."

Once inside the apartment, Chase led me to the bedroom. I crawled on top of the bed, and sprawled out on my back.

"I need to take a shower. Do you need anything?"

"I'll be fine once this bed slows down," I mumbled with my eyes closed.

I heard him chuckle as he headed for the bathroom. Several minutes later, he reappeared in the bedroom. I had not moved.

I opened one eye to look at him, and realized he had nothing but a towel wrapped around his waist. I clumsily sat up and folded my arms behind my head to enjoy the view.

He grinned, dropping his towel. My eyes lowered, slowly taking in every inch of protruding muscle down his abdomen, until they settled just a bit lower on something else that was now protruding.

He took his time making his way on top of me on the bed. I watched as his biceps and triceps took turns bulging as he walked himself across the mattress. Reaching out for him, I slid my fingers through his damp hair.

His lips brushed against mine ever so lightly. "Are you too tired?"

"Never for you," I breathed, running my hands down his back. My eyes begged for him to continue.

He lifted one hand off the mattress to caress my face, then cradled the back of my neck as he kissed me passionately. His movements were deliberately slow, as he peeled my dress up and over my head. The intensity in his eyes matched his kiss, and I could have stared into them all night.

We didn't know it then, but this would be our last night together.

Chapter Six

NIGHTMARES AND MIMOSAS

"*Help!*" *I shouted. "Can anybody hear me?"*

Just moments ago, there were over one hundred people on the other side of the wooden door. I listened now, but heard nothing. I pounded on the door as hard as I could.

"Chase! Are you out there?" No response. Nothing but silence. Tears began to fill up in my eyes, though I tried to remain calm. A sickening, familiar sensation ran throughout my body. I had been stuck once before, and I remembered the feeling all too well.

My hands were sore from banging so hard. I tried kicking, but it was no use.

"Please," I whimpered, resting my head against the door. "Not again."

I jolted awake, sitting straight up in bed. The room was dark, except for the sliver of light shining through the door from the window in the living room. I looked beside me, and Chase was fast asleep. I covered my face with my hands, trying to catch my breath. My cheeks felt wet from crying.

"It was just a dream," I quietly reminded myself. After a few minutes of deep breathing, my heart rate finally came down. I curled myself around Chase's broad back, hooking my arm around his stomach.

Feeling me touch him, he turned around. "What's wrong?" he asked sleepily.

I buried my face in his chest. "Nothing. I just want you to hold me."

He wrapped his arms around me, and we intertwined our legs. His warm body enveloped me, as I listened to his steady heartbeat. I tried to fall back to sleep; I tried to think of anything but the nightmare. The minutes passed, turning into hours, and I could not shake the short scene from my mind. I watched the sun come up, and finally fell back to sleep just in time for Chase's alarm to sound. He showered, and kissed me goodbye before he left for a meeting with at the record label.

I tried to occupy myself by reading and watching movies. When I looked at the clock and realized it was only noon, I decided to take a walk outside, wandering up and down the nearby streets to get familiarized with the area. Being alone in a new city was more of a culture shock than I had prepared for. I knew it would be different, and I expected to miss my friends, but I found myself missing small things: the yappy dog next door to the Brooks' house; Brody's pancakes in the morning; the sound of car horns beeping aggressively; and how I craved the taste of New York pizza.

Towards the end of any vacation growing up, I always felt ready to go home, missing my own bed and familiar surroundings. Being in California was like being on a permanent vacation, unable to land back in my own life of comfort. To add insult to injury, I was anticipating when the next earthquake would be. Since I had felt the tremor, any small vibration, including my phone, tricked me into thinking that it was happening again. The nightmare I had only made me more on edge.

I walked until it was time to get ready for training at the bar with Dave. I was relieved to have something to do, and I was even more relieved knowing alcohol would be involved.

"Dude!" Dave exclaimed when I walked in that night. "You're a genius!"

"I take it your text to Colorado went well?"

He grabbed me by my shoulders. "We talked all day! Well, we texted, but... same thing."

"What was his response?"

"Here." He took out his phone and handed it to me. "I can't believe I never thought of it before," Dave continued. "I just wish he would have told me how much having kids meant to him."

I scrolled to the end of the text thread. "You broke up?" I shouted. "That's it?"

"I know in my heart that I don't want kids. He knows in his heart that he wants kids. There's no point to stay together if we both want different things in life."

"And you're okay with that?"

"When I didn't know why he was breaking up with me, it was torture. Now, we've talked and we have closure." He looked at me over the top of his black rimmed glasses. "Do you and Chase ever talk about your future?"

I shook my head. "We're flying by the seat of our pants right now." After the amazing night Chase and I had, an unsettling feeling had made a home inside of my stomach. I told myself it was due to the nightmare, and tried to forget about it.

I spent the next hour training in my crash course behind the bar to prepare for tonight's shift. For the most part, everything was relatively easy; I learned the computer in less than five minutes, and learned where everything was located within ten. I needed more time to study the names and recipes of drinks – the ones that I had never heard of made me especially nervous. Luckily, Dave would be by my side to help. It would be fun working with him, and I was thankful to feel like I had made a real friend.

"Can I get a Corona," a customer asked.

I flipped the cap off into the garbage, and slid the bottle to him.

"Can I start a tab?" the man asked.

"Sure." I looked to Dave. "Just watch me to make sure I'm doing this right."

Dave stood over my shoulder while I tapped the information on the computer screen.

"You're a quick learner." He handed the receipt to me after it printed out, and I shoved it into a glass on the bar.

I stifled a yawn.

"Oh, no. You can't be doing any of that. We just started our shift!"

"I didn't get much sleep last night."

He stared off into the distance. "I miss having hot Valentine's Day sex. I need a new boyfriend."

"I'm not tired from the sex." I let the grin spread across my face while I recalled how mind-blowing it was. "Although, it was pretty damn good."

"Stop! You're making me jealous. Why are you so tired then?"

"I had a bad dream. It really bothered me. I couldn't fall back to sleep after that."

Four men strolled up to the bar, sitting on the stools directly in front of us. "Can we get a round of tequila?"

I began lining up shot glasses in front of them. "What are we celebrating?"

"My baby brother is getting married!" the loud one shouted. He slapped his brother on the back, several times too hard judging by the look on his face.

"Congratulations!" I poured the tequila over all four glasses, the way Dave had showed me earlier.

"You have to do one with us!" the loud one shouted.

I looked at Dave to find him sliding two more glasses my way. "The more you drink, the less annoying he gets," he whispered.

I chuckled as I poured, excited to begin drinking. I handed one glass to Dave, and held the other up above my head. "To the groom, and his wife-to-be!"

The four men raised their shots with ours, threw them back, and slammed the empty glasses onto the bar. "Another!" they cheered.

I tried to hide my contorted facial expression as I choked the liquid down. "Are we doing another with them?"

Dave nodded. "You can just Coyote Ugly it if you don't like the shot choice."

I raised my eyebrow. "You want me to dance on top of the bar?"

"No!" He slapped his face with his palm. "It's in the movie. The trick is to make them think you're taking the shot. You pour it into your mouth, then make like you're take a swig from a beer bottle – but you spit it out into the bottle, and nobody notices."

"That's disgusting, yet ingenious."

"Watch me."

I handed the men their shots, and watched as Dave backwashed his beer with tequila. It was flawlessly executed.

"Turn around when you do it," Dave warned. "It can get messy the first few times you try it."

I took the shot, but when I tried to spit it back out into the beer bottle, it sprayed all over the place like a busted garden hose. I ended up swallowing half of the tequila, and wearing the other half of it.

Dave laughed as he handed me a clean rag. "Maybe you shouldn't do that again until you practice. I guess it's safe to say you're not a spitter."

I tossed the rag at him. "My man has no complaints!"

"I'll bet he doesn't!" He twirled the rag and slapped my ass with it before turning back to the customers.

Dave and I were like a well-oiled machine, slinging drinks and making tips. I broke a sweat when the ten o'clock rush came in. We had taken two more shots, one with a birthday boy, and the other with a bachelorette. I was definitely feeling it more and more as the night went on, but the people in the bar were double as drunk, so no one noticed.

"I love this song!" Dave yelled. He pumped his fist in the air as he danced over to me. He took my hand, and twirled me around.

"Whoa," I said, steadying myself as I gripped the bar. "No more twirls, or I'm going to hurl."

He threw his head back as he laughed. "Are you drunk, New York? We've got to work on your tolerance!"

"I feel great. I don't know what you're talking about." I did feel great. My body felt loose and warm. It was then that I realized: my mind was defenseless when I was sober. Any and all thoughts could enter whenever they pleased, crowding my headspace and making me anxious. Alcohol acted like a bouncer, dragging them out and showing them the door. It protected me. All I had to do was drink until security showed up.

After I rang the bell for last call, Chase walked into the bar. He smiled when his eyes settled on me.

"That boy always looks like he stepped right off the Abercrombie billboard," Dave swooned.

I attempted to walk towards him, but my feet felt like they had been replaced with lead balls. As I got closer, one foot tripped over the other, and my ankle wobbled in my wedges. Chase caught me before I fell any further.

"First day with the new feet?" he chuckled.

I rolled my eyes. "Dumb shoes. How was your day?"

"It was good. Long, but good. How was yours?"

"Same." I wrapped my arms around his neck, pulling his lips closer. "Are you heading up now?"

"I'm going to jump in the shower. I'll meet you up there when you're done."

Dave showed me how to close out the cash register, and we cleaned up the glasses and beer bottles that sat empty atop the bar.

"Here you are," Dave said, handing me a stack of cash. "Two hundred and sixty dollars."

My eyebrows shot up. "Two hundred?"

"Wait until the weekend."

"Night, Colorado."

"Night, New York."

I groaned as I looked up at the stairs before me. "There has got to be a better way," I muttered. I slipped out of my shoes, and held onto the railing with both hands.

When I finally made it into the bedroom, Chase was already passed out on top of the covers. I clumsily crawled into bed, wrapping myself around him. Within seconds, I was passed out, too.

The next day, Chase was gone before I woke up again. I had another nightmare, and adding insult to injury, I was majorly hungover. Needless to say, I did not sleep well. With a pounding headache and puffy eyes, I popped two aspirin, and chugged a water bottle. I was not looking forward to another day left to my own devices.

My phone beeped when a text from Brooke came in. She told me to meet her and her friends for lunch, and I jumped at the chance. I needed to keep myself busy, and my mind occupied. I longed for that blissful calm feeling from the alcohol the night before, and counted the hours until I had to be at work.

"Looks like someone had a rough night," Brooke exclaimed as I approached her.

I quickly put my sunglasses back on. "Do I look that bad?"

"You just look tired. A little concealer and nobody will be able to notice." Brooke dug into her purse and pulled out her makeup bag.

I peered inside at what looked like an entire makeup warehouse. "You're like Mary Poppins with that bag. Do you have a sandwich in there? I'm starving."

Brooke giggled. "Aha! Here is my magic under eye eraser."

I stood still while she smeared concealer underneath my puffy eyes.

"Now I just have to blend it," she murmured, patting my face with her ring finger. "There. All better."

I took the compact mirror from her bag, and looked at my reflection. "Wow. You're good. You have to teach me how to use that stuff one day."

We were seated at a table outside under an umbrella. The sun was shining, as per usual, and mostly everyone sported giant, expensive sunglasses.

I was the only brunette at the table. I knew Michelle, but was meeting the other two girls for the first time. Their nails were perfectly manicured, hair flawlessly coiffed; I looked down at my own short unpainted nails, and wondered if I would end up like them if I stayed here long enough.

"This is Merritt." Brooke pointed to her two friends. "This is Lauren and Stacy."

"Merritt, that's such a unique name," Lauren said.

"Thanks." I laughed. "I don't have a cool story about it or anything. I don't even know where it came from."

"Ask your mom," Stacy said matter-of-factly.

"Dude, her parents passed away." Brooke looked at me apologetically.

"Way to go, dude." Lauren shook her head.

"It's fine. Don't worry about it," I said quickly, seeing Stacy's embarrassed expression.

The waitress approached us, pad in hand. "Good afternoon, ladies. Can I get you something to drink?"

"Let's do Mimosas!" Lauren suggested, her eyes wide with excitement.

"Five Mimosas, coming right up." The waitress left our table in a hurry.

"So, did you live in Manhattan?" Michelle asked.

"No. I was about twenty minutes away in Staten Island."

"That's one of the four boroughs, right?"

"Five, yes."

"What's it like there?" Stacy asked. "We've been dying to plan a girls' trip to New York for the longest time."

I shrugged. "It's hard explaining it when it's your home. The things that excite tourists don't seem all that awesome to us. Manhattan is definitely full of things to do. Staten Island is much more residential."

"You don't look like you're from Staten Island," Lauren stated. "I thought everyone there looked like Snooki."

I laughed once. "No, she's definitely one of a kind."

The waitress returned, placing a tall champagne glass in front of each of us. After she took our lunch orders, conversation bounced around from New York, to makeup, to hair extensions. I stayed quiet mostly, sipping my drink that continuously got refilled each time it was found empty. It was only when I stood to make a trip to the restroom that I realized how much I had actually drank.

"Whoa," Brooke said as she steadied herself. "How long have we been sitting here?"

"Five Mimosas too long," I replied. We walked arm-in-arm to the bathroom, giggling all the way.

"I like drunk Merritt," Brooke called out in the stall next to mine.

"Why's that?"

"You loosen up more, you laugh more. It's nice to see you like that."

"Geez, am I that awful to be around when I'm sober?"

"That's not what I meant, and you know it." She flushed, and began washing her hands. "I can tell you've been through some shit in your life. It makes me feel sad. I like seeing you happy."

I emerged from the stall, and looked at her in the mirror. "Thanks. I appreciate you inviting me out with your friends. It's nice to feel like I have someone out here."

She put her arm around my shoulders. "I got your back, dude."

"Ditto," I replied.

An hour later, I clomped up the stairs to my apartment. Tiredness had swept over me, and I could not wait to crawl into bed to take a nap being that I had a few hours until I had to be at work. I pushed open the door and made a beeline for the kitchen to grab a water bottle. I chugged half the bottle, and rummaged through my purse for aspirin. Suddenly, a shadow looming behind me startled me.

"Oh my God, Chase!" Water spilled all over me as I squeezed the bottle in fear. "What are you doing here?"

"I live here," he laughed. "I'm sorry. I didn't mean to scare you."

"Well, you failed." I continued looking through my purse.

"What are you looking for in there?"

"Aspirin. My head is pounding."

"Where did you guys go for lunch?"

"Tutto... tutta... I don't know. Tutta-something."

"The place with the red umbrellas?"

"Yep. That's the one. Aha! Found it." When I flipped open the cap, the bottle slipped out of my hand, and pills spilled all over the floor. I groaned, covering my face with my hand.

"Why don't you take these," Chase handed me two pills from the floor. "Go lie down, and I'll clean these up."

"It's okay. I can help." I crouched down next to him, picking up the small pills that were scattered everywhere.

"Maybe you shouldn't drink tonight."

A knot formed in my stomach. "What are you talking about?"

"I don't know. You're taking up day drinking now, for starters." He half-smiled, trying to appear casual.

"The girls ordered Mimosas with lunch." I tried to sound just as nonchalant.

"Hmm."

"Why the furrowed brow?"

"It's weird seeing you like this."

My head jerked left to look at him. "Like what?"

"Drunk."

"I only had a few glasses. I didn't realize how badly they were going to hit me until I stood up."

He wore a hint of a frown. "That happens when you're sitting the whole time you drink."

"I'm just so grateful to have Brooke and her friends taking me under their wings." I put the cap back on the bottle and stood, tossing it into my purse. "It feels like I belong."

Chase sighed as he stood, and put his arms around me, hugging me to his body. "I know it's hard being here without Shelly."

I nodded against his chest.

"Are you taking a nap?"

"Yeah. I need to have all my energy for later. Lie down with me?" I took his hand, but he pulled back.

"I can't stay. I have to head back out to the studio. We took a lunch break. I figured I would see you for a little while, since I won't see you tonight."

"You're not playing here tonight?" I whined.

"No. I'm sorry, babe. The next night we have off, I promise I will take you on a nice date."

"I don't want a date. I just want to be with you."

He tucked a curl behind my ear, and kissed my lips. "And I just want to be with you, too." He looked into my eyes. "Try to take it easy tonight, okay?"

My eyebrows pushed together. "Take it easy?"

"You already had drinks at lunch. I know customers at the bar can get pushy wanting you to take shots with them, but you don't have to."

"I know."

"Good." He kissed my forehead.

I thought about saying more, but I bit my tongue as I looked into his beautiful, concerned eyes. I did not want him to worry about me with all that he had going on.

I knew I didn't have to drink with everyone who offered to buy me one; I knew I didn't have to drink at all... but I wanted to. A small voice inside my head tried to warn me that I was in trouble, but I was able to silence it once I laid down on the bed.

Everything would be fine once I slept it off.

Chapter Seven

GOING UNDER

*W*eeks passed since Chase brought up my drinking. I had barely seen him; we were like two ships passing in the night. He would come home from recording at the studio, or a meeting with the record label, while I was leaving to start my shift. I often came home to an empty apartment, and woke up in an empty bed. He had been playing at various bars around LA, and would slip in sometime after three in the morning. I knew he had to stay after his shows ended to socialize; I knew our relationship would take a back seat to his music career; I knew it would be difficult not spending time together. What I did not know, however, was how dangerous it would be for me to be alone.

Before my accident, I had spent seven years focusing my time and energy on taking care of my father. There was no time to sit around and wallow in my sadness; I never experienced feeling carefree, or let loose with my friends. I went to school, babysat in the evening, and came home to cook, clean, and pay bills. I was a child living an adult life. After the accident, when grief reared its ugly head, Shelly and Chase were there to take turns occupying my time – I was never left alone for long. Falling in love with Chase made me so happy that I never found the need to numb my pain with anything else.

Now, I found myself craving the one thing that I had learned could soothe my entire nervous system in just a few gulps. I had found a way to detach myself from any and all emotions – and I did not want to stop. Reality would sink in the next day when I woke up sober, but I knew it would only be a few hours until I could drown my demons all over again.

Hiding it from Chase was easy, but it was the worst part. I wanted to prove to him that he had nothing to worry about, but the temptation was difficult to resist, as I was around it every night. At the beginning of each night, I told myself that I would stop, only to break that promise to myself less than an hour into my shift. Just one shot, I told myself. Before I knew it, I was on my third or fourth. The water level was rising quickly, and I was about to go under.

"Bottoms up, bitches!" Brooke shouted.

Dave and I, along with her entourage of friends, clinked our shot glasses with Brooke's.

"You're working on my birthday," Brooke complained. "Philip's working. This sucks!"

"You've got all of your friends here with you!" Dave offered. "Don't frown. You're too young for Botox."

"We're in LA. You're never too young for Botox," she replied with a smile.

"I'll be on the dance floor in spirit." I poured her and her friends another round of shots. "Take this as your parting gift. Go have fun!"

It was a busy night. I felt good turning down three requests to do shots with customers. At eleven o'clock, I felt my phone buzzing in the back pocket of my jeans. Shelly had texted me three times, and was now calling. Something had to be wrong.

I pointed to my phone, motioning to Dave that I would be back. I closed the door behind me as I stepped into the stairwell.

"Shell, is everything okay?"

"Good thing I wasn't dying. I texted you a million times."

"I'm at work. What's going on?"

She took a breath, hesitating before she spoke.

"Just tell her," I heard Brody in the background.

"Shelly," I warned.

"I saw your mother today."

Acid instantly pooled into my stomach. "Where?"

"I was coming home from class, and I saw her waiting outside of my apartment."

"How does she even know where you live?"

"I don't know. It's freaking me out, though. Thank God Brody was home."

"What did she want?"

"She was looking for you. I told her you didn't want to talk to her. I told her she had a lot of nerve coming back here."

I rubbed my forehead, trying to breathe through my anger. "I guess that means she's staying somewhere on the island."

"I took her number down. I know you don't want to call her, but it was the only way she would leave."

"Did you tell her I don't live there anymore?"

"I didn't know what you wanted me to say, so I just told her you moved out of state. She was surprised."

I laughed once. "Not as surprised as we all were to see her! Why won't she leave me alone? She ruined everything when she came back!"

"What did she ruin? You're living in The Golden State with the man of your dreams."

"Yeah. It's really golden here."

"What's that supposed to mean?"

"Nothing." I squeezed my eyes shut, feeling annoyed.

"I knew I shouldn't have told you."

My temper flared. "You absolutely should have told me! You're supposed to tell me everything!"

"Am I? Like you're telling me everything?"

"What are you talking about?"

"Nothing. Go have another drink. Forget I even called."

The phone beeped in my ear. When I looked at the screen, the call had disconnected. Shelly hung up on me.

When I returned behind the bar, Dave was pouring Brooke and her friends another round of shots. I slid another glass over to him.

He raised his eyebrows at me. "You okay?"

"I'm fabulous." We clinked glasses, and I succumbed to the desires of my rage.

Three shots later, I was feeling better. I kept checking the time, wondering when Chase would step through the door. The customers shouting drink orders had finally died down, all of them now bumping and grinding against each other on the dance floor. This was the perfect time to take my break. It was stifling in the packed bar, and I needed some air.

"Dave," I called. "I'm going outside."

"Take your time," he shouted back.

It was difficult getting through the crowd, and the buzz from the shots did not help as I was unsteady on my feet. I used my elbows to push people aside, clearing a path for myself until I reached the front door. Outside, the warm breeze felt cool against my dampened skin. I watched as half-naked girls puffed on their cancer sticks, laughing and shouting at each other as they passed by. I missed hanging out with Shelly, and I felt guilty for arguing with her earlier. She was calling to let me know what happened with Claire, and I had no right taking my frustrations out on her. I tapped out a text, but then deleted what I had typed; it was late, and I would call her in the morning to smooth things over.

I felt calmer than before with the alcohol now numbing my senses. I knew it was wrong, but I preferred this version of myself. Why feel wound-up and anxious, when I could feel relaxed and at-ease? Maybe this is why everyone living in LA seemed so laid-back – they allowed themselves to have fun and feel good.

Five minutes later, I was back inside pushing my way through the mob again. I felt like a pinball, knocked around from side to side by everyone dancing to the beat. There were no openings to squeeze through. As I shoved people aside, a fight suddenly broke out next to me. One man swung at another, but he missed. The other man rammed into his midsection, and I was thrown to the ground as they fell down on top of me with their beer bottles in hand. I shielded my face from the broken glass, and all the pairs of feet stomping around me. I tried to push myself off the floor, but a sharp pain went through my left hand.

"Get off!" I screamed at the men who continued the scuffle on the floor.

The next thing I knew, I was being lifted off the floor. Two familiar arms scooped me up and carried me behind the bar, setting me down into a chair. I looked up to see Chase.

"Oh my God! Merritt!" Brooke's shriek was loud as she came running.

I stared at my hand that was now throbbing, and saw a large glass shard sticking out of the puffy skin under my thumb. After my father's suicide, I did not do well with blood. The room started to spin, faster than it already was due to the alcohol. I felt very faint as I watched the blood drip down my wrist. Moisture filled the back of my throat, like it often did right before I was about to throw up.

"Do you think she needs to go to the hospital?" I made out Dave's concerned tone behind me.

"No hospital," I managed to get out. I could not take my eyes off of the deep read streaks against my skin.

Chase pulled the glass out of my hand without warning, and wrapped a clean rag tightly around my wound. I winced as he finished the knot.

"Sorry, baby. It has to be tight." His hand cupped my chin, gently raising it until my eyes focused on his. "Are you alright?" He offered a halfhearted smile. His lips were inches from my face, and they served as a pleasant distraction from the pain.

"There's blood..."

"Take her upstairs," Dave ordered, for me more than Chase.

"N-no," I stammered. "My tips..." I attempted to stand, but my knees refused to cooperate.

"Easy, girl. Dave's got your tips. You've lost some blood – you're coming with me." Chase put his arm around my waist, hoisting me out of my seat, and carried me up the stairs to our apartment.

"Please don't take me to the hospital." My voice sounded small, like a child.

"You might need stiches if the bleeding doesn't stop."

Several minutes later, Chase was kneeling on the bathroom floor, while I sat on the lid of the toilet. I squeezed my eyes shut to avoid seeing the bloody mess on my hand when he unwrapped the towel.

"You must think I'm such a baby," I shook my head, feeling embarrassed.

"Stop. There was a lot of blood coming out of this tiny hand. I'm sorry I couldn't get you out of there sooner."

"I'm just thankful you did. I was getting trampled. That must be what it feels like shopping on Black Friday."

He raised my hand to his lips, planting a kiss over the bandage. "There ya go. All better."

"Thanks, babe." I went to stand, but felt lightheaded. I held onto the towel rack to steady myself.

"Alcohol thins your blood. That's why your hand was bleeding so much," he said.

I put my hand on my stomach. "Seeing that blood made me feel so sick."

"You sure it wasn't the shots making you queasy?"

I looked down at the floor, guilty and unable to make eye contact with him. I did not want to see the look of disappointment on his face. The checkered tile squares began swirling together, and I had to squeeze my eyes shut to keep the spinning at bay. Saliva reappeared in the back of my throat.

"Merritt, I'm concerned–"

Dropping to my knees, I lifted the lid to the toilet seat as quickly as I could. Waves of vomit began erupting from my stomach. I felt Chase pulling my hair back from my face while I heaved my guts up into the toilet. I wanted to shoo him away, though I knew he would not listen. This was not something I wanted him to witness.

When I finally finished, I kept my head down. "Can you give me a minute, please?"

He sighed behind me, and then I heard the bathroom door close. I tied my hair up, brushed my teeth, and washed my face, all while completely avoiding my reflection in the mirror. I couldn't look at myself. I shuffled into the dimly lit bedroom to change into my pajamas, and slipped into the bed beside Chase. His eyes were open, staring up at the ceiling.

"We need to talk about this," he began. "But it's late... you're drunk, and I have to get up early tomorrow."

"I know," I replied.

To my surprise, he wrapped his arm around me, and pulled me over to his side of the bed. I rested my head on his chest, and tried to match his breathing. After I was sure I wouldn't throw up again, my eyes finally began to close.

I woke up the next day hugging Chase's pillow. My head felt as if someone had taken a sledgehammer to it, and my throat felt dry and scratchy. On the nightstand sat a water bottle with two aspirin, signaling that Chase had already left for the day. I reached for the pills, and felt a sharp pain slice through my hand, as I remembered being slammed to the ground the night before.

"I'm a mess," I mumbled against the mattress.

My phone buzzed with a text from Dave, asking about my hand. I typed a reply, and scrolled to find Shelly's name.

"Are you calling to apologize?" she answered. "Because I don't want to talk to you unless you're going to tell me that you're sorry."

"I am sorry, Shell."

"I'm listening."

"I am sorry for being so short with you last night. You know how I get when it comes to my mom, and I can't help that reaction. I'm sorry that you had to deal with her yesterday. I know you felt like you were being stalked, and it freaked you out."

"You sound like shit. Are you sick?"

"No. I had a rough night."

"You've been having a lot of those lately, haven't you?"

"Please. Not you, too."

"Why, has Chase said something to you about your drinking?"

"He's been hinting at it."

"He sees it. I'm not even there and I see it. This isn't like you. Is it because of the new friends you've made?"

"No," I whined, rubbing my head.

"So then what the hell is going on with you? You're spiraling."

"I'm not spiraling. I called to apologize, you know. Not for a lecture."

"I'm not giving you a lecture. I'm asking you to talk to me. Every time I call, you glaze over everything and tell me how it's all good and fine. I know you better than anyone else, in case you've forgotten, and I know you are not okay. I just need you to tell me why."

"I don't know why!" My voice strained to get louder.

"Merr, maybe you need to come home."

"I can't come home. Don't be ridiculous."

"Why not? You're not a prisoner. You're clearly going through something, and you're going through it alone. I know you have Chase, but he isn't exactly around very often."

"If I leave, Chase will want to leave with me. That was the deal. I can't make him throw everything away just because I want to come home. Not after everything he's done for me."

"Everything he has done for you is because he fell in love with you. You don't owe him for the rest of your lives. You have worried about everyone else your entire life. You need to worry about yourself for once. Chase is a big boy. He can handle himself. You're not responsible for him."

"No. I can't ruin this for him. I'm going to get a handle on things. It will all be okay."

"Not when you're working in a bar every night. That's not exactly the best environment for you to be in, clearly."

"This is coming from the one who told me to have a drink to take the edge off."

"Oh, so this is all my fault now? I turned you into an alcoholic because I told you to have one drink?"

"I'm hardly an alcoholic. There are people in that bar every night, doing the same thing I'm doing. You forget, I've seen you wasted more times than I can count."

"Maybe I should come out there sooner. Another few weeks seems so far away."

"No. Don't be crazy. You have school. I'll be fine. I promise."

"Look, I have to get to class now. I'm going to call you back later, and we can finish this conversation."

"Okay. I have work later tonight."

"Maybe you should take the night off."

"I just started working there. I can't take off."

She sighed. "I'll call you later, okay?"

"Okay. Bye." I gulped down the rest of my water, and pulled the covers over my head. I needed to sleep the headache away before work.

When I awoke, the sun was already setting. My hand was still throbbing, so I popped two more aspirin into my mouth and tried not to get the bandage wet in the shower. All the practice with one arm in a sling was finally good for something.

Chapter Eight

A HOLE IN THE CHEST

"Hey, Captain Hook," Dave called as I walked behind the bar at eight o'clock.

I smirked. "Have you been dying to say that all day?"

"Oh, I came up with a couple one-liners for your one-hander. In the end, it was a toss-up between Luke Skywalker, and Hook."

"I'd rather be Skywalker than Hook!"

"Skywalker wouldn't have let those guys knock him to the ground like you did."

"Dude, he let Vader chop his hand off."

"Did you just dude me?" he asked with a wry smile. "My little New Yorker is turning into a Cali girl!"

I laughed. "Okay, one: no, I'm not. Two: don't ever try to do a New York accent again."

Dave grinned. "Does it hurt?" he motioned to my hand.

"It does. The aspirin isn't doing much to help the pain."

"You know what will help with that?" He reached for a bottle of whiskey, and set it down on the bar in front of us.

I shook my head. "Not tonight."

He raised his eyebrows. "Suit yourself."

I watched as he poured himself a shot glass full of amber liquid. My mouth salivated at the thought. I quickly uncapped a water bottle and took several swigs, though it did not quench the kind of thirst I was experiencing.

"What happened to your hand, New York?" Jake appeared on the stool in front of me.

I stuck a Heineken bottle in between my knees, flipped the cap off with my good hand, and slid the bottle to him "I got cut with a piece of glass."

"At least you're resourceful."

"Just call me MacGyver."

The pain got worse the more I tried to use my hand. I gave up trying to stay away from alcohol. I needed something to take the edge off. Once my hand healed, I told myself, then I would stop. I poured Dave a shot along with mine. One turned into two, as it usually did, and by the end of the night, I had lost count. My hand felt great, though, and the battle wound earned me more tips than usual. Three hundred dollars richer, I stumbled into my apartment after closing.

I kicked my shoes off in my nightly ritual, and tried to navigate in the darkness. Halfway to the kitchen, I tripped over something on the floor, and crashed into one of the bar stools, letting out an involuntary yelp. I was sitting on the floor holding my foot in my hands when Chase came out of the bedroom, flipping on the kitchen lights.

"Are you okay?" His eyes were half opened, and his hair was smooshed up on one side.

"I stubbed my toe."

"Let me take a look." He crouched down and took my foot into his hands. He pushed gingerly on my second toe to see if it would move.

"That hurts," I said through gritted teeth.

"Are you drunk right now?" He undoubtedly smelled it on my breath.

"No!" I said defensively.

"What did you have tonight?" His tone was especially pointed.

"I had a couple of shots. That's it."

"I thought you were going to take it easy with that."

"No, you *told* me to take it easy." I pulled my foot away from him, growing more furious by the second. "I'm sorry I woke you up, but I can't help it if I tripped. It was an accident."

He stood, crossing his arms over his bare chest. "You could have helped it if you were sober."

I looked around until I spotted a pair of his shoes lying on the floor nearby. "I tripped over these!" I hurled one of his size twelves at him. "And that's why I fell into the stool!"

His expression wavered for a moment, realizing his part in the incident. "It doesn't change the fact that you're drunk. Again." He sighed. "You know, I told myself to let it go, but I can't watch you do this to yourself anymore, Merritt!"

My eyes rolled. "You make it sound like I'm an alcoholic. Everybody drinks when they go out, including you! Stop making a big deal out of this. Everything is fine."

"Everything is not fine!"

He shouted so loud, it made me jump. I felt tears threatening to make an appearance. I held my breath, willing them to stay behind my lids. "What do you want me to say?"

Chase ran his fingers through his hair, frustrated. "I want you to talk to me."

"I am talking to you. You're not listening."

"I hear what you're saying, but it doesn't match your actions. I know this move has been hard for you, but don't go down this path. I don't want you to turn..." He stopped before finishing his sentence.

"You don't want me to turn into who?"

"Look–"

"No, finish your sentence! You don't want me to turn into who? Say it, Chase!"

"I don't want you to turn into your father!" His shoulders fell after he let it out. "Is that so bad?"

I looked down at my toe. It was beginning to turn a deep shade of purple. "I need to put ice on my toe." I began to stand. Chase leaned down to help me up, but I swatted him away. "I don't need your help!"

The old familiar words just slipped out. He looked so hurt that it nearly broke my heart. I wanted to jump into his arms and tell him that I was sorry; I wanted to make it better, but in order to do that, I had to tell him the truth.

"Fine. I don't need this shit! I have an early meeting tomorrow." He turned his back, and walked into the bedroom.

The tears I had been holding in finally surfaced. I remained on the floor, covering my mouth with my hand in an attempt to muffle the sound.

Several minutes later, Chase came back out of the bedroom. He rushed over to me when he saw that I was crying. He wrapped his arms around me and held me while I sobbed against his warm skin. "Please talk to me. I just want to know what's going on with you."

"I just... I'm having a hard time lately."

"With what?" He pulled me away so he could look at me. He brushed his fingers over my forehead lovingly. "Please tell me what is going on in there."

"I've been having nightmares again."

"About your accident?"

I shook my head. "It's different. I'm stuck at the bottom of our staircase. I can't see upstairs, but I know that I can't go up that way. I try to open the door to get into the bar, but it won't open. I bang and kick and scream, but all I hear is complete silence. I call for you, but you're not there. There's nobody there, and I can't get out."

His eyebrows pushed together. "You're all alone."

I looked away as a tear rolled down my cheek. "Shelly called me tonight. She said my mom was waiting for her outside of her apartment."

"What did she want?"

"To talk to me. Shelly took her number so that she would leave her alone. I guess she didn't get the hint when I screamed in her face." I covered my face with my hands. "I just wish she would have left me alone. Everything was fine before she came back."

"You need to talk to her, Merr. You can only run for so long. Maybe once you talk to her, all of this will finally stop."

I wiped my tears with the back of my hand, and looked into his eyes. They were filled with desperation and worry, and it killed me to know that I was the one causing all of it.

"Maybe this is all too much."

"Too much?" I asked nervously.

"The gigs, the meetings, always recording in the studio. You're left alone all day and night."

I took a deep breath before I said my next words. I had to be strong, as I had once been not so long ago – like I was before coming to California. "It's not you, Chase. I think I have a problem."

"I know it's difficult to face your mom, but maybe if you just –"

"No," I interrupted. "I think I have a problem. With drinking."

A dozen emotions flashed across his face. "Okay. We can fix this."

I shook my head. "You can't help me with this."

"Stop pushing me away. You don't have to go through everything alone. Look at all we have been through together. We have always helped each other get through tough times in the past. Let me help you."

I took his beautiful face into my hands. "Chase, this is not me pushing you away. This is me telling you that you need to focus on your life here. You're in the middle of becoming what you have dreamed of being your whole life."

"None of that matters if you're not okay. I can cut back on gigs and meetings. I'll talk to George. I'll figure it out."

"No. You need to be doing all of those things in order to get where you want to be."

He looked down at my hand as he intertwined his fingers with mine. "I want to be with you. That's where I want to be."

Another tear rolled down my cheek, and his face became blurry. "I will always be with you. Even if we're not physically together. I just don't think I can stay here in this environment. I won't be able to stop."

"Well, try. How will you know if you don't try?"

"I have been trying." I reluctantly met his gaze. "I can't stop."

"You're leaving, aren't you?" His voice was low.

I did not answer. He already knew. I pressed my lips against his, as the tears continued to drop from my eyes. In one fluid movement, he scooped me up off of the floor and carried me into the bedroom. He laid me on the bed, pulling the covers over the both of us. We faced each other in the darkness, our bodies entwined, until we could no longer keep our eyes from closing.

When I woke up the next morning, Chase had already gone in to the studio. His text read that he planned to return around five o'clock. He cancelled his evening gig to spend our last night together. I quickly texted Dave that I had a stomach bug to get out of work. I couldn't bring myself to tell him that I wouldn't be at work, or in California, ever again. Then, I called Shelly.

"So, you're going to have to cancel your plane tickets to come out here," I began.

"What?" Shelly screeched. "Why?"

"Because I'm coming home."

It was silent on the other side of the phone.

"Shell?"

"What do you mean you're coming home... like, for a visit?"

"No, like, for good. I booked the flight before I called you, and now I'm letting you know."

"When?"

"Tomorrow. Maybe you could pick me up from the airport?"

"I will," Brody chimed in. "Just text me the info."

"Thanks."

"Is Chase coming with you?" Shelly asked, though she already knew the answer.

I hesitated a moment as my heart wrenched out of my chest for the third time that morning. "No. He is staying here."

"Did you guys have a fight?"

"Yes, but that's not why I'm leaving."

"It's your drinking." It was a statement, and not a question.

I choked back a sob. "I'm scared, Shell. I started something and I don't think I can undo it."

"You will. You can do anything."

"How do you know that?"

"Because I'm your best friend. I know you can do anything. You just need to get your mind straight again. How is Chase handling this?"

I closed my eyes, trying to get the image of his crestfallen face out of my head. "He's..."

"Heartbroken," Brody stated.

"Yeah."

"Well, text me your flight information, and we'll be there tomorrow," Shelly said quietly.

"Okay."

"Love you, Frog."

"Love you, too, Toad." I pressed the red button on the screen, and let my phone fall onto the mattress. I pulled the covers back over my head, and closed my eyes. I spent my last day in LA alone, alternating between sleeping and crying. It was fitting, I guess.

———

As I rolled my luggage towards the security guard, the knot in my stomach made its way into my throat.

"Sir, you can't go past this point without a boarding pass."

I sat my luggage upright, and turned to Chase. This was the part I had been dreading.

His usual spirited eyes looked so dull today, like all the color and life had been drained out of them. All that remained were two cold grey stones staring back at me. He had not said a word to me since we woke up this morning.

I wrapped my arms around his neck, inhaling his scent in the hopes that I could take it with me. "Chase Brooks, I love you more than you can ever imagine."

Reluctantly, his hands wrapped around my midsection. "I don't want to do this." His voice was low. "I don't want to say goodbye to you."

"Don't say goodbye. Just say that you love me. Say that everything will be okay, even though we're going to be millions of miles apart. Say that you'll call me and text me whenever you can. Say that you won't forget about me."

A tear slid down his cheek. "I could never forget about you."

"What about all the other stuff I just said?" I mustered a smile, but he did not.

"Please don't be funny right now."

"Okay."

"I don't want anything to change. I don't want things to be different." His grip around me got tighter with every word he spoke. "I don't want to lose you."

Every tear that dropped from his eyes was like a gunshot to my sternum. I tried to breathe through the pain. "You will never lose me. Not now, not ever. Do you understand? My heart is yours." I took another breath. "For as long as you still want it."

He dropped my duffle from his shoulder and slammed his lips into mine. Our tears mixed together on their way down to our lips. He kissed me with such a sense of urgency, as if it was the last time he would ever kiss me. Though he did not want to say goodbye, his kiss certainly did.

"Sir," the security guard said. "I'm sorry, but you'll have to leave her here now."

When his lips pulled away from mine, he took my breath with him. I felt like I was about to faint, as I begged my knees to stay strong just a few more minutes. I had to keep it together until Chase left. My heart pounded out of my chest as we looked into each other's eyes one last time, unsure of when we would see each other next.

"Don't go," he whispered, squeezing his eyes shut as he pressed his forehead against mine.

"I have to. But I will straighten myself out."

He kissed my cheek lightly, and then my lips. "I know. I love you."

"I love you."

I watched as he hung his head, and turned away.

"You can stay until he turns the corner," the security guard said gently. "Then you need to board your plane."

I nodded. "I know."

"Are you going to be okay?" she asked.

"That I don't know." I saw Chase look back over his shoulder one last time before he turned the corner. His eyes were red, his shoulders slouched. It was the last glimpse I had of him before he was gone.

I cried throughout most of the plane ride. I ignored the stares, and prayed that no one asked me if I was okay. I stared out the window, until my eyelids felt heavy. The turbulence shook me awake right before we landed.

Walking through the airport on my home turf, I was reminded of how happy Chase and I were as we held hands on our way to board the plane to California. Now, I rolled my suitcase alone, with a broken heart.

"Oh, God! You look like shit!" Shelly cried, as I approached her outside.

"Shelly!" Brody scolded.

I half-laughed. "I did just take a plane ride from the other side of the country."

Shelly threw her arms around me. "You look like you haven't eaten or slept in days. How was the flight?"

I tossed my duffle bag into Brody's trunk with her still hanging onto me. "I slept most of the plane ride."

Brody touched my arm. "How was he when you left?"

I tried to swallow the lump that had not left my throat. "I've been through a lot of pain in my life. I lost my mom, I lost my dad, and I've been trapped inside of a burning car. This... this was worse."

He gently pulled Shelly off of me. "I'm so sorry, Merr. This separation is only temporary. You guys are going to make it through everything, and you'll be together again."

The tears brimmed over my eyelids again. "When?"

He wrapped his arms around me. "I don't know."

A car waiting to pull up beeped its horn behind us.

"Relax, buddy!" Shelly screamed. "We're having a moment, here!"

"Let's get out of here," I said, pulling away from Brody. "Before she kills somebody."

I fastened my seatbelt in the backseat. I swiped open my phone to tap out a text to let Chase know I had landed safely. I stared at the blinking cursor, unsure of what to say. Words seemed futile when compared to the pain I had just caused him.

Shelly talked the entire ride home, which I did not mind for once. I needed something else to focus on other than the giant hole in my chest. When we arrived at my apartment, I stared up at the Brooks' house.

Shelly turned around in her seat to look at me. "I already spoke to Beverly. She's expecting you. I figured you wouldn't want to explain it after a day like today."

"Thanks. I hadn't quite figured out what to say to her. I'm so embarrassed."

Brody's eyes looked at me in the rearview mirror. "You have nothing to be embarrassed about. She will understand all of it. She'll be thankful you're okay, and that you're making the right choice."

"Am I?" I asked.

"Did you stay in California and turn into a raging alcoholic?" Shelly asked rhetorically. "You're making the right choice."

I unbuckled myself. "Thanks for picking me up, guys."

"Want me to stay over tonight?" Shelly asked.

"No. Thanks, though. I'll call you in the morning."

Khloe was waiting at the door as I walked up the driveway. Beverly was behind her, with her usual warm smile spread across her face.

I walked through the door as Tanner trotted down the stairs. "Welcome home, sis."

Khloe jumped into my arms. "Merry! I missed you so much!"

I squeezed her so tight that she let out a puff of air from her tiny mouth. "Not as much as I missed you!"

"Mommy said I have to go to bed now because it's late, but I will see you soon, right?"

"Right."

Tanner held out his hand. "Let's go, squirt."

"Can you give me a piggyback ride, Tan-Tan?"

"Only if you stop calling me Tan-Tan." He knelt down, and she jumped onto his back like a koala bear. It was comforting to know that everything was exactly the way I had left it.

Beverly watched and waited for her two children to disappear into Khloe's bedroom. As soon as the door closed, she turned to me and opened her arms.

Without hesitation, I flung myself into her embrace. She hugged me as I sobbed.

"I'm so sorry I let you down," I said.

"Are you crazy? You didn't let me down. Why would you say such a thing?"

"You were counting on me to take care of Chase, and I failed."

"I don't want you to take care of Chase if it means that you don't take care of yourself!"

While she was hugging me, my eyes settled on the wine rack in the dining room. A knot in my stomach formed, and twisted with desire. I knew that if I had something to drink, it would help to calm me down. I told myself that I needed something to get me through the first night without Chase; I just needed something to make me feel better I told myself this would be the last time.

I pulled away from Beverly, wiping my nose with the back of my hand. "Can I please have a few tissues?"

"Of course." She disappeared into the hallway.

I ran as quickly as I could, and grabbed a bottle of wine off the rack. I concealed it in my duffle bag, and swung it over my shoulder as Beverly returned.

"Thanks." I blew my nose, and wiped my eyes. I said goodnight, too guilty to stay and continue looking her in the eyes.

Inside my apartment, I wheeled my luggage into the closet and shut the door. I grabbed the bottle opener from the kitchen, and climbed into bed, wine bottle in hand. I remained in my clothes because they smelled like Chase. It was insane – when I was in California, all I wanted was to be back home; now that I was home, all I wanted was to run back to California.

I drank until I could no longer feel the throbbing pain in my chest, which was most of the bottle. The only time I picked my head up was to check if Chase responded to any of my texts. He hadn't.

Chapter Nine

THE DRUNK GIRL CRYING THING

"*S*omebody, help! Get me out of here!" I screamed.

I put my ear up to the door again, straining to hear any sign of life on the other side. I balled my hands into fists and pounded on the door for a second time.

"Somebody, please! Chase! Can you hear me?"

My throat burned from screaming so loudly. I kicked the door with all of my might. Something was blocking the door, and I could not push it open. After several more failed attempts, I sat on the stairs in defeat. I could not go back up, and I could not get through down here. I was stuck.

I covered my face with my hands, and began to cry.

MY PHONE BUZZED AND I OPENED MY EYES.

"Hello?" I answered groggily.

"I'm outside. Open up, I'm freezing by buns off!"

I quickly unlocked the door, and returned to my bed under the warm covers.

Shelly stomped the snow off of her boots, and hung her jacket in the closet. "I'm so over this snow. It's April, for God's sake!" She made a beeline for the bed as soon as she entered my room. "You've been lying in this bed for two days. Enough is enough." She ripped the covers off of me, and bounced onto the bed. "Rise and shine, bitch."

I grumbled while I sat up.

"You're not going to get better lying here."

"I know." I checked my phone for the millionth time.

"Has he called at all?"

"Nope."

"He's probably just busy with work."

"I just feel so guilty for leaving him."

Shelly eyed the empty bottle of wine, but said nothing. I was glad, because I didn't want to admit that I stole it from Beverly. "Just because it's his dream to be there doesn't mean it has to be yours, too. You need to figure things out. I'm sure he feels just as guilty for bringing you there in the first place."

"I can't get his face out of my head. He looked crushed when he left me at the airport." I squeezed my eyes shut to keep the tears at bay. "I feel like I ruined everything."

"You didn't ruin anything. Lots of people live apart from each other. This is only temporary."

"Until when, though? I hate not knowing – I hate that there's not an end in sight. What if he doesn't ever want to come back? What if he doesn't want to be with me anymore? What if... what if he finds someone else?"

"That boy loves you, Merritt. His heart belongs to you, and you will both figure everything out together. It's just going to take some time."

"Time. Why can't it ever be, like, ice cream or something? How come we can't just say, "It's going to take some ice cream to make everything better,"? Why is it always time?"

A smile crept onto her face. "Why don't you come out with us tonight? Brody and the guys are having a party at the house."

I shook my head before she even finished speaking. "No. I'm not ready to go out yet."

"You've been in bed long enough. You need to get some fresh air... and a shower."

I covered my face with my hands. "You're not going to leave me alone, are you?"

"Nope!" She skipped over to my closet and gasped. "Merritt! You haven't even unpacked?"

"Look at me, Shell. Does it look like I unpacked?"

Her eyes gave me a once over. "Fine. I'll bring my steamer over later and we can get the wrinkles out of some of these clothes. You'll look great tonight."

"I don't care what I look like. I'm only going out because you are as relentless as a squirrel."

"I'm not getting that analogy – how is a squirrel relentless? Like, that wasn't even funny."

"I just went through a lot. I guess I'm off my game."

"Maybe you're just not funny anymore. Maybe you've hit your sarcasm quota for life."

I clutched my heart. "Don't say such a thing! Sarcasm is all I have left in this world."

She giggled as she walked to the side of the bed, and threw her arm around my shoulders. "And me!"

"Hurry up and get to school. You're going to be late for class."

"I'll come by later to get ready for tonight." She grabbed her things and bounced out of the apartment.

Alone again. I laid back down on my pillow, pulling the covers up around my chin. I typed out yet another text to Chase. Staring at my phone, I waited for him to respond. After twenty minutes, my eyes began to close again.

It was getting dark when I opened my eyes. I frantically searched for my phone in the covers, hoping to see a response from Chase. All I found was a text from Shelly stating that she was on her way. Looking at the time, she would be here any minute. I unlocked the door, texted her to let herself in, and turned on the water in the shower.

Shelly came into the bathroom when she arrived. "You don't have anything picked out for tonight."

"I didn't know what to wear." I popped my head out from behind the shower curtain. Shelly was wearing brown boots with jeans, and a navy sweater. "I'll just do jeans and a long sleeve tee. I'll wear my Uggs. I want to be comfortable."

"I'll steam a few shirts so you can pick which one you want."

I breathed a sigh of relief that she did not argue with me about what I should wear. I did my hair, and made enough of an effort to put mascara on my lashes. That was all Shelly would get out of me tonight, and she knew it. She didn't complain once.

I surveyed the three tops she laid out on the bed for me, and pulled the black V-neck over my head. I tucked my jeans into my black knit boots, and spritzed perfume on. Lastly, I fastened the necklace Chase gave me around my neck.

"You look nice," Shelly said. "You're looking a little thin these days, but we'll get some food in you soon."

"I'm just not hungry." I checked my phone one last time before tossing it into my purse. Still nothing. I wondered why he was not responding to my texts. I knew he was upset, but I didn't expect him to ignore me for days at a time. I almost wished he was sending me angry texts instead. I already had abandonment issues from my mother – the last thing I needed was complete radio silence.

Shelly linked her arm with mine as we walked into the living room. "He will come around. I promise."

When we arrived at the party, we searched for Brody.

"Hey, bitch!" I heard someone shout behind me. I turned to see Tina and Kenzie making their way over to me through the crowded living room.

"I forgot to tell you," Shelly leaned in. "The girls were pissed you didn't say goodbye."

"Don't you roll your eyes at me," Tina pointed as she took her stance in front of me. "You left, and you didn't even tell us you were leaving! Who does that?"

Kenzie's eyes were wide with curiosity. "Tell me everything! How is it in California? I'm so jealous."

"Don't be." I spotted Brody in the kitchen, and nudged Shelly. "There he is."

Shelly took off bounding into the next room.

"What were you, on the Hollywood diet?" Tina asked, eying my body.

"More like the liquid diet."

Kenzie looked around. "Where's Chase?"

I ignored the stabbing pain in my chest. "He's in California still."

"Okay. Enough with the cryptic bullshit." Tina put her hands on her hips. "What the hell is going on?"

"Cliff's Notes version: My mom showed up at my door asking for forgiveness, Chase asked me to move to California with him, we were there for about five days before I decided to take up alcoholism. Now I'm back, and he's still there. The end."

Both of their jaws dropped open.

"Oh, good," said Shelly, returning with Brody. "You told them."

"What did your mother want?" Tina asked.

"I don't know."

Kenzie's eyebrows were still pushed together. "Did you guys break up?"

"I didn't think so, but he hasn't answered my texts in five days, so that's been a good time."

"Brody!" Jack, one of Brody's frat brothers, called from the staircase. "Game's starting. Let's go!"

"Let's go, babe." Brody took Shelly's hand.

I raised an eyebrow at her.

"We're playing against Jack and Melanie," she said apologetically. "Brody bet them that we were better at pool then they were. Want to come watch us take their money?"

"No," Tina said, linking her arm with mine. "She doesn't want to watch. She's staying down here with me."

"Rob and I are playing the winners," said Kenzie. "I'll see you guys a little later."

As soon as they disappeared up the stairs, Tina dragged me into the kitchen. "We're doing shots."

I shook my head. "No, Tee. I can't do shots. I need to stay away from alcohol."

"No one needs to stay away from alcohol. What you need is to learn how to remain in control." She spun the cap from the bottle of tequila and poured two shot glasses filled to the brim. "And I'm the professional at that."

I hesitated.

"Who drove tonight?" she asked impatiently.

"Shelly."

Tina handed the glass to me. "Then you're good." She clinked her glass with mine, and downed her shot.

Tanner appeared in the doorway, searching the room until his eyes settled on me. He looked down at the glass in my hand. "I came by your apartment before, but you had already left."

"Why, what's wrong? Is Chase okay?"

"He's fine. I just spoke to him an hour ago."

It felt as if someone poured lighter fluid on the fire in my stomach. "Well, at least he's talking to somebody."

"What do you mean?"

"He hasn't responded to any of my texts."

"He's just having a hard time."

I put my hand on my hip. "So it's okay to ignore somebody when you're having a hard time?"

He raised his hands up in surrender. "Hey, don't kill the messenger."

I looked down at the light brown liquor in my glass. I raised it to my lips, tilting my head back to let the liquid burn its way down my throat.

Tanner elbowed Tina. "Watch her tonight." He turned to walk out of the kitchen.

"I don't need anybody to watch me!" I called after him.

He shot me a look before turning the corner.

"You fell for the wrong brother," Tina murmured. "That boy is pure fire."

"You know what happens when you play with fire." I held up my empty shot glass. "Another."

She smiled. "Atta girl!" She poured us another round, and we slammed them back.

I immediately felt better as the tingling sensation began to flow throughout my body. If Chase was going to ignore me, then there was nothing I could do – except drink until I forgot about him.

Tina tugged on my wrist, motioning to the dance floor back in the living room. I looked down at her colorful arm of tattoos as I followed her out of the kitchen. She had a tough looking exterior, and an even tougher interior. I often wondered how she was able to be so detached from everything. She wore a cropped top with low-sitting torn jeans, and combat boots. Her black bob atop her head now had a bright red color streaking through it.

"I love the red in your hair," I yelled into her ear as we took our spots on the makeshift dancefloor. "It suits you."

"Thanks. Let me know when you want to spice up your look."

I laughed. It was a foreign, yet natural feeling all at the same time. The loud music helped drown out any thoughts that tried to threaten my good time. Tina and I danced until there was sweat glistening on our chests. Several partygoers tried dancing with us, but we danced away from them. I felt angry again when I saw Tanner watching us from the other side of the room, as if he perched himself there to keep lookout for Chase.

"I'll be back," I shouted to Tina. I stomped over to Tanner, who was now wearing an amused expression on his face. "Did they promote you to supervisor here, or are you just watching me so you can report back to your brother?"

He laughed once, ignoring my question. "So, I came by earlier to see if you wanted to come boxing with me."

I scrunched my face up. "Boxing?"

"You've got fight inside of you. You just don't know how to channel it yet. Come to the gym with me tomorrow. I'll introduce you to my coach."

I rolled my eyes. "Is this where you give me the I-used-to-be-you speech?"

He shrugged, unfazed by my attitude. "I don't need to give you a speech. When you're ready to see what I'm talking about, you can let me know."

"I'm glad you like the gym membership I got you for Christmas, but I don't really think boxing is for me."

"Suit yourself. Just know that drunk isn't really a good look for you."

"I am not drunk." I spun on my heels, and stomped away from him. I was going to return to dancing with Tina, but I decided to make a quick left into the kitchen. I poured myself another shot of tequila, and downed it quickly. When I arrived back on the dance floor, Shelly and Brody were dancing alongside Tina.

"Where were you?" Shelly asked.

"Talking to Tanner."

"Has he heard from Chase?"

"Yup."

Her face crumpled when she realized what that meant. "Oh, Merritt," she began.

I held my hand up. "Don't. I'm over it."

"Have you been drinking?"

"I'm pacing her," Tina interjected. "Relax, gingersnap."

Shelly opened her mouth to protest, but thought better of it. Instead, she wrapped her arms around Brody's neck and continued dancing. Tina was the only person Shelly would bite her tongue for.

I had snuck a fourth shot a little while later, and by the end of the night, I had thrown back a fifth. By the time Shelly realized what I was up to, it was too late. She was furious.

"Why don't you guys get out of here," Tina suggested. "I'll take her home."

"You're just trying to make me go home so she can continue to drink!"

"Look at her. She's not continuing anything."

I put my hands on my hips. "What's that supposed to mean?" I slurred.

Tina and Shelly exchanged glances. "Fine," Shelly said. "But you're going to have to hold her hair back when she starts to puke."

"I'm not gonna puke." I held onto Tina's arm. "Just stop rocking – you're making me dizzy."

"Let's go." Tina motioned to the door. "You're done."

"No!" I yelled. "I don't want to be done!"

"You've had enough for tonight," Shelly yelled back.

I crossed my arms in defiance. "I'm not leaving."

All of a sudden, Tanner appeared beside me. The next thing I knew, I was being lifted into the air. "Hey!" I screamed. Then, everything turned upside down. His hands held on to my legs as we moved towards the door. "Tanner! Let me go!"

"If I let you go, you'll crack your head open on the floor." He swung the door open with one arm, and walked down the stairs outside.

"You know what I mean!"

I saw an upside down Shelly running after us, with Brody and Tina not far behind. "Are you taking her home?" she called to Tanner.

"Yup," he responded.

"Maybe you shouldn't hang her upside down," Brody called.

"I've got this," he said. "You guys have done enough for one night."

"Hey!" Shelly snapped. "You'd better watch your tone!"

Tanner spun around to look at her.

"Wee!" I laughed as I flew around in the air.

"Oh, for God's sake," Tina muttered.

"You are the one who took her to a party," Tanner growled. "Do you really think that was a smart idea?"

Brody looked like he wanted to say something, but hesitated. He was a peacemaker, and Tanner was known for knocking guys out with one blow to the jaw. "Are you going to stay with her, or are you just dropping her off?"

"I'm not gonna puke. Don't you guys listen to me?" I repeated.

"I'll watch her tonight. I'm taking her to the gym with me in the morning." Tanner turned back around and continued walking to his car.

"Night!" I waved goodbye to my friends. "Wait, you know I'm not going to the gym with you, right?"

"Can you just shut up right now?"

I balled my hand into a fist and punched his left ass cheek, which was the only thing I could reach while hanging from his shoulder. "Oh, that's firm."

I heard him chuckling as he swung open the door to his Mustang, and tossed me into the back seat. His smirk faded when he looked down at me. "If you puke back there, I'm going to leave you for dead on the side of the road."

I burst into laughter, and watched as he shook his head and slammed the door shut.

We were home within minutes. I was feeling less giggly after being knocked around due to Tanner's reckless driving.

"Let's go," he motioned once we arrived at the house.

I groaned. "You drive like a maniac. How does Charlotte get in the car with you?"

His eyes dropped from mine. "She won't be getting in my car anymore, so it doesn't really matter."

I gasped as I jolted upright. "Oh, no! Did you guys break up, too?"

His gaze returned to mine. "You and Chase broke up?"

"I left, and now he won't talk to me."

He sighed. "Charlotte won't talk to me, either." He held his hand out for me. "Come on. I'm freezing my balls off."

I slid out of the car, and Tanner scooped me up in his arms.

"Why won't she talk to you?" He kicked the door shut with his foot and made his way up the driveway.

"I screw everything up. It's what I do."

I rested my head against his shoulder while he carried me up my apartment stairs. "You screw things up because you're scared. If you know you love her, you don't have to push her away."

He set me down on the top landing, and turned the key in the door.

"Hey, how did you get my keys?"

"Get inside."

I searched for pajamas while Tanner made himself comfortable out on the couch. I tossed my hair into a bun, and stumbled into the living room. "Where's my purse?"

He held it up. "Go get some rest."

"I just want my phone."

He shook his head. "You're not getting it tonight."

I put my hands on my hips, swaying from the unsteady feeling inside me. "I said I want my phone."

"And I said you're not getting it tonight."

I felt anger burning in my stomach, and it began to make its way up into my chest. My hands were in fists, and my jaw clenched under my skin. "Why can't I have my phone?"

"Because you don't need to text Chase in the state you're in right now."

"You're not in charge of me. I can text him if I want to."

"He's not answering you. Do you think drunk texting him will make him change his mind?"

We remained in a stare down. Suddenly, I realized that it wasn't anger churning inside of me. My eyes widened.

He sat up and pointed to the bathroom. "Go!"

I ran to the toilet, and flipped the lid open just in time. The tequila that burned going down hours before burned even worse coming back up. I felt Tanner's hand on my back in an attempt to comfort me, and I was thankful to not be alone. The waves of vomit lasted what seemed like forever. When I felt like I had nothing left inside of me, I hovered over the bowl to catch my breath.

"How many shots did you have tonight?" Tanner asked, crouching on the floor behind me.

I held up five fingers, spitting into the toilet.

I heard him exhale as he leaned against the bathtub.

I clutched the sink, pulling myself up. I swished my mouth out with mouthwash, and plopped back down beside him. Tears began spilling down my cheeks, as all of the emotions I had stuffed down inside began to surface.

"Please don't do the drunk girl crying thing." Tanner closed his eyes and rubbed his forehead.

"I'm sorry," I sniffled, wiping my nose with the back of my hand. "I just don't understand why my life has to be like this. My mother ruined everything! Everything was fine before she left us. My dad was happy. I was happy. When she left, everything went to shit! Then, Chase came along and everything was great again. Chase and I were great, and then she knocks on my door to ruin everything all over again. She must have radar or LoJack on me or something. Every time I'm happy, poof! There she is!"

"You can blame her for everything if you want to, but eventually you have to take responsibility for your own actions. You are the one who chooses to let her consume your life. You are the only one who can make it stop."

I looked at his blurry face through my puffy, tear-soaked eyes. "Why is everyone in your family so insightful?"

"I can't take the credit for that one. My boxing coach helped me with a lot." He looked down at his lap. "And Charlotte."

I covered his hand with mine. "You will get her back. If she loves you, she won't be able to stay mad at you for long."

"How do you know that?"

"Because no matter how mad I am at your brother, it's always worse to be without him."

He looked down at my hand, and his face suddenly twisted in disgust.

"What?"

He picked my wrist up, holding my hand up to my face. "You have puke on your hand, and now it's on me."

I pointed. "The soap's on the counter."

He stood, frantically scrubbing his hands in the sink.

I laughed, until I felt another eruption make its way up my throat.

In between heaves, I heard Tanner sigh as he sat back down on the tile. "It's going to be a long night."

Chapter Ten

THE FIGHTER

The tile felt cold under my face when I woke up. I picked my head up, and looked for Tanner. He had made a bed inside the tub with my pillow and comforter. His bulky body looked funny crunched inside the small space. I would have laughed if my head didn't hurt so badly.

I stood, looking at my reflection in the mirror. Black mascara streaked down my cheeks, and my eyes were almost swollen completely shut from crying so much. I wanted to take a shower, but I did not want to disturb Tanner, no matter how uncomfortable he looked. He had stayed up listening to me cry for the duration of the night. I felt sad for him that Charlotte was not speaking to him, but knew in my heart that she would come around soon enough. Though he was a self-proclaimed screw-up, he had a good heart. Like his brother.

Walking into the living room, I searched for my purse. I needed aspirin and my phone, in that order. Swallowing the pills, I chugged an entire bottle of water. I swiped open my phone to find a plethora of texts from Shelly, Brody, and Tina. I did a double take when my eyes settled on Chase's name. He had texted and called me at around ten this morning. It was now noon.

I immediately called him, as my heart pounded in my chest, hoping that he would answer.

"Where the hell have you been?" he asked as soon as he picked up.

"Me? You're the one ignoring me for days."

"Are you okay? Tanner stopped texting me last night, and I haven't heard from him since."

"He's asleep in my tub right now. He's fine."

"Why is he in your tub?"

"Is that why you called me? To find Tanner?"

It was quiet before he responded. "I wanted to find Tanner because..."

"Because he was keeping tabs on me for you?"

I heard him exhale, and I wondered if he was running his fingers through his hair. "It sounds bad when you put it that way."

"What way would you put it?"

"I miss seeing your face when you're annoyed with me."

My heart nearly jumped out of my chest. "So, you don't hate me?"

"No, I don't hate you. I'm sorry I never responded to your texts. I just miss you so much. It's killing me."

"So why ignore me if you miss me? How is that going to help anything?"

"I don't know. I was just trying to get you out of my head."

"I don't want to be out of your head. Keep me in there."

He chuckled. "How are you doing? I heard you had a rough night."

I closed my eyes. "I did. But only because you weren't talking to me."

"I'm sorry."

"Tanner wants to take me boxing today."

He sounded amused. "You're going to box?"

"He said his coach helped him a lot with his anger. I figure it's better than a shrink."

"I think you're going to be glad you did this. Maybe not right away, but in the long run."

"I'd like to tell you about it afterwards... if you'll actually answer."

"Of course you can call me after."

"I never heard from my mom for eight years. You can be mad at me all you want, but please don't ignore me like that. It's too much for me to handle."

"I promise I won't do that again. If I don't respond right away, it will be because I'm in a meeting or recording."

"How's that all going?"

"It's great. I just wish you were here with me. This place is lonely without you."

"It was lonely when I was there, too."

"This isn't how I pictured everything."

"Me neither."

"Dave is pissed, by the way. Brooke, too. They're mad you never said goodbye."

"Just tell them that I don't do goodbyes very well. I'm sure I'll see them again one day."

"When?"

"I don't know. My plan is to help your family out at the shop. I will give Tanner a chance with this boxing thing. Whatever will help me, at this point."

"How are they doing?"

"Your mom's holding it all together. Khloe is her usual self. Tanner's in a fight with Charlotte, but I know they'll work it out. He'll be fine."

"What are they fighting about?"

"He didn't say. She's not speaking to him, so he probably did something dumb. I told him she'll come around."

"How do you know she will?"

"Because when you fall in love with a Brooks brother, there's no alternative. Once you know them, you can't ever go back to life without them."

It was quiet on the line. The silence reminded me of how our relationship was when it started; we always found comfort in our silence, as long as we were together.

"You know, the hardest part wasn't saying goodbye to you. It has been waking up every day without you, realizing that it wasn't just some bad dream. You're not here, and there's nothing I can do."

I covered my face with my hand, willing the tears not to surface. My head was pounding too much to cry. "We will be together again."

"I love you."

"And I love you."

"Call me later."

"Don't ignore me."

"I won't."

"Good."

"Bye."

I listened for the click on his end, and took a deep breath. I was happy that we got to talk, but that didn't change the pain radiating from the hole in my chest. The hole would remain empty until I was in Chase's arms again.

Tanner emerged from the bathroom, his hair smooshed up on one side, like Chase's often was when he woke up. "I don't recommend sleeping in a bathtub."

"I told you to sleep in my bed last night. You're stubborn."

"Chase would have killed me if I let you choke on your own vomit and die in your sleep."

"You're the best little brother a girl could ask for."

"Yeah, well... this was a one-time thing. Don't think I'm going to continue carrying you out of harm's way every time you put yourself in front of it."

"Thank you, Tanner. Seriously."

"Do you plan on showering before we leave?"

"What's wrong?" I patted the octopus of curls on top of my head. "You don't think this is a good look for me?"

"Sure, it is. On Halloween."

I held up my middle finger and grinned. "How much time do I have?"

His eyebrows shot up. "You're coming willingly?"

"You did say you weren't carrying me around anymore."

He smirked, as he walked to the door. "You've got twenty minutes." He swung the door open, and turned back to look at me. "You really think Charlotte will come around?"

I nodded. "I know she will."

I closed the door behind him, and made a beeline for the shower. I scrubbed my face and body, without enough time to bother with my hair. I quickly changed into grey sweat pants and a matching hoodie. To say my eyes were puffy and red was an understatement, but with Tanner waiting outside, I had no time to fuss with my appearance.

In the passenger seat, I tapped out texts to Shelly and Tina, letting them know that I was alive. Tanner drove in silence, and I was grateful. Within five minutes, we had arrived, and he zipped into a spot.

When we stepped inside the gym, I was hit with the musty smell of sweat. There were dozens of punching bags hanging around the spacious room. To the left, large men grunted as they flipped over giant sized tires; to the right, muscular women took turns slapping thick ropes against the ground. My eyes finally settled on the caged-in ring that sat in the center of the gym.

Inside the ring were two men. The shorter of the two wore padded headgear, and a mouthpiece that made his lips protrude; he was wearing a t-shirt with the gym logo on the front. He was sweating profusely, and breathing heavy. Just by looking, I could tell that he was the one being trained.

The taller man, towering over his opponent, wore no headgear. His dark hair was buzzed on the sides, matching the stubble on his face, and longer on the top. He sported a scar over his left eyebrow. Tattoos covered every inch of his bare upper body, including one that twisted up onto the side of his neck. He looked every part the fighter, mean and tough, with the menacing muscles to match. As we got closer, I noticed how puffy and disfigured his ears were from being punched one too many times – they were the only imperfect things on him. He moved so fluidly around his opponent, it was almost graceful. I could not take my eyes off of him.

"That," Tanner said, pointing, "is T.J."

"That's your coach?" I asked, slightly intimidated yet slightly intrigued.

"Yup. I'll introduce you when he's done."

We waited at the bottom of the ring for him to finish. T.J. acknowledged Tanner with a nod as he swayed from side to side. He glared down at me with his piercing blue eyes, then smiled wide to reveal the words "FUCK YOU" scrolled across his mouth guard. I grinned, and he turned his attention back to his opponent, who was taking this time to catch his breath. The two circled each other for another minute, until the man in the shirt swung his fist.

T.J. stepped back, dodging the swing with ease. Then, he lunged forward, and tackled the man onto his back. They crashed into the floor of the ring with a loud thud. Every muscle in T.J.'s shredded body stretched and tensed as he unleashed a series of punches into the man's abdomen. In the time it took me to blink, T.J. took hold of the man's arm, spun around, and locked his arm in between his legs. The man furiously tapped T.J.'s leg, begging him to release his arm before it snapped in half.

My mouth was left half-open. I closed it when I noticed Tanner smiling at me.

"I knew you'd love this place," he said, leaning in.

After helping the winded man up, T.J. shook his hand. He hopped out of the ring, and pulled his mouth piece out as he came down the stairs. My eyes were fixated on his tattoos, each one flowing into the other, as if they were telling a story.

"T.J. Cutler, this is Merritt Adams. Merritt, this is T.J., my coach."

T.J. stuck his hand out. "Nice to meet you. I like your name."

"Thanks. I like that Ninja Turtle spinny thing you did to that guy's arm."

He grinned, surprisingly revealing a full set of teeth. "That was called an arm bar, though I like Ninja Turtle spinny thing better."

I smiled, and breathed a sigh of relief that he had a sense of humor.

Tanner placed his hand on my shoulder. "Take care of her, Teej. She's stubborn, but she's got fight in her."

T.J. raised a skeptical eyebrow at him. "More stubborn than you?"

Tanner grinned as he backed away. "She might take the cake."

I crossed my arms over my chest. "I mean, I'm standing right here."

T.J. gestured to the stairs leading into the ring. "Alright, Merritt Adams. Let's see what you've got."

My eyes widened. "We're starting in there? Don't you think that's something we need to work up to?"

"You can leave your socks and shoes down here," he replied, as if he did not hear my question. "Take off your hoodie, and put your hair up."

I quickly complied, slipping out of my sneakers, and stuffing my socks inside. I threw my sweatshirt over them, piled my curls at the top of my head, and made my way into the ring. I was not crazy about being on display in the middle of the entire gym. I fussed with my tank top, nervously awaiting whatever was about to happen.

T.J. had gone to the far corner of the gym, collecting gloves and pads. My stomach churned while I watched him trot back over to me. He jumped up and over into the ring, dropping the pads at my feet. "Hold out your hands."

I held my hands out in front of me. He slipped my fingers into the gloves, and wrapped the Velcro straps around my wrists.

"Make a fist. How do they feel?"

"Tight," I replied. "But it's fine."

His eyes narrowed. "Well, are they tight or are they fine?"

"It's fine that they're tight," I countered.

One corner of his mouth slowly turned up. He began bouncing from side to side in front of me. He held up a black rectangular pad in front of his chest. "Okay. Hit me."

Unsure of how exactly he wanted me to hit him, I threw a punch at the pad.

"Okay. Now, hit me like you mean it."

I exhaled, and tried again.

"Come on. You punch like a girl."

I tightened my fists in front of me, and threw another punch – harder this time.

"There ya go. That's how I want you to keep punching. Alternate between your left and your right. When you punch, I want you to twist from the waist," he demonstrated, "and put your back into it." He pointed at me. "Don't stop until I tell you to."

I nodded, and began mimicking what he had done, slowly at first. I picked up speed once I became more comfortable with the twisting motion. Immediately, I understood why he had told me to use my back; my punches landed with much more force than before.

"Yes, good!" T.J. exclaimed. "Harder! Let's go!"

I started to break a sweat, and I could feel my breaths becoming shorter with each punch. My arms were burning from shoulders to wrists. I wanted to take a break, to drop my arms, but I would not dare say so. I continued slamming my fists into the pad as fast as I could.

I was so focused on landing my punches, I did not hear T.J. shout, "Time!" He lowered the pad as I was in the middle of hurling my next punch. My knuckles plowed into his cheekbone.

My hands flew up to my mouth in horror. "Oh my God! I'm so sorry!"

He chuckled and wiggled his jaw. "It's been a while since someone's clipped me."

"Are you okay?"

"I'll live."

"Guess it's a good thing I punch like a girl."

"Take a look at where we are standing."

I looked down, realizing that we were no longer standing in the middle of the ring. We were about two feet from where we started.

"Is that bad?" I asked.

"You pushed your opponent backwards. That's what you want to do. It means you punched with force. It means you're in charge – you're on the offense, and your opponent is merely defending himself."

I shrugged one shoulder, trying to act nonchalant. "I meant to do that."

"Now, imagine how much better you could have done if you weren't so hungover."

I felt my cheeks flush instantly. "I'm not hungover."

"Bloodshot, baggy eyes," he pointed at my face. "You look tired and weak. Plus, you're sweating a lot."

"Maybe I just sweat a lot."

"Or maybe you drank until you puked."

We stared into each other's eyes, neither one of us wanting to break first.

He grinned. "Tanner is right. I see it in your eyes."

"See what?"

"The fight. You've got passion inside of you. That's only the first step."

"Okay. So, what's the second step?"

"You tell me."

I lifted an eyebrow. "Aren't you supposed to be the one teaching me?"

"Think about it. What else do you need besides passion to do what I do?"

I chewed my lip as I thought. "I need to know how to fight."

"Right. Over the next few months, I'll be training you how to channel your anger – to hone your emotions. You'll need to do two things, though."

"Let me guess – you want me to tell you what those two things are?"

He crossed his arms over his bare chest, wearing an amused expression. "You catch on quick."

"Okay, let me see," I said, thinking aloud. "I need to be dedicated to your training."

"That's one."

"I need to..." I looked around at everyone in the gym. "Build muscle?"

"Nope. You don't need huge muscles to be a good fighter. This one is going to be a bit of a challenge for you: you need to trust me."

I laughed once. "What makes you think that would be hard for me?"

"Call it a hunch."

I put my hands on my hips. "What exactly did Tanner tell you about me?"

"He said you went through a lot of shit, and you needed help. I plan on getting the rest of your story from you." He picked up the pad. "You're going to tell me everything I need to know."

I wondered what it was that he would need to know.

"Oh, and one other thing. Don't ever show up here hungover again."

"What does that have to do with anything?"

"If you feel like shit, you fight like shit. Plus, you look like shit."

"What does it matter what I look like?" I asked defensively. "Maybe you don't look so great yourself."

"Of course I do." He grinned as he smacked the pad several times. "Let's go."

I rolled my eyes at his arrogance, but raised my fists in front of my face. All of my focus was concentrated on hitting my target, and my mind could not wander anywhere else. The more T.J. yelled, the harder I hit. I enjoyed feeling the impact of my fists on the pad, as it rippled up my arms and jolted my body.

After a while, T.J. ditched the pad, and put his hands up to block my punches instead. We circled around each other, watching and waiting for the other to make the first move. A devious smile crept onto his face while his eyebrows lowered. I watched his body movements, trying to anticipate his plan of attack. I flinched with every step and jerk he made.

"Do you trust me?" he asked, his eyes locked on mine.

"Not for one second," I replied from behind my fists.

"I'm going to take you down," he informed. "I just need you to go with it."

"Should I be wearing headgear?"

"No, because you trust that I won't hurt you."

"How do I know you won't?"

"You don't know. That's what trust is − you give someone the chance to hurt you, and hope that they don't."

I inhaled deeply, and signaled that I was ready.

I did not even see him move. One second, I was upright on my feet, and the next second, my back smacked against the floor of the ring. T.J.'s body was pressed against mine, one hand hooked around my leg, and the other supporting the back of my head. He stared into my eyes, barely out of breath, and awaiting my reaction.

"Well, I can feel my legs," I said, wiggling my toes. "That's a good sign."

He laughed, and pulled me up to my feet as he stood. "That wasn't so bad, being vulnerable, was it?"

I tilted my head from side to side. "I'd much rather be the attacker than the one being attacked."

"That is a very informative and revealing statement." He patted his left leg. "You're going to come at me, and lift this leg up. If you ram your shoulder into me at the same time, you'll be able to tackle me to the ground. You ready?"

Now, I was the one wearing the devilish grin. "Ready." I did as he said, and slammed my left shoulder into his stomach. My right arm hooked around the back of his leg, lifting his foot up off the ground. We crashed onto the floor, though not as gracefully as when he had tackled me.

I laughed as I sat up, rubbing my shoulder. That was the most physical activity I had done since the shoulder surgery, and the dull ache was a reminder. "That was awesome."

T.J. reached out and ran his thumb over my surgery scars. Though his hands were used for causing pain, they were soft and gentle on my skin. "What happened here?"

"Shoulder surgery. Last year."

"From the accident?"

I jerked back from his touch. "You know about my accident?"

"It was all over the news. It's not exactly a secret."

I quickly stood, adjusting the waistband of my pants around my hips. "Can I hit the pad again?"

He grabbed the pad without question, and jumped to his feet. "Go."

We spent the remainder of the hour in silence, with the exception of T.J.'s commands.

Our time came to an end when Tanner stood outside of the ring, leaning against the cage.

"How'd she do?" he asked.

"I have to say, I'm impressed. Once she learns to trust me, she'll do even better." T.J. winked at me. "See you tomorrow, Adams."

"Tomorrow?" I looked to Tanner.

"In the beginning, you'll be training here every day," Tanner answered. "You can leave straight from work. That's usually when I come."

"How much does this daily training cost?"

"Thirty a month, but you don't pay until you finish your sessions."

At least it would give me something to do in the evening, other than stare at my phone and wait for Chase to call.

"There's one more rule," T.J. called as I made my way down the stairs. "No alcohol for eight weeks. You need your mind and body sharp for practice."

Clearly, Tanner had told him more than I thought. I felt embarrassed. Someone as strong as T.J. probably looked down on weak people like me. That was not the version of myself that I wanted him to see – or anyone else, for that matter.

"What did you think?" Tanner asked when we were back in his car on our way home.

"I loved it. It feels good to hit things."

"Yes, it does. That's something Chase will never be able to understand."

"He doesn't have that anger inside, like..."

"Like I do," Tanner finished.

"Like we do," I corrected. I shook my head as I stared out the window. "My friend, Tina, once told me that I didn't belong with Chase. She said I was too dark for him. I can't help feeling like he's too good for me – like maybe he deserves to be with someone... better."

"I think people like us will always feel that way. We know we're a mess, and we know we're going to make mistakes. Growing up, I always looked up to Chase. I wondered how he could be so good all the time. But I've learned: he needs people like us, just as much as we need people like him. We can't drive the darkness out with more darkness, and they can't live in the sunshine all the time. It's not real. Life is a mixture of ups and downs. That's why they say opposites attract. You need that counterpart – someone who can balance it out with you."

I watched him as he spoke, his turbulent eyes focused on the road ahead. "You should say that to Charlotte."

He looked surprised. "You think it would make a difference?"

"I think it would make all the difference."

Chapter Eleven

DAY TWO

"How was your day? Are you famous yet?"

Chase chuckled, and I felt a pang in my heart. Seeing him on FaceTime was better than only hearing his voice; still, it was not as good as seeing him in person. Though he had interrupted my last few hours of sleep, I did not mind; our time was precious, and worth it, despite the early morning wakeup call.

"Not famous yet. Just exhausted. We've been practicing by day, and performing at night."

"You're a musical superhero." I stifled a yawn.

"You should go back to sleep. You don't have to be up for another couple of hours."

"I'd rather stare at you."

"I wish I was lying next to you."

"Me, too."

"So, what do you think of this T.J. guy? Tanner raves about him like he's the second coming."

"I'm really glad we got him that gym membership. He loves it." I yawned again. "T.J. was nice, I guess. He seems really good at what he does. I like that it gives me something to do after work."

"I just want you to be happy, and feel good."

"Punching things definitely made me happy. Who knew?"

He grinned sleepily. "My warrior."

"I wish I knew when I was going to see you again."

"I'm sorry, Merritt. I feel like this whole thing is my fault. If I didn't make you come to California, none of this would have happened."

I sat up on my elbow. "You did not make me do anything. This not your fault. This did not happen because you made me go to California. This happened because..." I tried to find the words to explain what had happened to me while I was out there. "I have issues. I don't know."

He sighed, running his fingers through his hair. "I just miss you."

"Ditto, babe." I watched his eyelids begin to close, and I knew he would be asleep momentarily. "I love you," I said softly.

"I love you," he whispered back.

I watched him as he drifted off, my thumb refusing to press the button to end the call. His perfectly plump lips parted, and I wished more than anything that I could kiss them goodnight. Being apart from the person I loved had shown me how much I had taken for granted; every kiss, every touch, every scent that I once had the luxury of experiencing were now moments that I yearned to have. My heart ached in ways I never knew it could. I wondered just how much of this we could endure.

———

"YOU CAME BACK," T.J. SHOUTED FROM INSIDE THE RING AS I entered the gym.

"How else am I going to learn that Ninja Turtle spinny thing you did?"

He laughed. "That's going to take some time. We've got a lot of hurdles to jump before we get there."

I kicked off my socks and sneakers, and climbed the stairs. I tossed my sweatshirt onto the ground before swinging myself into the ring.

"Hair up, Curly Sue."

I grimaced. "Everyone used to call me that when I was little."

"Take it as a compliment. She was adorable."

"Fighters aren't adorable." I swept my hair up, and held my hands out in front of him.

"Sure they are." He slid the gloves onto my hands. "Just look at me."

I rolled my eyes. "Arrogant, much?"

He grinned. "Says the girl who rolls her eyes constantly."

I set my fists in front of my face when he picked up the pad, and prepared myself for the next hour.

"Go."

My punches started quick and forceful. Though my arms were sore from yesterday's session, I welcomed the burning sensation in my muscles.

"Today," T.J. began. "I'm going to ask you questions while you punch."

"Trying to throw me off?"

"It will help improve your concentration. It's easy to hit when there's no distractions around."

"Okay."

"What was the scariest moment in your life?"

I froze. "That's your opening question?"

"Did you expect me to ask you what your favorite color is?"

I continued punching. "Being trapped inside my car."

"What was so scary about it?"

"I thought I was going to die, and I knew it was going to hurt."

"Was it the dying part, or the pain?"

"The pain." Punch.

"You weren't afraid to die?"

"Nope." Punch, punch.

"So, you're afraid to feel pain."

"Who's not?"

"Some people like pain."

"I don't think anyone enjoys being burned alive." Punch.

"That's fair. What about love?"

"What about it?" Right, left.

"When did you have your heart completely broken?"

"When my mom walked out on me and my dad."

"Ah, see? I've struck a nerve. Your punches just got weaker."

"My mom lives on that nerve."

"Why?"

"She ruined everything when she left."

"Like what?"

"My dad killed himself." Right, left. "I crashed my car." Right, left.

"What if I told you that the only thing your mom ruined was her own life?"

"How so?"

"Your father had two choices when your mom left: fight, or flight. Those are the choices everyone gets in life. You can either fight through whatever happens to you, or you can run away from it. He chose flight. He gave up. He was weak."

My jaw clenched as I swung my fists.

"You got drunk to escape the pain. That's why you crashed. You are weak, too."

I swung even harder.

"Your mother didn't love you enough. So what? You weren't enough of a reason for your father to stay. Tough shit."

I hit the pad with all of my might.

"That feeling inside you – that twisting in your gut – that is pain. It feels like you're angry, but the anger is only there to cover up the pain. You need to learn to embrace it."

My arms fatigued, and I dropped them to my sides. "How do I embrace something that I don't want to feel?"

"You have to feel it. That's the only way through it. Allow yourself to accept whatever you're feeling in that moment. Be honest with yourself, and admit what's really bothering you. Stop rolling your eyes at everything; stop trying to run away from it all; stop trying to bottle it up; stop evading responsibility for every situation you find yourself in."

"I was in some pretty shitty situations. What the hell else was I supposed to do?"

"You are not in control of the things that happen to you, but you can control how you choose to deal with them. You always have a choice."

I held his gaze as he stared down at me. I had always thought that I was stuck suffering from the tragedies in my life – you play the hand that you're dealt, and there's nothing else that you can do because it's all out of your control. But I was not convinced of everything T.J. was saying. Not yet. I was not ready to accept responsibility for it.

"You don't know what I have been through. You don't know what it was like. I didn't have a choice in anything. She left. She made the choice for me. She should take responsibility for what she did. Not me."

"You can't take responsibility for anyone's actions but your own. If she's not ready to take responsibility for her shit, then that's on her. Don't be like your parents. You need to get up and fight. You can't stay on the ground curled up in a ball every time something bad comes your way."

"I'm still here, aren't I?"

"Drunk and barely surviving is not the same as living and overcoming."

"No, but it's easier," I retorted.

"It takes more courage to stay and face your problems than it does to run away from them. Right now, you need to decide something: are you a coward, Merritt? Or are you a fighter?"

I tightened my fists. "I'm a fighter."

"Saying it, and being it are two different things."

"That's why I'm coming here every day, with you. So you can teach me how to fight."

"Okay, then." He lowered the pad, and his eyes narrowed. "One last question for you."

I inhaled, preparing myself for what he was about to ask.

"Do you like pizza?"

My face twisted into a confused expression. "Pizza?"

"You came here from work, and it is now seven o'clock. Are you hungry?"

"I am a little hungry," I admitted.

"Let's go grab a slice next door. We can continue this conversation there."

"I don't want to take up your time. I can just eat when I get home."

"I didn't say you were taking up my time, did I?" He looked at me expectantly.

"No."

"So, let's go."

T.J. was so confident in everything he said, he left no room for anything else. If he said it, he meant it. Cut and dry. I liked that about him.

While I stepped back into my sneakers, he threw a shirt on over his head. I tried to keep from laughing.

"What's so funny?" he asked, giving me the side-eye.

I gestured to what was once a t-shirt that would now barely qualify as a tank top because of how much material he had cut off. "Why even bother putting a shirt on?"

"Listen, Merritt. You're cute and all, but I think we should keep it strictly professional for the sake of my program. You can't be telling me to take my clothes off."

My jaw dropped open as he walked towards the front door.

He spun around to see my reaction as he walked backwards. "What? No snarky comeback? That's disappointing, Adams!"

I huffed and stomped past him out the door.

As soon as I stepped into the pizzeria next door, the aroma of delicious New York pizza filled my nostrils, causing me to salivate on the spot.

"I forgot how much I missed pizza," I murmured.

"Why did you have to miss it?" T.J. asked. He stood beside me in front of the glass counter, surveying the different pies on display.

"I was in California for the past month and a half. Nobody else does pizza like we do."

"What can I get ya?" the man in a white apron asked.

"Two plain slices. Well done, please."

"The usual for me," T.J. responded. "And one of those with everything on it."

"You got it, boss."

I followed T.J. to a booth at the far end of the restaurant. It was fairly crowded, and he seemed to know everyone there. I watched the two high school girls working behind the counter giggle to each other after T.J. waved to them.

"So, why did you go to California?" He leaned his elbows onto the table while we awaited the arrival of our food.

"My boyfriend is a singer. Tanner's brother, Chase. He's getting a record deal."

He stared at me blankly. "That doesn't answer my question."

"You asked me why I went to California. I said I went because my boyfriend had to go there." I returned the blank stare. "How does that not answer your question?"

"I asked why you went. You told me why your boyfriend went."

"I went because he went." I crossed my arms. "He said he wouldn't go unless I went with him."

"Well that doesn't sound very fair. I'm surprised you even went."

My eyebrows pressed together. "What are you talking about?"

"He pressured you to make the choice that would be in his favor. It's like an ultimatum."

I laughed once. "No. You don't know him. It was nothing like that."

"Okay. If he's so wonderful, why did you come back?"

One of the giggly school girls brought out T.J.'s tray of food, followed by her giggly friend who was carrying mine. "Let me know if there's anything else you need," she cooed.

"Everything looks great here. Thanks." Completely oblivious, he took a giant bite out of his grilled chicken sandwich while the girls scampered off, whispering to each other the entire way back.

"You're a real ladies' man."

"Those aren't ladies. Those are kids." He held up his sandwich. "Want to try a bite?"

"No, thanks. I'm all about my pizza right now." I shoved the end of the slice into my mouth, and closed my eyes to savor the moment.

"When you're done chewing, you can tell me why you left California."

I frowned. "You're ruining my pizza."

"The sooner you stop trying to avoid this conversation, the sooner it will be over."

I put my pizza down, and stared at him while I finished chewing.

He grinned his boyish grin, patiently waiting, with part of his sandwich balled up in his cheek.

"You want to know what happened? Chase asked me to go with him to California. I said I'd think about it. The next day, my mom knocked on my door, after being gone for eight years, and completely caught me off guard. I left for California several days later, got a job as a bartender, and started drinking a lot. I told myself I would stop, but I couldn't. So, I left." I shrugged. "The end."

"You want to know what I just heard?"

"No, but you're going to tell me anyway."

"You were unsure about going to California with your rock star boyfriend, but your mom came back into your life and threw you for a loop. So, you ran to get away from her. Once you got to California, your feelings caught up with you – and you ran from them, again. You tried numbing your pain with alcohol, but my guess is Chase caught on, and wasn't happy about it – and what did you do? Ran from that problem, too. All that running. How is that working out for you?"

"Do you think I should have remained in California? I'd probably be a full-blown alcoholic by now. I had to get out of there."

"Don't you see what the root of all your problems are? The one thing that connects everything in your life?"

"It's my mother. I told you – she ruined everything!"

"You're right. It is your mother. She is the root where all of the issues you've created stem from. So, what are you going to do about it?"

I rolled my eyes. "If you're going to tell me to talk to her, you can just save it. I have no interest in talking to her. Ever."

T.J. set his sandwich down on his plate. "Your attitude is doing nothing for you. You're only going to continue to spiral downward if you don't stop this unhealthy pattern you've created. You have to be ready to stand up and say that you've had enough. If you're not ready to change, then there's nothing I can do for you."

"You know what?" I rummaged in my purse for my wallet, and tossed a five dollar bill onto the table. "I have had enough. I've had enough of your interrogation and your verbal abuse. Enjoy the rest of your sandwich." I slid out of the booth, and stormed out the door.

I had made it back to my car before T.J. ran out into the parking lot. I was just about to back out of the spot when my passenger door opened.

"Get out of my car, please."

T.J. swung the door closed, and fastened his seatbelt. "I'm going to show you something. Drive."

I hesitated. "I'm tired, T.J. I just want to go home."

"We won't be out long. I promise."

"Where are we going?"

"Take Arthur Kill Road, and I'll tell you when to turn off."

I exhaled, and reluctantly followed his directions. I drove in silence, growing more curious with every turn I made.

"Pull in here." T.J. pointed to the parking lot on my left.

"Uh, that's a prison."

"Kill the engine. I'm going to tell you something."

Without the headlights from my car, the former correctional facility looked eerie in the darkness. Now closed down, the abandoned building was surrounded by nothing but barbed wire and trees.

T.J. removed his hat, and pointed to the scar above his left eyebrow. "You see this? This was from my dad. I was twelve."

I raised my eyebrows. "Was he a fighter, too?"

"No. He was a drunk. He beat the shit out of my mom whenever he had too much to drink. He got me good a few times, too. He drank, and he turned into a different person – not that he was so great when he was sober. I was five when I saw him hit my mom for the first time. Needless to say, I had a lot of fear, and a lot of anger growing up."

"Why did your mom stay?"

"That was the choice she made. She didn't feel like she could get away from him. She didn't think she could make ends meet without him. There's a laundry list of all the excuses she told herself."

I chewed my lip before asking my next question. "Why are we here?"

"My dad used to be in there, before they closed down and transported all the prisoners upstate." He looked out the windshield as he spoke, and his eyes glazed over as if he was somewhere else. "I was trying to get him off of her one night. He was beating on her real bad.

I was a scrawny twelve-year old. I punched him in the back a few times, but he elbowed me in the head," he recalled, rubbing his scar. "I was knocked out for a few minutes. When I came to, he was holding my mom up against the wall by her throat, and there was nothing I could do. Her feet twitched, and then they just... dangled. I watched him choke the life right out of her."

My hands covered my mouth to hide my mortified expression. "Oh my God."

"After that, I was placed into foster home after foster home. Nobody wanted to deal with an angry, disturbed teenager. I got into a lot of trouble. I was mad at the world."

"How did you end up where you are now?"

"The last home I went to was the home of an old boxer. He straightened me out, and taught me everything I know. I had to learn how to work through my anger, and stop running from it. I learned that my childhood would always be a part of who I am, but it didn't have to be the only thing that defined who I would become."

I looked down at my lap, feeling foolish for being so upset about my problems when T.J. had been through an even worse hell. I could not even imagine what that must have been like for him. He had been through tough times – he had once been weak. If he could survive everything he endured, and come out stronger on the other side, then I should be able to do the same.

He lifted my chin with his finger. "Don't feel sorry for me. I don't. Not anymore."

Looking into his blue eyes, my frustration with him melted away. He was not being hard on me to be an asshole. He knew exactly what I was going through, and he knew he was capable of getting me through it. All he needed was for me to believe that he could – to trust him.

"Thank you for sharing that story with me."

"I hope that you want to keep training."

"I do. I just don't know how to do this."

He smiled. "That's why you have me."

Chapter Twelve

THE WAY YOU NEED TO BE LOVED

"Do you have to train today?" Shelly whined. "It's Friday night. Can't you just say you're not feeling well, or something?"

"No, Shell. It's important and you know it."

"I know. Can we go get dinner when you're done? I'm starving."

"Sure. No Brody tonight?"

"Nope. He's doing poker night with the guys."

"Okay, I'm just pulling up now. Think about where you want to eat. I'll call you when I'm done." I quickly jogged from my car to the gym doors.

"You're late, Curly Sue."

"I know, I know. It was crazy at work today." I tore off my sweatshirt, and kicked off my sneakers as quickly as I could.

"Excuses, excuses." T.J. wagged his finger at me from inside the ring.

"I texted you that I got held up at work."

"Drop and give me ten." He stood with his hands on his hips, a smug expression on his face.

I rolled my eyes, and saluted him. "Sir, yes sir." Dropping to the floor, I began my set of push-ups.

"You can give me five extra for rolling your eyes at me."

"My eye roll is totally involuntary. I have no control over what they do."

"You have control over everything you do. The sooner you realize that, the better off you'll be."

I stopped in the middle of my push-up and stood.

"You're not done. What are you doing?"

"You said I have control over everything I do." I put my hands on my hips. "I'm not doing another push-up."

He stared back at me, with a slow smile creeping across his face. "Okay. You win."

I grinned triumphantly.

"Don't get too ahead of yourself. You still have to follow my rules."

I raised my fists up near my nose. "Let's go."

For the next hour, we circled each other in the ring. We fell into our rhythm, like we were long-time dance partners. My body anticipated his movements, and reacted to them accordingly. My energy was calm, and my mind was focused; I thought about nothing more than throwing my next punch.

I had now trained with T.J. for a week. Every day had felt like Groundhog's Day: work, train, sleep, and repeat. Though it was monotonous, the routine was healthy for me. Training with T.J. was therapeutic. We had bonded on a level that I had never bonded with anyone else; he was the first person I knew who had suffered in life the way I had. I understood him, and he understood me.

"Hey, T.J.!" someone called, braking my concentration. "Where do you want these?" Two men were carrying a long table through the front doors of the gym.

"Right over there by the front desk," T.J. called. "Sorry," he said turning back to me. "I lost track of time."

"What are those for?" I asked.

"I'm having an open house tonight. Anybody that is interested in joining can come check the gym out, and meet our trainers. I invite other vendors from the area to come promote their businesses; that brings more potential customers that wouldn't normally be here. There will be food and music. It's a good time. You should come."

"Can I bring my friend?"

"Of course. It's from seven to ten."

"Okay. I'll be back."

Once I was inside my car, I hit Shelly's name on my phone.

"Finally! I'm withering away to nothing over here!"

"Why couldn't you just eat a snack while you were waiting for me?"

"I'm so weak from hunger, I couldn't get off the couch."

I rolled my eyes. "Dinner's at seven. I'll be at your place by 6:45. Dress casual."

"Oh!" she exclaimed. "We're going on a date!"

I laughed. "Goodbye."

After a quick shower, I threw on jeans and a light sweater. The end-of-April weather was finally warming up, and I was grateful to slip into my flats instead of boots. I missed the California sunshine and perfect temperatures; I missed Chase even more. I checked my phone while I waited for Shelly to come out of her apartment. No new messages or calls.

Shelly emerged from her apartment with a big smile, excited to begin our night. Her red hair bounced around her shoulders as she skipped to the car. "Where are we going?"

"T.J. is having an open house tonight. He said there will be food and music. I figured we could eat for free."

"In the gym?" she crinkled her nose.

"Yeah. It seems like a big event. He was setting up when I left earlier."

"Will there be shirtless, muscular fighters there?"

"I don't know if they will be shirtless, but there should be plenty of muscles."

"I suppose that will have to do." She checked her makeup in the visor mirror.

"How's everything with you and Brody?"

"Fine," she sighed.

I looked at her out of the corner of my eye. "Want to try that once more, with feeling?"

"Can we just discuss it later?"

"Sure." I wondered what was going on between the lifelong love-birds. I pulled into my usual spot in front of the gym. Red and black balloons were now tied to the door handle, and I could see how crowded it was through the glass windows.

Inside, a DJ was spinning current dance songs in the middle of the ring. Trays of food lined the wall to the right; vendors from the neighborhood were at their booths to the left.

"It's huge in here!" Shelly said. "It doesn't look this big from outside."

"I know." I scanned the room for T.J., but could not find him.

Shelly made a beeline for the food line, and handed me a plate. "I wonder where the food is from."

"I would assume somewhere nearby. It looks great." We piled out plates high with chicken, pasta, and vegetables, and stood over to the side.

Shelly grabbed my arm. "Holy hotness. Look at him!"

When I turned my head in the direction of Shelly's gaze, I smiled. T.J. was walking towards us from the far side of the gym. His red baseball cap was on backwards, and he was wearing his usual black t-shirt with the sleeves cut off, exposing his tattoos and shredded obliques.

"That's T.J."

Shelly's mouth dropped open as she looked at me. "That is T.J.? That is the guy you've been training with for the past week?" She looked back at him, and then at me. "He is gorgeous!"

I looked down at my plate of food. "Stop making it so obvious that you're staring at him."

"I'm not."

"Your eyes are so wide, they might pop out of your head, and I could use a shovel to scrape your jaw up off the floor. You're right – totally discreet."

"Is he walking in slow motion, or is it just me?" Shelly whispered, as T.J. walked within earshot.

"I think your brain is in slow motion," I muttered.

Shelly burst out laughing.

"What's so funny?" T.J. asked as he crossed his arms over his chest.

"Why don't you ask Shelly?" I gestured to my left with an innocent smile.

"Hi, Shelly." T.J. extended his hand for a shake.

"Hi, Shelly. I'm T.J.," Shelly said. "I mean... Shelly. I'm Shelly. You're T.J. But you know that. Of course you know that. It's your name." She laughed nervously, and I watched her cheeks turn the same color as her hair.

"We don't let her out much," I joked, leaning in.

T.J. grinned. "It's a pleasure to meet you, Shelly." He turned his attention to me. "I'm glad you came."

"The place looks great. There's so many people here."

He nodded proudly.

Suddenly, I heard a high-pitched squeal. "Merry!"

A tiny human was running at me, full-speed. Tanner was not far behind, walking towards us with his usual strut.

"Khloe!" I exclaimed. I handed Shelly my plate, and scooped her up as she crashed into me. "What are you doing here?"

"Tanner said I could hit the punching bags if I was a good listener." Her eyes were wide with excitement as she pointed to the bags across the gym.

"Who is this adorable young lady?" T.J. asked, amused.

"This is Khloe. She's Chase's little sister." I gestured to Tanner. "Tanner's sister, too."

T.J. stuck his hand out for Khloe to shake. "It's so nice to meet you, Khloe."

Her hand looked even tinier than usual inside of his. She wrapped her arms around my neck after shaking his hand. "I missed you so much, Merry. Mommy said I had to give you some space until you were feeling better. Were you frowing up?"

"I was sick, but I'm feeling much better now."

"Yay! Can we have pancakes tomorrow?"

"I have to work in the morning, but we can absolutely have pancakes on Sunday."

"Merry lets me help her make pancakes," Khloe said to T.J. matter-of-factly.

"I bet you make the best pancakes." His eyes sparkled as he looked at her with his huge smile. Khloe had the ability to make everyone happy.

Tanner held out his arms and took her from me. "Let's go hit the bags. Let Merry finish eating."

She waved feverishly. "Bye, Merry! See you later!"

"That is one adorable kid," said T.J. "She loves you."

"Merritt has that effect on people." Shelly wrapped her arm around my hips.

"I don't doubt that," he said with a wink. "If you ladies will excuse me, I am going to make my rounds and say hello to everyone. There are some tables over there," he pointed. "You don't have to stand while you eat."

"Thanks." I tugged on Shelly's elbow. "Let's go sit."

"I cannot believe I sounded like such an idiot!" Shelly whined when she plopped into a chair.

I shook my head. "I can't believe it either. I've never seen you get like that before."

"I've never been in the presence of such a beautiful man! How do you even concentrate when you're training?" Her eyes widened. "Have you seen him without a shirt on?"

I laughed. "Yes, I have. He's good-looking, but that's not what I'm focused on while I'm throwing punches."

"I'd let him throw me around that ring any day," she murmured, her eyes following him through the gym.

"Okay, spill. What is happening with you and Brody?"

She shrugged, suddenly at a loss for words. "It's nothing."

"If you guys break up, I don't think I can handle it. My mental stability relies on the two of you, so you better work your shit out."

"We've just been together forever. What if he's not who I am supposed to end up with? What if I never know what else is out there? How can I be sure if I've never dated anyone else?"

"Where is this coming from, all of a sudden?"

She pushed her vegetables around in her plate. "He keeps talking about getting engaged after graduation."

"Shelly, that's great!"

"I don't know. I feel like we're too young to be engaged."

"Says who? Society? If you love each other, and you want to spend the rest of your lives together, who cares if you're young?"

She shifted her gaze as she took her last sip of water.

"I'll get us more water, and a few of those chocolate chip cookies. We will talk through this, and you will feel better."

She nodded. "Maybe a slice of that cake will help, too."

"You got it." I made my way to the dessert tables, deep in thought about what to say to Shelly when I returned. It was unlike her to imagine a life without Brody in it. They had been inseparable since they were ten.

"Leave some dessert for everyone else," T.J. said from behind me.

"Shelly's having a boy emergency. This is the standard amount of sugar that's needed for these types of things."

"And how's everything going for you with California?"

"Fine, I guess. We don't really talk much. He's so busy all the time."

"I'm still so surprised to hear that you're with a guy like that."

I raised an eyebrow and turned to face him. "A guy like what?"

"I didn't expect you to be with the all-American, Mr. Perfect type."

I half-laughed. "I don't know if I should be offended right now."

"I just meant that you seem like you'd go for someone with a little more..." he trailed off while he searched his mind for the right word. "Substance."

"Chase has a lot of substance," I defended. "I used to think the same way you did, but then I got to know him. He's amazing."

He raised his eyes to meet mine. "As long as you're happy, and you're getting treated right. That's all that matters."

"I am."

"Long distance is hard. It takes a lot of dedication."

"Well, I'm dedicated." I shoved his shoulder playfully. "I'm here every night of the week with you, aren't I?"

He laughed. "Okay. Go bring the cookies for your sugar emergency. We'll continue this tomorrow."

"Oh, goodie," I rolled my eyes.

T.J. grinned. "I should make you drop and give me twenty."

"But you won't." I smiled innocently over my shoulder as I walked back to Shelly. Tanner and Khloe had joined her in my absence. Khloe was resting her head on Tanner's shoulder, which was the signal that she was getting sleepy.

"We're going to hit the road," Tanner said. "Squirt wanted to say goodnight to you first."

I knelt down beside Tanner's chair and stroked Khloe's golden hair. Looking at her was like looking at a mini-sized Chase. It made my heart hurt.

"I'll see you on Sunday for pancakes, okay angel girl?"

She nodded. "Can we make chocolate chip pancakes?"

"Of course we can."

Tanner stood with her in his arms. She waved to us one last time before he carried her out the door.

"I wonder what your kid will look like. You're so dark, and Chase is so light," Shelly mused, resting her chin in her hand.

"Eat your cake, and tell me what has gotten into you."

"I really don't know. Everything going on with you and Chase lately really has me thinking."

"About what?"

"About life. How are you and Chase going to make this work when you're on opposite sides of the country? Is your relationship strong enough to withstand the distance? What if you guys grow apart? What if he meets someone else? What if you meet someone else? You know the saying: out of sight, out of mind."

"Get to your point quickly, please," I warned.

"When I think about your future, it makes me think about mine. Where will life take me? Where will it take Brody? We've always been in the same spot our entire lives. We've never had to go through any hardships. What if this isn't it for us? What if we're meant to be with other people?"

"You've been in love with each other since you were ten. There's no one else in this world that you're meant to be with. You've withstood the test of time, which is so hard to do. You're perfect for each other."

"How can you be so sure?"

"Because I know how much he loves you. I have watched it my entire life. He stood by you through everything with your dad, and he's stood by me through everything with mine. He is the best person I know – nobody else out there could ever compare to Brody. I've seen how much you love him, too, Shell. You would be lost without him."

Tears began to well up in her eyes. "Am I awful for thinking this way?"

"Not at all. It's normal to wonder about all the what-ifs in life. It's especially normal to worry when you're nearing the end of college. It means that your childhood is officially over, and you have to be a grown-up. It's terrifying."

"All my life, I've never imagined being with anyone else. It's always been Brody. Now, he's talking about getting engaged, and taking the next step... what if I'm not ready to be married, yet?"

"You live together. What's the difference if you have a ring on your finger? It's all the same. Just with a different last name."

"It's just so... final."

"Death is final. Marriage is reversible. But you don't need to worry about that. If you're truly not ready to get engaged, then tell Brody that. He'll understand."

"Will he, though? It's part of our plan – we get engaged after we graduate."

"You're not graduating for another year. You have time. Maybe you will feel differently, then... and if you don't, you adjust the plan."

"I guess so." Her eyes scanned the room, and settled upon T.J. "If things with Chase don't work out in the end, you have to go for him."

I laughed. "I'm still dumb enough to hope things work out with Chase."

"Don't call my best friend dumb." She picked up a chocolate chip cookie for herself, and handed me another. "Whatever happens in our love lives, at least we have each other."

I tapped my cookie against hers, and took a bite. "I'll cheers to that."

———

IT FELT ODD, YET NATURAL BEING AT CHASE'S HOUSE WITHOUT Chase. I was comfortable there, but it felt like something was missing. It didn't help to remember that Chase wasn't the only one missing. I kissed my fingertips and placed them on Tim's urn in the living room.

"Miss you," I said softly.

"I'm ready!" Khloe called from upstairs.

I met her at the bottom of the staircase, and she took my hand to lead me into the kitchen.

Beverly, still in her Sunday morning robe, looked up from her pile of papers at the dining room table. "I left everything on the counter for you, Merritt."

"Thank you," I called back to her.

I lifted Khloe's tiny body and sat her on the counter. "What would you like to be in charge of?"

"I want to crack the eggs, and I want to help flip the pancakes!"

I handed her two eggs, and slid the bowl across the countertop. "Get crackin'!"

She giggled as she tapped the egg against the bowl. I measured and poured the rest of the ingredients, and handed the whisk to Khloe when she had finished. We were a good team, and I could never feel anything but happy whenever I was around her.

"T.J. has so many tattoos," she said while I poured the first pancake onto the griddle.

"He does. Do you like them?"

She scrunched her nose up. "I don't know."

"No is the correct answer," Beverly called from the other room.

I stifled a smile. "Do you know how people get tattoos onto their skin?"

Khloe shook her head.

"They carve it on with a needle," Tanner said, joining us in the kitchen.

Khloe's eyes widened. "Doesn't that hurt?"

"Yup." He leaned on the counter next to us. "I think I'm going to get one later."

I raised both eyebrows at him. "Of what?"

"I haven't figured it out yet."

"Oh, God. Tanner!" Beverly yelled. "Please don't get something spur of the moment. It's going to be on your body for the rest of your life."

"Can I come with you?" I whispered.

Tanner's eyebrows shot up. "You want one, too?"

"I want to see what it's like first."

"Sure, thing, sis. I'll be your guinea pig."

"I want a guinea pig!" Khloe exclaimed.

"Those things are rats, you know," he replied.

"But they're so cute!"

"We are not getting any pets right now," Beverly answered.

I giggled. "Okay, flipper. It's time."

I guided the spatula while Khloe did her best to flip the pancake. They never actually flipped successfully, but it made her so proud to do it that I didn't mind the mess.

Tanner made a face when he watched the batter go everywhere.

I raised my finger to my lips. "Make yourself useful and set the table, would ya?"

He stuck his tongue out at me, and began pulling plates out from the cabinet.

When the pancakes were ready, we sat down to eat. Beverly pushed her pile of papers to the empty space where Tim once sat.

"What's all that?" I asked, motioning with my fork.

"I'm trying to figure out if we can afford to hire another person at the shop." She took a sip of coffee from her World's Best Mom mug. "We need help, but I don't want it to stretch us too thin."

"I keep telling you," Tanner groaned. "We're fine. We don't need to hire anyone new."

"I don't want my kids being worked to the bone. You're already there way past closing, and I'm drowning in paperwork." She gestured to the papers next to her. "Your father used to help me with everything."

"I can help you with the paperwork," I suggested. "I'm good with computers."

"We can't take you off the floor," Tanner chimed in.

"It wouldn't be during my normal work hours."

"No way." Beverly waved her hands in protest. "You're not doing this on your free time."

"Why not? I think it's a great idea."

"It's too much." She rubbed her eyes, and ran her fingers through her hair. Another shot to my heart as I was reminded of Chase.

We finished eating in silence. I would convince Beverly to let me help her, but I needed a little help. I devised a plan while we ate. After we cleaned up, I caught Tanner in the kitchen.

"Charlotte is a business major, right?"

"Yeah. Why?" He flinched at the sound of her name.

"Is she talking to you, yet?"

He shook his head. "What are you thinking?"

"Your mom won't let me help her, but I wonder if she would let Charlotte." I looked in his eyes, hoping to see a spark of understanding.

"Why would she let Charlotte help and not you?"

"Because she would be under the impression that she was helping you get back together with Charlotte." I began to smile at my clever plan. "Plus, it would force you and Charlotte to spend more time together, which in turn would inevitably cause you two to actually get back together... for real."

Tanner's eyes narrowed as he tried to understand what I was proposing.

"Just give me her number. I'll handle it."

"If it will get us back together, I'll do whatever you say."

"Good. I'm going to work on step one of my plan." I walked back into the dining room and sat down next to Beverly.

"What was he whispering about?" she asked quietly.

I sighed for dramatic effect. "He's in a fight with Charlotte, and they aren't speaking to each other."

"Is that why he's been so mopey lately? I knew something was going on between them. I hate seeing him like this."

"I know. He's head over heels in love with her. They're just young and stubborn."

She nodded. "He got all the stubbornness out of the three kids. It wasn't evenly rationed at all."

I laughed. "I think I have an idea about how to get them talking, though." I chewed my lip to build the anticipation. "I would need your help."

"Oh?" She swiveled in her chair to face me. "I'm intrigued."

"Tanner knows you're swamped with paperwork. So, what if I

talked to Charlotte, and got her to agree to take a part-time managerial position as part of an internship for her business experience? It's a win for her, because she could gain hands-on experience; it's a win for Tanner, because she would be around the shop while he's there; and it's a win for you, because you'll get free help."

She looked at me with knowing eyes. "Merritt, you are an extraordinary young woman. Do you know that?"

I shrugged. "Maybe you could even invite her to come for dinner once or twice."

"That would get them talking again. How are we going to get her to agree to this idea, though? What if she turns it down?"

"Then you'll just have to let me help you with the paperwork – and I won't take no for an answer."

She sighed in defeat. "Fine. You have a deal, Miss Adams." She held her hand out, and we shook on it. "I'm so glad Chase found you."

I looked down at the table. "Yeah. I can fix everyone else's problems except my own."

"Everything is going to be okay in the end. I promise you. The love that Chase and you have for each other will carry you through anything. Look at how far it has gotten you both already. It seems like just yesterday he was driving you to physical therapy, and telling me how incredible you were."

My eyebrows lifted. "Really?"

Tanner waltzed into the room. "Please. We'd have to sit through an entire dinner and listen to every detail about your conversations. I wanted to stab myself in the eye with my fork just to put myself out of my misery."

Beverly laughed. She placed her hand on my shoulder. "When Chase fell in love with you, we all did, too."

"Clearly," I joked, gesturing to Tanner.

He grinned. "Come on. Let's go hit the bags."

I leaned over and gave Beverly a hug. "Everything is going to be okay for you, too, you know. You are not alone in this."

She squeezed me tightly before letting me go.

Once we were inside Tanner's car, I dialed Charlotte's number on my phone.

"You're calling her now?" he asked, nervous and excited at the same time.

I nodded, waiting for her to answer.

"Hello?"

"Hi, Charlotte. It's Merritt."

"Uh, hi, Merritt. What's up? Is everything okay?"

"Yeah, everything is fine. I'm calling because I have a business proposition for you."

It was silent on the other line while she tried to figure out what I was talking about. I covered my mouth, trying not to giggle, as Tanner hit my leg.

"What do you mean?" she asked.

"Beverly has been having a hard time with the shop ever since Tim passed."

"Oh, no. That's terrible."

"We need an extra hand in there, but she can't afford to hire someone. I remembered that you are a business major, and I figured I would take a shot in the dark to see if you would be interested in gaining some experience running a business. Tanner and I have the labor handled, but you would be helping Beverly behind the desk with her end of things. Think of it as an internship in a manager's position."

"Wow. A manager? That's a lot to take on."

"It's really not, because you'd simply be assisting Beverly. You'd be like her right hand woman, and you'd oversee everything she does. It would be a great learning experience for you."

It was silent again.

I knew I almost had her. "Look. I know you and Tanner are broken up, and I know you probably don't want to see him. But you don't have to worry about that, because he would be in the garage, and you'd be in a totally different area inside the office."

I heard her blowing air out. "This would be a great opportunity. My dad doesn't exactly involve me in what he does at the bakery."

"Great. I'll let Beverly know. Can you start tomorrow?"

"Tomorrow? Wow, so soon. Uh..."

Tanner and I held up our hands, crossing our fingers while we awaited her response.

"You'll be there, too, right?"

"Yep. Monday through Saturday."

"Okay. I'll do it."

Tanner smacked the steering wheel in excitement.

"Thanks so much, Charlotte. This is really going to save their business. Beverly will be so thrilled."

"I'm glad I can help. It broke my heart watching what Tanner had to go through when he lost his dad."

"He loves you. You know that, right?"

She paused before answering. "It's hard. We're just so different. I don't think he's capable of change."

"That's not your call to make. It's up to him if he wants to change. Change is hard, but if he sets his mind to it, then he will. I know it's killing him not being with you. He's heartbroken."

"Is he?"

"He is. Whatever he did, try to forgive him for it. Let him make it up to you. We all deserve second chances."

"Thanks for calling, Merritt. I'll see you at work tomorrow."

"See you."

Tanner pulled into the gym parking lot and killed the engine. He stared out the windshield, deep in thought.

"I've got your back, little brother." I patted his giant shoulder before hoisting myself out of the car. I was eager to get into the ring.

T.J. was waiting for me inside, as usual, checking his watch.

"You're early."

"Maybe you should have to drop and give me twenty this time," I countered.

He grinned. "It would be a cold day in hell if I let that happen."

I kicked off my sneakers, and tossed my hoodie onto the floor. "I just might make you eat your words someday."

T.J. flung his hat outside the ring, and pulled off his t-shirt.

I remembered Shelly's incoherent babbling from the other night, and tried not to smile. "You made quite the impression on my friend Friday night."

He held up the pad. "Is that so?"

I began throwing my two-punch combination to warm up. "I've

never seen her get so tongue-tied before. You must get that all the time."

"I do alright, I guess."

"The fighter covered in tattoos with the rippling muscles is modest?"

He chuckled while he blocked my punches. "I'm actually not as much of an arrogant asshole as you think I am."

"I don't think you're an asshole."

"Oh, just arrogant, then?"

I smiled, and continued punching.

"Alright, Curly Sue. Let's change it up."

I followed him out of the ring, and over to a massive tire that I had seen grizzly men toss around.

"You're going to flip this before I let you leave."

I blew air out of my mouth, and knelt down, scooting my fingers underneath the hard rubber edges. I pulled upward, but the tire barely budged. I now understood why those men grunted so loudly while they did this. "This is too heavy. I can't do this."

"If you think you can't, then you can't."

I resisted the urge to roll my eyes, and stuck my fingers under the tire for a second time. I pulled until my fingers were sore.

"Lift with your legs," T.J. yelled. "Push through your heels."

I dug my heels into the floor.

"It's like a squat. Push up."

Following his commands, I felt the tire begin to rise. I had lifted it up to my waist when it went smashing back down to the ground. "This is so dumb," I grumbled.

"Again," T.J. commanded.

I lifted the tire to my waist for a second time, and tried desperately to get enough leverage to flip it over.

"Get under it!"

"I'm trying!" I yelled back.

"Try harder!"

The more he yelled at me, the angrier I got; the angrier I got, the stronger I felt. I walked myself underneath the tire, bent my knees slightly, and pushed up through my legs with all of my might. The tire finally left my hands and went crashing to the ground onto the other side.

I dropped to the ground and sprawled out on my back, gasping for air. "That... sucked... so bad," I breathed.

T.J. chuckled and stretched out beside me. He folded his arms back behind his head, and his tattoos stretched with his skin. I allowed my eyes to travel over his body while I caught my breath.

"So, I'm thinking about getting a tattoo."

His eyebrows shot up. "Out of the blue?"

"I stare at yours every day. It's not exactly out of the blue."

"What are you thinking of getting?"

"I don't know, yet. Tanner's getting one. I told him I'd go with him to watch."

"I told him to see my buddy, John. He did all of mine. If you decide to get one, you should have him do it. He's the best."

"Do yours all mean something?"

"They do. I got them at different points throughout my life."

I pointed to the woman's face imprinted onto his ribcage. She was beautiful, with dark eyes and long wavy hair. Her lips were turned up into a slight smile. "Who is that?"

"That's my mom."

"Wow." I leaned in and ran my fingertips over his slightly raised skin, following the ink swirls in her hair. "She was beautiful."

"She was." He stared up at the lights hanging high above us. "What was your life like before your mom left?" he asked.

I laughed. "My life was what you would call normal. My parents went everywhere together, and did everything together. I never saw them fight. My dad loved my mom more than anything; he adored her. They were high school sweethearts. I would always ask him to tell me the story of how they met. No matter how many times I heard it, I was amazed at how he certain he was that she would be the person he would marry one day – just from talking to her one time.

When she left, it was so out-of-the-blue, it didn't even seem real. She kissed me goodbye as I left for school that morning; by the time I got home, she was gone. I was scared, confused, hurt – but when I watched the breakdown of my father, I had to put my feelings aside. It was like he couldn't function without her. Over the years, his drinking got worse, and he sank deeper into his depression. I had to do everything. I was paying the water bill and studying for my algebra test. I always tried to make him feel better – like maybe if I do this one thing, he will snap out of it... but he never did. I found him bleeding out in the tub last year. I think that's when the switch flipped in me. I just shut down."

"It makes sense," T.J. replied. "You held it together for so long because you had a reason to. You were busy taking care of your father – your mind was preoccupied, and your feelings were on the back burner. When you lost your father, you had no one to take care of but yourself. All of your focus was on you, and you didn't know how to deal with the things you felt because you had bottled them up for so long."

"I was so angry. It came on all of a sudden – like a tsunami of rage."

"Rage is like that. It's an addictive thing."

"I blamed my mother for everything. How could I not? She was the first domino to fall, and she knocked down all of my other dominoes. If she never left, none of this would have happened."

"You don't know that, Merritt. There is no way for you to know what could have happened. Sometimes, we are led to the same path no matter which route we take. If your father relied that heavily on your mother for his happiness, there's no telling what would have happened down the line. That's why it is so important for you to take responsibility for your own actions, and create your own happiness, independent from anyone or anything else." He sat up on his elbows. "I have to be honest with you. I'm a little worried about your long distance relationship, and how it will affect you."

I rolled onto my side to face him, propping my head up with my hand. "What do you mean, how it will affect me?"

"When you've gone through the kind of shit we've been through, you need stability; you need someone who can be there for you when you need it – someone you can count on. I worry that you will be left with more disappointments than happy moments; more loneliness than affection; more sadness than laughter; more emptiness than fulfillment. I know you love him, and I'm sure he loves you, too; but, you need someone to love you the way you need to be loved."

"How do I need to be loved?" I was almost too afraid to ask, unsure if what he said would compare to what I currently had.

T.J. was about to say something, but stopped himself. He shook his head as he sat up. "I can't tell you that. That is something you need to ask yourself."

"You two are supposed to be fighting, not sleeping," Tanner called from several feet away.

I sprang up onto my feet. "Are we going to get your tattoo now?"

"Yup. You getting yours, too?"

"Not yet. I need to think of something good, first."

"What are you getting done?" T.J. asked him.

"John is drawing something up for me. I told him I wanted something for my dad."

"Does Beverly know?" I asked, raising an eyebrow.

"No, but I'm hoping once she sees it – she will be happy with it."

"If she kicks you out, you can always ask Charlotte to crash at her place." I dug my elbow into his ribs as I waved goodbye to T.J.

T.J. shook his head at me. "Goodbye, Curly Sue."

Tanner looked nervous as he sat in John's chair ten minutes later. I sat in a chair beside him, anxiously waiting for the skin branding ritual to begin.

T.J.'s friend, John, was prepping his needle, and set up the ink on his tray. His earlobes were stretched out with enormous black gauges; his bald head was offset by his long braided beard; his arms were covered in colorful tattoos, sprawling out onto the tops of his hands. Though his exterior was loud, his voice was low and even.

"How do you know T.J.?" he asked, peering at me over the rim of his thick black glasses.

"I'm training at his gym."

"You're training to be a cage fighter?"

I laughed once. "Just the training part."

"A fighter that doesn't have any fights." He stretched a pair of latex gloves onto his hands, and began wiping Tanner's shoulder with disinfectant. "Do you have any tattoos?"

"Not one."

"She's interested, though," Tanner chimed in. I noticed his leg was bouncing nervously as John placed the sketch onto his arm.

"Look through those." John gestured to three thick binders sitting on the table beside me. "Maybe you'll see something you like."

I picked up a binder, but it remained closed on my lap. The sound of the needle sounded like the dreadful dentist's drill, and I cringed as it dug into Tanner's skin for the first time.

Tanner's eyes tightened, and his jaw tensed under his skin, though I knew he would never admit to the pain.

"The outline is the worst part," John murmured, deep in concentration.

For the first thirty minutes, I was completely engrossed in watching John's steady hand as he followed the lines he had sketched. After that, I began flipping through the binders of artwork, searching for something to peak my interest. Pictures of roses, skulls, and hearts all blurred together. John's work was incredible, but nothing jumped out at me.

Two hours later, Tanner's shoulder piece was finally done. Tim's tombstone was etched onto his arm, surrounded by clusters of small roses on either side.

"Wow," I said when Tanner stood up. "That's beautiful."

John wiped the excess ink and blood from Tanner's shoulder, and lightly dabbed the ointment on top. "Keep this covered for a couple of hours." He walked us to the register in the front of the shop, and rattled off care instructions.

"Do you love it?" I asked once we were inside Tanner's car.

He was grinning from ear to ear. "I do."

"I wonder what your mom will say."

He shrugged. "Too late now."

"Yes. Yes, it is."

When I got home, I called Chase. I needed to hear his voice. I needed to know that he was still there – still in love with me. The days were adding up, and soon it would be two months since we had seen each other. The more days that passed, the harder it was to remember how it felt to be held; to be kissed; to look into his eyes; to fall asleep wrapped up in his arms. I called him, knowing he would not answer.

The conversation with T.J. occupied my mind. I had never thought about what I needed in order to feel loved. For so many years, I had forgotten what it felt like to be loved by someone – by anyone – until Chase came into my life. I did not have a list of prerequisites needed to date me. All I knew was that Chase loved me, and in whatever way that was, it was exactly what I needed.

Chapter Thirteen

HE DESERVES BETTER

*M*onday morning, I was eager to get to work. I knew Tanner was, too. Charlotte would be starting her first day of training with Beverly, and my plan would commence.

"You look nervous," I whispered to Tanner as we walked to the front door of the shop. "What's your plan?"

"I haven't decided yet. I'll know when I see her."

I gave his arm a reassuring squeeze. "All you have to do is smile and say hi. It's only the first day. Ease into it."

He did not respond as he held the door open for me.

Charlotte was already sitting behind the counter with Beverly. Her long blonde hair was curled at the ends, cascading down over her shoulders, and her makeup was perfectly done. I noted her efforts, and took them as a positive sign. I saw her eyes light up for a split second when Tanner stepped inside, right before they quickly averted to a pile of papers in front of her.

"Morning, ladies." I waved as I grabbed a water bottle from the refrigerator.

"Good morning," Charlotte said, overly cheerful for seven o'clock in the morning.

"Your hair looks great curled like that." I hit Tanner in the arm. "Doesn't her hair look nice?"

He barely looked up at her. "Her hair always looks nice."

Charlotte's pale cheeks turned bright pink within half a second, but she was smiling.

I felt like Shelly as I stared at the two awkward lovers before me. I now understood the enjoyment she got out of matchmaking, as I could feel my plan working already. I winked at Beverly, whose amused expression mirrored mine, before walking into the garage.

My happiness turned to longing as I set my tools up for the day ahead of me. Tanner and Charlotte did not know how lucky they were to be in the presence of each other – to be in the same town, in the same state, on the same coast. My buzzing phone in my back pocket startled me out of my thoughts, and when I looked at who was calling, my smile spread from ear to ear.

"A phone call in the middle of the day? To what do I owe this honor?"

Chase laughed. "I had a few minutes to say hello. How's your day?"

"My day is okay. The past week has been fine, as well."

"I know it has been a while since we talked. I've been sleeping every free moment I get. I'm exhausted."

"I know the feeling. Work has been crazy. So, listen to this: I hatched a plan to help your mom out, and get Tanner and Charlotte back together at the same time. I am a mastermind."

"What do you mean help my mom? What's wrong?"

"She's just stressed with work. She is trying to run this business alone, and she won't let me or Tanner help her. I got Charlotte on board, though. I really think it's going to help."

It was quiet on the other end of the line.

"You should try to call her more. She misses you." I paused. "I miss you."

"I'm trying to juggle everything as best as I can, you know. I don't need the guilt trip right now."

"Babe, I'm not trying to give you a guilt trip. I know how hard you are working over there. You don't have to explain yourself to me. Just tell me that you miss me," I laughed. "That's all I need to hear."

"Of course I miss you," he snapped. "You left me, remember?"

We were both silent as the smile disintegrated from my face. I had always felt comfort in our silences. Now, I only felt sadness.

He sighed. "I'm sorry."

"Don't be. I have to get back to work."

"Okay. I'll try to call you later. I love—"

"Yup. Later." I pressed the red button before he could finish his sentence, and tossed my phone onto the toolbox. I closed my eyes and tried to breathe through the mixture of emotions swelling up into my chest. I paced back and forth as I tried to regain my composure.

"You okay over there?" Tanner called.

I shook my head.

"Save it for T.J. later."

I stuck my ear buds into my ears, and turned up the volume on my iPod. I rolled under the car that needed work, letting the music drown out my thoughts for the remainder of the day. I worked straight through lunchtime, and did not even notice it was time to close the shop until I saw a pair of black slip-on shoes standing beside me.

Charlotte waved when I looked up.

I took out my ear buds, and managed a smile. "How was your first day?

"It was good. Beverly is amazing. I don't know how she's doing it all by herself."

"She's Super Woman."

"I just wanted to say thank you for getting me this pseudo internship." She glanced over her shoulder at Tanner, who had his back turned to us as he packed his tools away. "I thought it would be weird working with him, but it was fine."

"Have you guys talked at all today?"

She shook her head. "He stayed out of the office, like you said he would."

"You sound disappointed."

"It's the first day. We'll see how it goes, I guess."

I tilted my head in Tanner's direction as I stood. "He has a good heart, Char. I'm not saying you should give him a second chance, because I don't know what you're even mad at him for... just keep in mind that he has a good heart, and he loves you."

She looked down at her feet, twirling a strand of her blonde hair around her index finger. "Thanks again, Merritt. For everything."

I waved goodbye and left the two alone in the garage. If they would talk, at the very least, it was a start. I checked my phone as I got into my car: no missed calls or messages from Chase, but I had three from Shelly. I called her as I started driving to the gym.

"What took you so long to call me back? Did you get my messages?"

"I was working, Shell. What's up?"

"Have you talked to Chase today?"

"Briefly. Why?"

"I sent you pictures. Check your texts."

"I'm driving. Can you just explain what's going on? I don't want to be late for T.J."

She sighed. "I woke up this morning, and did my usual scrolling on Facebook while I ate breakfast. Chase was tagged in a few photos from some random chick. It looked like he was at a show."

"So?"

"So, it looked like he was hanging out... with this girl."

Acid trickled into my stomach, but I tried to remain calm. "What did she look like? Was she blonde? Maybe it was Brooke. Maybe he went out with the guys and their girlfriends last night."

"It wasn't Brooke."

I exhaled the breath I had been holding. "I'll look when I get to the gym."

"Merr, he had his arm around her in almost all of the pictures. I'm not trying to make you upset, but I thought you should know. You're not on Facebook, so you wouldn't see these things."

"Thanks for looking out, Shell. I gotta go."

"Call me later, okay?"

"Sure. Bye." I raced the rest of the way to the gym. When my car screeched to a halt in the parking lot, I opened Shelly's texts. The girl Chase had his arm around in the pictures definitely was not Brooke. I recognized Philip, and the rest of his bandmates, but did not know the other girls that were with them. I knew it was normal for fans of the band to snap pictures of them. I did not think he was cheating on me, or at least I hoped he wasn't. What upset me more was the fact that he was either too tired or too busy to talk to me, and when we finally talked earlier, he had given me an attitude. I didn't get so much as a text most days, yet this stranger got to have his arm around her. I could feel my cheeks getting hot as I stared at Chase's smile.

T.J. startled me out of my thoughts, leaning into my open window. "You coming in, or are we training in your–" he stopped when he saw the tears in my eyes. "What's wrong?"

I held up the picture of Chase and the blonde.

He took my phone from me to get a better look. His eyes were soft when he handed it back to me, but his voice was firm. "Get out."

I rolled my window up, and stepped out of my car. He held the gym door open for me, and I walked inside towards the ring.

T.J. pulled my arm. "We're going over here today." He motioned to the large black punching bags that were hanging in the far corner of the gym. Positioning himself behind one, he turned his baseball cap backwards. "Go ahead."

Without a word, I began hurling my fists into the bag, each punch landing harder than the one before it. Instantly, I began to sweat, all of the anger and heat coming to the surface of my skin. The picture of Chase and the blonde was burned into my mind. My arms were burning, but I did not stop. T.J. held the bag steady for me as I attacked it with all of my might. Droplets of sweat began dripping down my face. It took me several minutes to realize that the drips were not sweat, but tears.

"Okay," T.J. said gently. "You can stop now."

"No." My voice came out like a sob. My arms and shoulder felt weak, but I did not let them fall. I used every ounce of strength in me to muster another punch as the tears overflowed.

"Merritt, enough." T.J.'s voice was louder. He pulled the bag back when I did not listen, and I stumbled as my arm swung into the air.

"What are you doing?" I growled, the tears streaming down my face.

He stepped around the punching bag, and wrapped his arms

around me. My body stiffened at first, unsure of what he was trying to do. His embrace felt warm and inviting, and my muscles began to relax as I buried my head into his chest.

"Did you ask him who the blonde was?" he asked.

"Shelly sent me the pictures. I just saw them before I got here."

"You should talk to him before you get upset. I'm sure there's a perfectly good explanation."

"He was very short with me on the phone today. We barely talk. He has no time for me. The longer we're apart, the easier it will be for him to forget about me."

T.J. gripped my shoulders, and held me away from him so that he could look into my eyes. "He won't be able to forget about you. You're pretty unforgettable."

I frowned. "You're just saying that to make me feel better."

"When have you known me to blow smoke up your skirt?"

I crossed my arms over my chest, failing to think of a comeback.

"Exactly. Wipe your eyes, doll face. I'm going to teach you a new move today."

My eyes widened as I followed him. "The Ninja Turtle spinny thing?"

"Not yet. Have patience, grasshopper."

We left our sneakers on the floor before stepping into the ring. Once inside, T.J. peeled off his t-shirt, and I flung my sweatshirt over the ropes in our daily ritual.

"I'm going to teach you what to do after you get your opponent on his back." T.J. lunged forward and took me to the floor. His movements were quick, and before I knew it, he was sitting on top of me full-mount with his legs on either side of my hips. "Did you get that?"

"Uh..."

He laughed. "Once you slam the other person to the ground, you need to move quickly so they don't succeed in getting up." He stood and pulled me to my feet.

"You're going to have to walk me through this."

"Get in position, right before you knock me over."

I bent down, hooking my arm around his leg, and pushing my shoulder into his abdomen.

"Now, once I hit the floor, your left leg is going to come forward, and you're going to drop your knee on the outside of my hip."

I pushed into him, lifting his leg, and flipped him onto his back. My knee dropped down as he said it should, and I swung my right leg onto the other side of his body. It was exhilarating to be able to execute these maneuvers.

T.J. was laughing below me. "You're a natural at this."

"Damn right I am!" I lifted my arms above my head in victory, pretending to smile at the invisible crowd.

"The only problem with a full mount," he began. In one swift motion, he flipped us both over. I was whirled around onto my back, and now he was on top of me. "If you're not careful, the tables can be turned in the blink of an eye. You always want to make sure you're on top. From this position, you can do anything you want to your opponent."

"What would you do?"

"I like to take my time on top. This is my opportunity to weaken my opponent. He will tire out from trying to defend himself, and as soon as I see that, it's over. That's when I make my move."

"Show me."

His eyebrows lifted. "You want me to put you in an arm bar?"

I nodded feverishly.

"It might hurt a bit," he warned. "But I won't sink it in all the way."

"I can take it."

He smirked. "That's my girl." He grabbed my left arm, and swiveled around onto his back. His knees squeezed together, trapping my arm between them, as he lifted his hips up to lock my elbow. It was quick, and smoothly executed, and it hurt like hell.

"Ow!" I cried.

T.J. released my arm immediately, chuckling as he sat up. "Hurts, doesn't it?"

I rubbed my elbow. "You could break someone's arm like that."

"If you're trying to break someone's elbow, you could. The point is to bring your opponent to the point of surrender. He taps, and you win."

"Can you get out of an arm bar, so you don't have to surrender?"

His eyes narrowed as he grinned. "I like that question. What do you say we save that for your next session, and go grab some dinner?"

"I won't be very good company."

"Eh, I've had worse."

"Gee, thanks."

He chuckled, amused with himself. "So, pizza?"

"Pizza."

We walked next door, ordered the same food and sat in the same booth in the back as we did the last time we were here. T.J.'s high school fan club perked up as soon as they saw him.

"How old are you, anyway?" I asked while we waited for our food to come out.

"Twenty-five," he replied.

"You seem so... established."

"I'd like to think I am."

"That's so impressive. You're so young to have your life set."

"I wouldn't say it's set. I have a business that I'm thankful for, but there's more to life than just work."

"What else do you do with your time?"

"I said there's more to life than work. I didn't say I did anything else." He laughed.

"Now I see why you don't mind hanging around me so much. You have no life!"

"Curly haired girls in glass houses shouldn't throw stones."

I took my crumpled straw wrapper and tossed it at him and grinned.

The young girls bounced to our table with our food. "Hi, T.J." they said simultaneously.

"Hi. Thanks." He wasted no time in taking a mammoth-sized bite from his chicken sandwich. The girls scurried back behind the counter, whispering to each other.

"Okay, Curly Sue. You're halfway through training. Tonight, I'm giving you homework. You're not going to like it, but you need to complete it."

"What kind of homework?"

"You need to call your mom."

My stomach dropped. "Why though? How is talking to her going to make a difference?"

"You said it yourself – all of your troubles began with your mother. That means they will end with her, too. You have spent your life running around your problems. Now, it's time for you to learn how to cut through them, so that you can finally move past them."

I took a deep breath, and exhaled slowly.

"What are you afraid of?" he asked.

I thought for a moment, searching for the words to explain how I was feeling. "Honestly, I'm scared of hearing the truth. In my mind, she left because she was a bad person. It makes it easier to blame her, to hate her, if I keep telling myself that she left because something was wrong with her." I looked down at my feet, thinking aloud. "I'm afraid of hearing that she left because she wasn't happy with us... with me."

One corner of his mouth turned up, as he held my gaze.

"What?" I asked, suddenly feeling self-conscious.

"That was such an honest answer. Your progress and strength has made me so proud, Merritt."

"Thanks. I really couldn't have come this far without you."

"You could have. You just need to believe in yourself. You are your biggest obstacle."

"I think this will be my biggest obstacle." I pulled out my phone and texted Shelly for Claire's number. I knew she had saved it, in the hopes I would come to this very moment.

While we finished eating, I decided to text Chase, as well. I hoped I could catch him before he went on stage tonight; I hoped we could smooth things over.

As I stepped into my apartment later, my phone sounded from inside my purse. Chase was actually calling me. My stomach twisted nervously as I answered.

"Hey."

"Hey. I saw your call. I go on in a few minutes." He didn't sound any different than when we had spoken hours earlier, and my heart sank.

"I'll make it quick then. Shelly sent me the pictures from your show last night," I began. "You look so happy in them."

"Thanks."

"It's funny," I faked a laugh. "She called me freaking out, saying that you had your arm around some blonde chick."

"Why is that funny?"

"I... I guess it's not. I tried to explain to her that there was probably a perfectly good explanation as to why you would be... hugging another girl like that in pictures." I held my breath, waiting for his reaction.

"What is this about, Merritt?"

"It's about how you have no time to talk to me, yet you have plenty of time to hang out with other girls!" I blurted out, frustrated with his shortness.

"Other girls? I perform, and girls want pictures with the band. You know what it's like."

"You know, I was hoping you would feel sorry for the way you spoke to me this morning, but I can see that you clearly don't care."

"I told you I was sorry, but maybe you didn't catch that before you hung up on me."

"I was mad."

"Well, maybe I've been mad, too! Jesus Christ, Merritt. I am going through hell over here without you. You left. Part of me knows deep down you never wanted to come in the first place, and I know it's my own fault for dragging you here... but I like it here! I'm happy here. I just wish you could have been happy here with me."

I thought about the pictures. Chase's expression exuded happiness – he was happy. He was experiencing life, and living out his dream. Then, T.J.'s words entered my mind. He was worried that I was not getting the kind of love I needed; however, I was the one who wasn't giving Chase what he needed. It was selfish of me to try to hold on to him from afar – to drag him through everything I was going through here. I was screwed up. I was the broken one who needed fixing. Like an anchor weighing him down, I was only causing him pain. He didn't deserve this. Moreover, I didn't deserve him. Tears stung my eyes as the realization of what I had to do suddenly became so clear in my mind.

"I'm sorry, Chase. I know this isn't fair to you. You deserve to be free, and have the time of your life over there. You don't need all of my baggage bogging you down."

"Merritt, wait." He heaved a sigh. "That's not what I meant."

"You can admit it. I don't blame you for being angry with me. You should be able to do whatever you want with your life. I don't want to stop you." Silent tears fell from my eyes. "Your dad told me to make sure that I help you, because he couldn't. I thought that by going to California with you, I could help you become everything you've always wanted to become. But, I'm starting to see that there is only one way for me to help you."

"Please, I know what you're thinking." He began to scramble, sensing what I was about to say. "That won't help me."

"I'm a mess, Chase." I laughed once. "I'm a mess, and you're the Golden Boy. I am trying to get my act together here, I really am… but the truth of the matter is: you deserve so much better than this. You deserve someone who can love you the way you deserve to be loved."

"You love me, Merritt. You love me, and I love you. You're everything I need."

"I'm not. I wish I was."

"Chase! Let's go, man! We're on!" I heard someone shout from his side of the phone.

"I'll be right there. Just give me a minute," Chase shouted back. "Merritt, listen. I have to go right now, but I am going to call you the second I step foot off that stage. Please say you will answer. Please say we can work this out. I'm sorry I was so short with you today. I truly am. I'm just under so much stress, I'm tired all the time, and I hate being away from you. It won't happen again. That girl in those pictures Shelly sent you is just a girl. She's a fan of the band, and she asked for a picture. I don't even know her name. You have to believe me."

"I do believe you." I squeezed my eyes shut, mustering up the last few ounces of strength that I had left. I knew this would hurt him, but it would be better for him in the long run. "I have to let you go. I have to say goodbye."

"You're just letting me go perform, and then I'll call you back. Right?"

"No, Chase. I'm letting you go. You deserve better than me. You deserve to be happy."

"You make me happy!" His voice was strained, desperate to change my mind.

"I love you so much. I'm sorry... for everything." I ended the call, shut my phone, and stared at the blank screen. I had just walked away from the love of my life.

Chapter Fourteen

DOWN THE RABBIT HOLE

I did not sleep at all. I kept my phone off, knowing I wouldn't have the heart to ignore Chase's calls once he finished performing. I went through alternating hours of heartache and acceptance. It killed me to break up with him, especially right before he went on stage. Despite how much it hurt, I felt in my heart that I was doing the best thing for him. He would see it, eventually.

I had a full day at work ahead of me, and still had not done T.J.'s homework. I had to find a way to push the pain from the forefront of my mind and get out of bed. I knew I had to make the dreaded call to Claire before I saw T.J. Reluctantly, I turned on my phone, and tried to ignore the multiple alerts from Chase that came through.

I stared at Claire's number on my phone and listened to the sound of my heart pounding in my chest. My thumb hovered over the call button as I thought about each scenario that could happen when I called her. I thought about why I was here – how I got here; I had left the person I loved on the other side of the country in order to undo the giant knot I had entangled myself in. Perhaps, the sooner I hashed things out with my mother, the sooner I could move past all of the hurt and resentment I had built up inside. Maybe I could even turn myself into someone that Chase would deserve. My thumb hit the button, and I held my breath while I listened to the ringing. It rang, and rang, and I was just about to hang up when I heard the ringing stop.

"Hello?"

"Uh, yeah. Is this Claire?"

"Merritt?"

"Yeah."

"I didn't think you would call."

"I didn't want to, but... I'm doing this for myself. Not for you."

"I'm sorry. I just... I really need to talk to you. I'm not okay with the way we left things."

I chuckled. "The way we left things? Do you mean when I told you to go away, or when you disappeared for eight years?"

There was a pause on the other side of the phone. "I heard you're not in New York anymore. Is that true?"

"I wasn't. I'm back now."

"Oh, that's good news."

"Yeah, it's great," I said flatly.

"Do you think we could meet? I would really like to sit down with you, face to face."

"That's funny. You could have seen my face every day for the last eight years, but you chose not to. Why all of a sudden?"

"It's not all of a sudden. I've been trying to do this for a long time, now."

"Guess you didn't try hard enough. I've been in the same spot since you left."

"I'm here now. That's what matters."

"You're here, and Dad's not. Doesn't really seem fair."

"No. It's not fair. Nothing in this life is fair."

I was silent. I couldn't argue that fact.

"Maybe you're free tonight? We could meet somewhere – wherever you choose. Just name the time and I'll be there."

"We can do it at my apartment. I don't want to do this in public."

"That's fine. What time? I can bring takeout if you'd like."

"Don't bring me anything. Be here at seven."

"Seven. Got it."

I pulled the phone away from my ear and ended the call. Glancing at the clock, I went to the bathroom and got ready for work.

Everyone was silent when I walked into the shop. Beverly, Charlotte, and Tanner's faces all wore the same expression.

"Geeze. Who died?" I stopped and thought about what I had said. "Did someone die?"

"How are you?" Charlotte asked.

"I'm fine," I responded, lifting a suspicious eyebrow. "How are you?"

"Chase called me last night," Tanner blurted out.

"Oh." Now I understood the awkward silence. I immediately looked at Beverly. "Am I fired?"

I could tell she was trying not to laugh. "No, of course not! Do you think your job is contingent upon you staying with Chase?"

"I never really thought about it."

Tanner walked around the counter, and rested his arm on my shoulders. "I told you not to break my brother's heart."

I craned my neck to look up at him. "It won't be broken for long. He'll move on. You'll see."

"You're an idiot if you really believe that." He turned and walked towards the garage door. "Let's go. We've got work to do."

"You're not an idiot," Charlotte called after me.

As I stepped into the garage, I called T.J.

"What's up, Curly Sue?"

"So, I did your homework."

"Oh, yeah? What happened?"

"She wants to meet tonight. She's coming over at seven."

"So, you're calling to tell me that you won't make it to training tonight."

"Yes, but for good reason! I'm following through with my homework assignment."

"Fine. I'll allow it, just this once."

"I'll make it up to you. I'll train for an extra hour tomorrow."

"What makes you think I want to train you for two hours?"

"Oh. You're right. I'm sorry."

"Relax, I'm kidding."

"Oh."

"You okay? You're not firing your usual insults back at me."

"I... I broke up with Chase last night."

"Shit. All because of the girl in the picture?"

"No. That was nothing."

"Okay. Well, you can tell me about it tomorrow. Are you going to be okay with your mom tonight?"

"I have no idea. I just need to get through work, first."

"You know my number if you need to talk. I'll be here."

"I know. You have no life. I remember."

"There she is."

I cracked a smile. "Goodbye, T.J."

"Bye, doll face."

———

AT SEVEN O'CLOCK ON THE DOT, I HEARD A KNOCK FROM OUTSIDE.

My hand shook as I turned the knob to open the door. This was it.

Claire smiled nervously. "Hi, Merritt."

Without a smile in return, I took a step back and gestured for her to come in.

"Thank you." She walked into the apartment and took off her coat. "Where would you like me to put this?"

"Just lay it on the couch," I pointed.

"It's so nice in here." She looked around and draped her coat over the armrest of the couch.

"Yeah. The Brooks took care of me when I had nothing and no one left."

"They're good people."

We stared at each other in silence for a few moments, unsure of what to say next. I wanted to get this over with as quickly as possible, but I did not have a clue where to start.

"So," she began. "I don't know if I should start at the beginning, or the end."

I shrugged.

"I think if I start at the end, everything will make more sense. I can backtrack from there."

"Whatever." I sat on the opposing couch, and braced myself for what was about to happen.

She took a shaky breath, and her eyes remained on mine. "I am an alcoholic."

Stunned, as if I had been hit over the head with a bag of bricks, I said nothing.

"It took me so many years to finally be able to say those words – and to get up the courage to say them to you."

I remained silent, waiting for her to continue. Words had not yet formed into thoughts inside of my brain.

"Your father and I were young when we had you. Your dad went to work every day; I was left home alone with a newborn baby. I had no clue what I was doing. You would cry, and I would cry right along with you. I didn't know it then, but I was suffering from postpartum depression. Do you know what that is?"

"Yes, I know what that is. Everyone knows what that is."

"Well, back then, I didn't. All I knew was that I felt such a heaviness in my chest whenever I looked at you. I stayed up at night, worrying about every little thing that could possibly happen. I was sleep-deprived, and anxiety-ridden. I would beg your father not to leave me each morning, but he would just tell me that I was doing a great job and had nothing to worry about.

I didn't tell my doctor what I was going through because I was embarrassed. When I said it out loud, it sounded like I hated being a mother. It sounded like I hated my baby." She leaned in. "I never hated you. Not once. But, I was in pain, and I needed to find something to make the pain stop. It started with wine. I would drink a glass while you were taking your afternoon nap. Then, it increased to two glasses, and before I knew it, I was finishing a bottle each day."

"Didn't Dad see that you were drunk when he came home?" That was the first coherent question that had formed.

"Your father looked at me through rose-colored glasses. I could do no wrong, and even if I did, he would not have admitted it."

"That's the first thing we agree on."

She nodded. "I got really good at hiding it. I know it sounds terrible that I was drunk while taking care of a baby, but I was able to function. I didn't drink to black out, and I never threw up. I just needed something to numb the pain."

A knot formed in my throat as I listened to her explanation. As scary as it was to admit it, even if just to myself, I understood exactly what she was saying.

"Over the years, wine turned into cocktails, and cocktails turned into straight vodka. I was able to drink without anyone noticing a thing."

"So, you're an alcoholic. How does that explain why you left?"

"I went out to dinner one night with my friends from the law firm. My boss approached me at the end of the night about drinking on the job. He had found a bottle of vodka in my desk drawer. His ex-wife was an alcoholic, and he recognized the signs. He told me about a great rehab facility that I could go to. He offered to pay for it and everything. I was embarrassed, and I knew that going to rehab would mean that I would have to tell your father the truth... and that you would find out, too. I denied having a problem, and told him that everything was fine. After all, it was fine. No one was getting hurt from my drinking. Until the night someone did get hurt."

My eyes widened as realization set in. My mind raced to connect all of the dots. "You were drunk the night you picked me up from Shelly's house and crashed into the fire hydrant?"

Her eyes filling up with tears for the first time. "I was worried about losing my job. My boss threatened to fire me if I didn't tell your father the truth and get help. The drinking always seemed to worsen whenever I was worried about something. I thought I was okay to drive the night I went to get you from Shelly's. I ran a red light without even realizing that it was red, and another car almost smashed right into us. I panicked when I realized what I had done, and lost control of the car."

"You said a squirrel ran out in front of your car... but you were drunk." I shook my head in disbelief. "I had to get stitches from the broken glass that fell on me!"

"It was the first time I had hurt you, and I swore it would never happen again. The only problem was that I couldn't stop drinking. I tried." She wiped a tear that had escaped. "I couldn't stop. I checked myself into the rehab facility that my boss had told me about, but it wasn't that easy. I had to undo thirteen years of drinking. I fell off the wagon countless times."

I sat up in my chair. "Let me get this straight – you chose abandoning your family over simply telling them the truth, and letting them help you. How do you justify that?"

All she could do was shrug her shoulders. "I don't have an answer for you. I was an addict. I wasn't thinking clearly. I just knew that I couldn't allow myself to be around the people I loved anymore. If something would have happened to you that night... if that accident was worse..."

"I was in an accident that *was* worse!" I yelled, finally finding my anger. "You left, and Dad went off the deep end. I spent the rest of my childhood suffering because of you! Dad killed himself because of you! You might not have hurt me too badly in that accident years ago, but you still managed to cause the accident on the night of Dad's funeral!"

"Merritt, I know you're angry with me, and I understand all of the reasons why. But you need to see that you were the person who caused your accident. You were the one drinking, and you are at fault for that. It terrifies me to think that you're making the same mistakes that I once did."

"Are you fucking kidding me? I wouldn't have had to go through any of that if it weren't for you leaving like a coward!"

"When I learned about your accident, and your father's death, my heart broke into a million pieces. I never wanted anything to happen to the two of you. I thought I was protecting you by leaving. Then, I found out that you were drunk the night of the crash. Merritt, alcoholism is hereditary. It was passed on to me by my father, and I passed it on to you. I know you were drinking to numb the immense grief you were feeling. I know it because I've been there."

Fire exploded in my eyes as I stood. "Don't even begin to act like you understand what I went through! You weren't there! You didn't see the blood pouring out of his wrists! You didn't see how pale his skin was when I found him! You didn't see how the tub was permanently stained a deep red after that night! You weren't there while I held him in my arms, waiting for the ambulance to come!" I choked back a sob. "You know what I told him? While he was lying there, in a pool of his own blood, I told him that I forgave him... that it was okay to let go – that I wouldn't be angry with him." I stormed to my front door, and swung it open wide. "I can tell you that I won't be saying those same words to you. Now, please leave."

She covered her mouth with her hand, muffling her sobs, while she stood. "Merritt, can we continue this another time?" She swung her jacket around her shoulders. "I know this is a lot to take in. Please don't let this be the last time you talk to me."

"Right now, I just need you to leave."

She tried to reach her hand out for me, but I quickly backed away. She put her head down when she walked out the door, and I slammed it behind her. I paced around the living room, trying desperately to choke back the tears. It was no use. I collapsed onto the floor in the middle of my apartment, and let eight years' worth of tears come out. Waves of emotion crashed into me, relentless and unyielding, as I sobbed harder than I ever had before.

The happy childhood I once thought I had was a lie. My mother was a functioning alcoholic who had been suffering since she gave birth to me. My father was in denial, which only perpetuated her secret. All of my fondest memories were now tainted by the truth.

After some time, I picked myself up and went to the bathroom to splash water on my face. Looking at my reflection in the mirror, all I could see was Claire. Her eyes, her hair, and her addiction stared back at me. In California, Chase had been worried that I would become my father; now, for the first time, I saw that I had inadvertently become something much worse: I had become my mother. This realization hit me like a ton of bricks, and I could not bear the weight of it. I balled my hand up into a fist and smashed the glass, shards falling into the sink. I did not check to see if my hand was bleeding; I did not care if it was – something had taken over me. I stormed into the kitchen.

Rummaging through my cabinets, I remembered that Tina and Kenzie had brought over housewarming beverages when I first moved into my apartment last year. My eyes finally settled on what I was searching for: a brand new, unopened glass bottle of tequila.

Before I could come to my senses, I unscrewed the cap, and took a long swig from the bottle. The familiar burning entered my throat, and I quickly took another gulp to accompany the first. More tears spilled out of my eyes. I carried the bottle into my bedroom, leaving the cap behind on the kitchen floor. Again and again, I drank from the bottle, until the wonderful numbness began to set in. After I felt like I had drank enough, I placed the bottle on my nightstand and curled up into a ball under my covers until I fell asleep.

Chapter Fifteen

A SECOND CHANCE

My head was pounding. The sun was bright as it streamed through my window. I squeezed my eyes shut and yanked the blanket over my head. I tried to ignore the pounding in my brain, but it only seemed to get louder.

"Merritt! If you don't open this door, I will!"

I immediately sat up. The pounding was not in my head, but on my front door.

"Okay, Merritt! That's it! I'm coming in!"

I tore the covers off of me, and stumbled over my feet as I ran to unlock the door.

Tanner shouldered past me, letting himself into the apartment. "What the hell, Merritt?"

I shielded my eyes from the sunlight, and quickly closed the door behind him. "I'm sorry. I have a bad migraine." I shuffled back to the bedroom, collapsing onto the bed, and not wanting him to see me.

"Are you sick or–" Tanner froze in the doorway. His mouth dropped open when he laid eyes upon my nightstand. "What the fuck did you do?"

Though I had cried an ocean last night, tears still managed to find their way to the surface. "I... I messed up, Tanner."

Without missing a beat, he began opening my dresser drawers, frantically searching for something. I watched him rip open my closet door and disappear inside; he emerged two seconds later, tossing my sweatshirt and a pair of sweatpants at my face. "Put these on. We're leaving in five."

"I can't," I began. "I can't face T.J. like this"

Tanner gripped my shoulders and lowered his chin to look at me. "Clean yourself up, and meet me in the car." He walked towards the door, and held up his hand. "Five minutes."

I spent two of the five minutes in bed, clutching my sweats in my hands, too afraid to move. Though I was embarrassed to let T.J. see me like this, I was even more upset about how much of a disappointment I would be to him. The last thing I wanted to do was let him down, after all the progress he had made with me – for me.

With only seconds to spare, I sat beside Tanner in his Mustang. I tried as hard as I could to not look hungover, but I knew my eyes would be a dead giveaway.

We rode in silence, staring straight ahead out the windshield. I could hear my heart thumping inside of my chest, as every turn Tanner made brought us closer to the gym.

Once inside, I spotted T.J. making his way to the ring. His grin faded as I approached him.

"What's wrong, Curly Sue? You look like–"

I looked down at his sneakers, too ashamed to bring myself to look him in the eyes.

He stepped closer to me, lifting my chin with his finger. After he surveyed my appearance, his face crumbled.

My eyes welled up instantly seeing his disappointment.

His fingers left my chin, and pointed towards the exit. "Get out."

Tears spilled down onto my cheeks. "T.J., please," I tried.

He glared down at me with icy blue eyes and a look of disgust. "I said get out."

I gripped his t-shirt in my fists as a last resort. "Please don't kick me out, T.J. Please don't make me leave."

He pried his shirt out of my hands, and released me as he stepped back. "I warned you. You knew the rules. Now go."

Tanner was at my side, knowing T.J. would react this way. He tugged on my elbow. "Come on. I'll take you back."

I hung my head as I turned away, and followed Tanner to the door. I did not care who saw me crying. All I cared about was the person who now hated me. I looked back once, and saw T.J. hurl the pad and gloves against a shelf, sending everything crashing to the floor. He stormed into his office, and slammed the door shut.

Back in Tanner's car again, I covered my face with my hands and sobbed. "What am I going to do?"

Tanner heaved a sigh from the driver's seat. "Give him some time. Maybe he will come around." He turned his key in the ignition.

My head shot up. "Tanner, wait." I flung open the passenger door, and ran towards the gym.

"Where are you going?" he yelled out his window.

I swung open the gym door and ran to T.J.'s office, his door still closed. I knocked on the door, and then pounded harder when he didn't open.

"T.J. open up!" I yelled.

Finally, the door opened. "I told you to get out."

I pushed past him before he could stop me, and let myself inside. "Well, I'm not leaving." I crossed my arms across my chest, and planted my feet where I stood. I did not know if this would work, but I had to try.

His eyebrows furrowed, and his jaw worked under his skin. He held my stare, neither one of us wanting to break first. "You have two minutes. Then, you have to leave." He gave the door a forceful push, and it slammed shut.

"I messed up last night. I know I am halfway through your training, but we are going to need more than a month to undo almost a decade's worth of my issues. I still need your help. I made a mistake, and I regret it. Please don't make me stop training."

He pointed to his chest. "I am not making you stop training. You did this. You did this to yourself. You keep blaming everyone else for your problems, but you're the one who needs to take ownership of it all!"

"Yes, I agree. I take full responsibility for last night. I was upset about breaking up with Chase, and then everything with my mother happened. Please give me another chance."

"Why didn't you call me? I was waiting by my phone hoping that you would call to tell me what happened with your mom. Instead, you get drunk? That's the same old weak ass bullshit that you have been doing. I thought you were making progress. I thought you were changing. Fuck me, I guess, right? I trusted you, and you broke that trust. You broke your trust to yourself!"

I stepped closer to him, but he took a step back. "T.J. I am so sorry. I didn't do this to hurt you. The last thing I wanted was to see the look of disappointment on your face."

"The last thing you should want is to disappoint yourself!" he shouted. "When are you going to get it, Merritt?"

"I feel it. I know I screwed up." My eyes were imploring him to let me stay. "Please, T.J. Just one more shot."

"Why? Why should I believe that you won't do this again? Why should I waste my time on another coward like you?"

I winced, accepting the verbal punch to my gut. I deserved it. "Because you taught me to keep getting back up every time I get knocked down. I'm making the choice to keep fighting."

He rubbed the back of his neck while he contemplated his decision. "It's hard to argue when you use my own words against me."

My eyes widened. "Are you letting me stay?"

He nodded once, but his eyes narrowed. "No more mistakes, though. Fool me twice, you're done."

I rushed at him and clutched his midsection tightly. "Thank you so much. I won't screw up again, I promise." I waited for him to return the hug, but grew impatient when he didn't. I lifted one of his arms, and tried placing it around me. "God, your arm is so heavy. Just hug me, dammit."

I heard him chuckle, and then his arms wrapped around my body. He rested his chin on the top of my head, and I breathed a sigh of relief.

"I can't lose you, too," I said quietly.

He held me out in front of him far enough to look me in the eyes. "Then don't do something like this again."

I stared up at him, and lowered my chin. "I won't."

His arms dropped to his sides, and he gestured to the empty chair beside me.

I sat, and watched him walk around his desk to sit in his large computer chair.

"So, tell me how it went with your mother."

I took a few deep breaths while I gathered my thoughts. "Apparently, my mother was an alcoholic."

His eyebrows lifted, though I knew he wasn't surprised. "That makes a lot of sense."

"She said she had postpartum depression after she had me, and she would drink in order to feel better." I averted my eyes, embarrassed to admit it out loud. "You can call me a hypocrite anytime, now."

"Do you think I would ever call you that?" T.J. waited for me to make eye contact with him before continuing. "Alcoholism is hereditary. With all that you've had to endure in your life, it's no wonder you looked for something to help you cope with the pain. I get it. I get you, and you're not a hypocrite."

"I just feel so mixed up inside." I rubbed my forehead. "I have hated her for so long, but now I don't know where to put that hate. How can I hate her when I did the same exact thing? I understood every word she said."

"We're all guilty of judging people and situations too harshly. Life comes full circle, and as we grow up, we're usually faced with the very things we swore ourselves against. It happens, and I'm glad it happens because it's a valuable lesson to learn. It's important for you to hear your mom's side. All that hate you carried around inside of you can now be turned into empathy. She was suffering long before you or your father suffered."

I listened, taking in every word he spoke.

"What made you start drinking last night?" he asked.

"I was looking at myself in the mirror, and all I could see was her. After hearing everything that she told me," I shook my head, cringing. "I became her, T.J. Somehow, I managed to turn into the person that I hate the most."

"So, in turn, you hate yourself."

"Shelly thinks I am a warrior. Staring at myself in the mirror, I realized that I'm not a warrior. I'm a coward. I was so mad at myself last night. I wanted to do the one thing that I knew would hurt me the most."

"That self-sabotaging behavior has got to stop, Merritt. You need to gain control of your emotions. Your mother did you a favor. She held up a mirror so that you could take a good hard look at yourself. If you don't like what you see staring back at you, then make a change."

"I want to."

"Then do it," he countered. "A warrior is more than someone who fights in wars. She is someone who shows courage and perseverance in those battles. I can teach you how to fight, but I can't throw the punches for you. Fighting takes heart. You either have it, or you don't. Your parents didn't have it; mine didn't either. Should we just lie down and accept our fate as cowards, or should we fight to become something more?"

"We should be warriors."

One corner of his mouth turned up. "There's my girl."

———

"Just dump it down the drain," I ordered.

"That is such a waste of money," Shelly replied from the kitchen.

"So then take it to the frat house. I don't care what you do with it. I just need it out of here."

"I can't believe you fell off the wagon." She loaded the bottles of tequila, vodka, and rum into a shopping bag, and carried it to the front door, setting it down beside her shoes.

"I can't believe my mother was an alcoholic my entire life."

"I can't believe you broke up with Chase."

"You win."

Shelly plopped onto the couch beside me. "Has he been calling you?"

"Yup. Funny how he suddenly has time to call me now."

"That is very true. How are you holding up?"

"I think about him every second I'm awake." I swallowed the lump that had now made itself at home in my throat. "I think that no matter what I do, no matter where I go, I will always be his. My heart will always belong to him."

"That will leave you very lonely in life."

"I guess that's what I get for falling in love with someone I didn't deserve."

"That's where I'm going to have to stop you." Shelly sat up to lean towards me, trying to look threatening by narrowing her eyes. "If you want to wallow in your heartbreak, I will sit here with you. If you want to cry your eyes out for days on end, I will sit here with you. But if you are going to talk about how Chase is too good for you, I will not sit here for that shit. You are a good person, Merritt Adams. You have been through worse than anyone else I have ever known; you protect the people you love like a mother bear with her cubs; you are beautiful; you are smart; you are a warrior princess, and anyone who knows you is lucky to have you. I know Chase is great, but don't act like he is God's gift to the world. He is a mere mortal just like the rest of us."

I rested my head on her shoulder, smiling and fighting off the urge to cry – again. "I don't deserve you, either, Toad. You're the best friend I could ever ask for."

She covered my hand with hers. "Forget the boys, Frog – you're the love of my life!"

I giggled. "Ditto."

"So, tell me," she said. "Have you made out with T.J. yet?"

I pulled away from her, my face contorting between variations of shock and appalment. "Have I what?"

Shelly rolled her eyes dramatically. "Don't act like you haven't thought about it."

I pinched the bridge of my nose between my fingers, and took a deep breath. "Shell, I literally don't have the energy for one of these conversations with you."

She put her hands up in surrender. "I'm just saying: you're single now, and if I was single, I would make a beeline right for that boy's lips."

I shook my head, but laughed. "How are things with you and Brody?"

"The same. He's still perfect, and I'm still an asshole for worrying about marrying him."

"You are not an asshole."

"And you're not undeserving of Chase."

"Fine. You're an asshole, then."

She giggled and smacked me with one of the decorative couch pillows. "It takes one to know one!"

"We'll forever be assholes together." I nudged her with my elbow. "Let's go out tonight. I'm tired of sitting in this apartment and sulking."

"Oh, no," she said, waving her index finger in my face. "You are not allowed anywhere where alcohol is being served. I won't get scolded by Tanner again."

My eyebrows shot up. "Oh! What if we invite Tanner? I'll tell Charlotte to come, too. That way, they'll end up in the same place together!" I jumped up, and ran to the bedroom to get my phone. When I reappeared in the living room, Shelly was already texting Kenzie and Tina.

"Tina suggested Big Nose Kate's." She looked up from her phone to see my reaction. "Are you going to be okay with that?"

"I can't not go places just because I've been there with Chase."

She agreed. "Are you sure you're going to be okay surrounded by alcohol?"

"I will be better than okay. I know I can do this." I grimaced. "Plus, I don't want to get on T.J.'s shit list ever again."

"I bet he's sexy when he's angry," Shelly mused.

I rolled my eyes. "Is Brody coming?"

"No. Let's have a girls' night. I haven't had one of those in ages."

"Okay. I'm going to tell Tanner that it's a girl's night, but I'm tipping him off anyway. Charlotte won't know any different."

"Forcing the hand of fate. I'm all for it." She stood. "I'm going to go home and change. I'll be back at nine to pick you up."

"I can drive. I'll be your D.D."

"If you're not drinking, then I'm not drinking." She stuck out her chin in an attempt to seem resolute.

"You don't have to do that. You're not the one with a drinking problem."

"You jump, I jump, remember?"

I chuckled at the reminder of our eighth grade pact. "Okay. See you at nine."

Though I still felt immense pain radiating from the hole in my chest, I was excited to prove to myself that I would be stronger than the urge to drink. Before I stepped into the shower, I tapped out a quick text to T.J. to inform him of my plan. Keeping him in the loop was part of my strategy to gain back his trust.

An hour and a half later, the girls' night was in full effect. The warmer weather was teasing us as the months got closer to June, which made just about everyone in New York break out their summer wardrobes. We traded our boots for open-toed wedges, and swapped out our heavy sweaters with strappy tank tops. Shelly, Tina, Kenzie, and I danced in a circle in the middle of a very sweaty dance floor. Not one of them held a drink in their hands.

Tanner was perched at the far end of the bar, keeping watch of the front door. Charlotte had agreed to meet us, unaware of her ex-boyfriend's planned presence. Part of me felt guilty for tricking her into crossing paths with Tanner; on the other hand, if she was half as stubborn as I was, she needed a helpful push in the right direction.

I spotted her as soon as she walked through the door. Blondes were far and few between on Staten Island. Instantly, I was brought back to the memory of being in California, and felt a wrenching in my heart. I put on a smile, and waved to Charlotte until she saw me. I quickly alerted Tanner with a text, reminding him to keep his distance until she had been here for a while. I didn't want to make it obvious to her that she had been set up.

We danced and took selfies in true girls' night fashion. Several guys kept trying to infiltrate our circle, but Tina was able to fend them off. Each time she did, Charlotte laughed and shouted, "I love her!"

I fanned myself after dancing for an hour straight, the sweat dripping down the middle of my back. "I'm getting us water!" I shouted to the crew.

Shelly and Tina exchanged glances. "Should someone come with you?" Shelly asked.

I shook my head, and held up my hand as I took my oath. "I promise I will be okay." I spun on my heels, and made my way to the bar. It was less crowded outside of the dance space. I leaned against the bar, trying to flag down the bartender. I thought of Dave, and felt another shot to my chest. I checked my phone while I waited, and noticed a text from T.J.:

YOU CLEAN UP NICELY.

SCRUNCHING MY FACE UP IN CONFUSION, MY HEAD WHIPPED AROUND to search for him. Finally, my eyes settled on a familiar pair of sky blue eyes across the room. He was standing next to Tanner, wearing a black t-shirt, camo shorts, and his usual boyish grin. Another text from him drew my eyes back to my phone:

I KNOW IT'S A GIRLS' NIGHT. JUST WANTED TO TELL YOU THAT YOU look great... and I'm proud of you.

I OFFERED HIM A SMILE BEFORE RESPONDING TO HIS TEXT:

YOU DON'T LOOK TOO SHABBY, YOURSELF... AND THANKS ;)

I ORDERED FIVE WATERS, AND CARRIED THEM BACK TO THE GROUP OF parched ladies. We chugged the water, and continued dancing.

Charlotte grabbed my forearm. "Tanner is here!"

"What? Where?" I looked in every direction except for the one I knew he would be in.

"He's by the back door." She pointed discreetly. "Do you think he's here with another girl?"

"No way." I craned my neck, pretending to look to see who he was with. "It looks like he's here with friends."

The girls looked where we were looking, already knowing my plan.

"You should go say hi," Shelly suggested.

Charlotte shook her head feverishly. "No way. What if he's here, looking to leave with someone?"

"Then he'll leave with you, instead." Tina's bluntness wouldn't go over well with someone as reserved as Charlotte.

Shelly punched my arm. "T.J. is here!"

I rubbed my arm. "Have you been working out?"

She stretched up onto her toes, waving Kenzie over. "You have to see Merritt's trainer."

"Stop making it so obvious," I hissed, as all four of them leaned over in unison to get a better view.

"How is it that you always manage to surround yourself with such hot, muscular men?"

I glared at Tina. "He's single. Knock yourself out."

"No! I called dibs first!" Shelly interjected.

"You're not single!" Tina retorted. "You can't call dibs."

"Technically, you're single now, too," Charlotte offered.

Kenzie and Tina both looked at me, waiting for me to deny it. "I'm not interested in him like that. He's my coach."

"Let's all remember what happened the last time she said that," Tina said, nudging Shelly in the ribs.

Shelly bit her bottom lip, stifling a smile.

I scowled at her for finding Tina's comment funny.

"Seriously, that's the kind of guy she should be with," Tina said. "I told her Chase was too vanilla for her."

"Tina!" Shelly was back on my side now.

"Come on," she continued. "I bet you he's been through some shit in his life. She needs someone who understands her problems because he's been through them himself. Chase couldn't handle all of the baggage that she came with."

"Do they always talk about you like you're not standing here?" Charlotte asked.

"Always," I replied flatly. My phone buzzed in the back pocket of my shorts. It was T.J. again:

TANNER WANTS TO KNOW WHEN HE CAN TALK TO CHARLOTTE. POOR bastard is dying over here.

I MADE SURE THAT CHARLOTTE WASN'T ABLE TO SEE MY SCREEN AS I quickly texted him back:

THE GIRLS ARE BUSY DROOLING OVER YOU AT THE MOMENT. TELL him to give me two minutes.

OVER ME?

YOU'RE SURPRISED?

OH, YEAH. I FORGOT. I'M SUPPOSED TO BE ARROGANT.

I'M ROLLING MY EYES AS I TYPE THIS.

I KNOW. I WATCHED YOU.

THAT'S NOT CREEPY AT ALL.

. . .

That did come out a little stalkerish, huh?

I giggled.

"Who are you talking to?" Shelly snatched my phone from my hands, and her eyes widened. "You're talking to him!"

"Who?" Kenzie asked, peering over her shoulder.

"I knew it." Tina wore a smug expression.

"You better watch yourself," I warned playfully. "I know how to fight now."

"Short stuff is a tough guy now!" Tina laughed.

"Come on." I pulled on Charlotte's arm. "Let's go say hi to the boys. I think we've been spotted."

She nervously fixed her hair as we approached Tanner.

"Hey, little brother." I slapped him on the back.

He and Charlotte wore matching smiles as they stared into each other's eyes.

"You're like a matchmaker," T.J. whispered into my ear.

I grinned proudly. "T.J., this is Tina and Kenzie. You already know Shelly."

Shelly waved, refraining from attempting to speak words this time.

T.J. acknowledged the girls, and returned the wave to Shelly. "How's your night going, Red?"

Shelly's cheeks now matched her new nickname. "It's good. We're having a girls' night."

"Well, we were," Tina said, nodding at Charlotte and Tanner.

"Nice ink." T.J. gestured to her colorful arm. "When are you getting yours?" he asked me.

"You're getting a tattoo?" Tina shouted. "You tell me nothing!"

"I haven't decided yet. Calm your tits."

"Wanna dance?" I overheard Tanner ask Charlotte.

"Uh... it's a girls' night. I don't want to break the rules."

I gently pushed her towards him. "We can make an exception."

Her face lit up. "Okay. Lead the way."

Tanner looked like a kid on Christmas morning. He took her hand, and walked to the dance floor.

"It's nice to see you smiling, baby doll." T.J. pushed me with his shoulder.

I caught Tina mouthing, "Baby doll?" to Shelly, followed by Shelly's exaggerated shrug.

"I don't feel like drinking at all. It feels great."

Kenzie hugged me to her side. "I'm glad you're doing better."

"Have you heard from your mother since you saw her?" T.J. asked.

"Nope. I was pretty upset that night. I think she's giving me some time to deal with everything she unloaded on me."

"What do you think you're going to do?" Shelly inquired.

"Truthfully, I don't know. I want to meet with her again, just so I can be done with her. I don't think I could ever have an actual relationship with her."

"Maybe you can't have the same relationship you once had," T.J. replied. "But you might be able to create a new one. One you feel comfortable with."

"Brain and brawn," Tina murmured.

T.J. looked down at his sneakers and smiled.

"Are you blushing?" I cried, poking the dimple in his left cheek.

He swatted my hand away, grinning. "Get out of here! Aren't you supposed to be having a girls' night?"

"We totally don't mind hanging with you," Shelly responded.

I laughed once. "Speak for yourself."

T.J. jabbed me in my ribs. "You couldn't handle hanging with me, Curly Sue."

Tina arched an eyebrow. "Prove it. Let's go dance."

"I don't want to intrude on your time."

Tina took one arm, and Shelly took the other. They pulled him to the dance floor, as Kenzie and I followed behind them. We were all laughing as they sandwiched T.J. in between them. He was being a good sport about it, and I was having fun. For the first time, I was happy to be back home, surrounded by my friends. I glanced at Tanner and Charlotte, who were dancing closely just a few feet away. They'd be back together in no time. Tanner winked at me when he caught me staring.

I glanced at the time on my phone, wondering what Chase was

doing for the tenth time today. He was most likely performing somewhere in L.A., with dozens of girls hoping to get a chance to talk to him after his set. I did my best to push the thought from my mind, but I could not help wishing he was here as I saw the way Tanner looked at Charlotte.

At one o'clock in the morning, we all waved goodbye and went our separate ways in the parking lot. T.J. walked me and Shelly to her car.

"Goodnight, Red." They high-fived each other before she got into the driver's seat. He touched his hand to my arm. "See you tomorrow, doll face. Good work tonight."

On the ride home, I leaned my head back on the headrest and stared off into the distance out the window.

"You really don't feel anything for T.J., do you?" Shelly's question broke the silence.

I shook my head. "I can't be interested in someone when I'm in love with someone else."

She placed her hand over mine. "I know how much you miss him. I'm sorry you're going through this."

"Me, too."

Chapter Sixteen
FORGIVENESS

"What do you think?"

"I think it's going to hurt," Tanner replied.

T.J. was grinning from behind his desk. "I think it's perfect for you."

I turned the piece of paper around to face me. On it was the head of a warrior princess that John, the tattoo artist, had sketched for me based on my description of what I wanted. She had long flowing hair, war paint under her eyes, and wore a headpiece that formed a V on her forehead; the whole tattoo would be done without color, with the exception of her piercing blue eyes.

"Where are you going to put it?" Tanner asked. He was leaning against the wall in T.J.'s office. We had just finished training, and I wanted to show T.J. the tattoo idea before we headed home.

I shrugged, looking at T.J. for his input.

He leaned his elbows onto his desk, rubbing his five o'clock shadow while he contemplated. "It would work on a number of places, like upper arm, shoulder blade, or ribcage."

"I think I would like it on my arm." I touched the shoulder that had been injured in my accident a year ago.

Tanner nodded in agreement. "That's going to look so badass."

"Let me know if you want company when you decide to go," T.J. offered.

I stood from my chair, and swung my purse onto my shoulder. "Ready, little bro?"

Tanner tossed me his keys. "I'll be out in a minute. Just have to talk to Teej for a minute."

I arched an eyebrow at him. "Okay." I waved to T.J. and closed the office door behind me.

Outside, the setting sun was still warm. May had gone by in the blink of an eye, and the summer was underway. I sat on the curb beside Tanner's Mustang, closing my eyes and tilting my face towards the sky. Though I had kept busy with work, training, and hanging out with the girls, I could not deny that there was still something missing from my life. Chase's calls came in less frequently now, but I woke up to the same text each morning: "Have a good day. I love you." I didn't know what I would do once those texts stopped. I knew eventually they would.

My training with T.J. was coming to an end. I wanted to get the tattoo as part of my celebration for completing his program. I had not thought about alcohol once since my slip up after meeting with my mother. I was on my way to recovery.

A shadow was now blocking my sun. I opened my eyes to see Tanner. "You ready?" he asked.

"Yup. Everything okay?" I asked, brushing the dirt off of my back-side as I stood.

"Yup."

We buckled our seatbelts, and he backed out of the parking spot. After driving a couple of minutes in silence, Tanner glanced at me out of the corner of his eye.

"What?" I asked.

"Is there something going on between you and T.J.?"

"What?" I half-shouted. "Are you seriously asking me that?"

"I see the way he looks at you. I just can't figure out if you're looking at him the same way."

"First of all, he doesn't look at me in any way that you're implying. Secondly, I most definitely am not looking at him like that." I twisted in my seat to face him. "Is that what that was about back there? Please tell me you did not say something like this to him."

His eyes remained on the road. "I don't want him taking advantage of you. I'm trying to look out for you."

"Take advantage of me? Tanner, what the hell? You know T.J. You're the one who told me about how great he is. He has been helping me. Nothing more." I looked down at my lap. "You know what I'm going through."

He nodded sheepishly. "You helped me so much with Charlotte. I want to be able to help you, too."

"You carried me over your shoulder out of a party when I was drunk, slept in my bathtub to make sure I was okay, and took me to train with T.J. so that I would get sober. You have helped me more than you can possibly imagine."

"I'll always look out for you. Even if you never get back together with Chase – which I think you will. My dad saved your life. Helping you makes me feel like I'm helping him, in some weird way."

I gave his arm a squeeze. "I think about your dad every day."

"Me, too."

When I walked into my apartment, I sat on the arm of the couch and stared at my phone. I knew I had to reach out to my mother one last time, but I had been putting it off. It was the final piece of my puzzle – all I had to do was snap it into place. I pressed her name on my screen, and lifted the phone to my ear.

"Hi, Merritt," she answered quickly.

"So, I've had some time to think, and I would like to meet with you one last time."

"Okay. When are you available?"

"Tomorrow at seven, again, if that's okay with you."

"Sure. Yes. Seven is good."

"Good. Bye."

"Merritt?"

"Yeah?"

"Thanks for calling."

"Sure."

———

"Harder! Punch!" T.J. shouted.

My shoulders burned as my fists fired furiously at the pad.

"Three! Two! One! Time!" He lowered the pad while I caught my breath.

"What time is it?" I gasped. "I need to leave here by six-thirty."

"You've got two minutes. Don't worry. I've been keeping my eye on the time."

"My stomach is in knots."

"I know. Just breathe."

"All your words of wisdom, and you just tell me to breathe?"

He grinned. "I have faith in you. You need to have faith in yourself."

"I'll be fine once it's over."

"Call me when she leaves. We can talk it out."

I inhaled deeply. "Okay. Here I go."

"You've got this, Curly Sue!" he called as I exited the ring.

I left the gym, and took a quick shower. After I finished getting ready, I paced in my living room, going over everything I planned to say.

Again, my mother arrived promptly at seven o'clock with a knock on the door.

I let her into my apartment, and she took the same seat on the couch as last time. This time, however, I sat next to her, leaving one cushion between us. She sensed the change, and shifted nervously in her seat.

"I just wanted to start by saying I'm sorry about upsetting you last time," she began.

I held up my hand to stop her. "You don't have to be sorry. I am sorry for how abruptly I made you leave. I have a habit of shutting down when I feel emotional. I'm working on it, and I will try to do better tonight."

She swallowed hard, and her eyes were wide. "Okay. Thank you. I understand."

"You shared a lot with me last time, so now I want to share some things with you. I have been struggling since Dad died, as I'm sure you can imagine. What you don't know is that I fell in love with someone who helped me put the pieces of my life back together after that."

"The blonde one that was here the day I came?"

I nodded. "He is a singer in a band. We went to California together in February to meet with a record label that wanted to sign him. It was right after you showed up out of the blue, and that brought back so many demons I had been running from for so long. While I was in Los Angeles, I started drinking... a lot. It just felt so good being drunk. It became something I counted on, something I needed, in order to shut off the constant thoughts inside my head. I craved that allover numb feeling from it."

I looked into my mother's brown eyes, and knew that she was not judging me; I knew she understood. She placed her hand on my knee, and though I flinched, I forced myself to allow her to keep it there.

"When I tried to stop drinking, I realized that I couldn't; or I didn't want to. So, I left. I came back home, and left Chase behind."

Claire swiped away a tear that had rolled down her cheek. "Merritt, you need to get help for your drinking. It can get so much worse."

"I have been working with someone for the past two months. I only made one mistake, and that won't be happening again. I'm learning to deal with my emotions, and I'm getting stronger every day."

"That's good to hear. You've always been strong-willed. If you say you're going to do something, then I know you will. And what about Chase?"

"We tried to make the long distance thing work, but after a while it hit me that he deserved someone better than me. I think I always knew, deep down, but I kept telling myself that I could be better – I could do more, or try harder." I shrugged. "I broke up with him. We haven't spoken in weeks."

She took both of my hands in hers. "Do you love him?"

"I love him more than anything in this world. That's why I had to let him go."

"No, Merritt," she shook her head fervently. "You can't let a love like that go. Believe me when I say: you will regret it for the rest of your life. I think you're making a huge mistake."

"When you love someone, you have to do what is best for him, even if he doesn't see it. Chase needs someone better."

"Better than you? I doubt that he could ever find someone that exists."

"You're my mom. Of course you're going to say that."

"I know I haven't been around for these last important years of your life, but I still know you. I know who you are, and I know what is in your heart. Chase fell in love with you because he saw it, too. He chose to be with you, despite knowing your flaws. Nobody is perfect. Even if you think he is perfect, I can guarantee you – he is not.

Don't beat yourself up because of the way you handled a situation. Mistakes are necessary for us to learn from. Learn from yours, and use it to become an even better version of yourself. You deserve all of the wonderful things this world has to offer. You are worthy of love. Let people love you, and above all else, love yourself."

I felt my lip tremble as the tears surfaced.

Claire touched the palm of her hand to my cheek. "My beautiful girl, stop punishing yourself. Even if you never forgive me, I beg you to forgive yourself. It is the most important thing you can ever do."

I wanted to remain tough – to not let her in – but I was exhausted. After all of the running I had done, my legs finally gave out. I had fought so hard to keep myself locked up in my fortress, and it was now time to let the gate down. "I am so sorry for everything," I choked out as I sobbed. "I have been so mean to you."

Claire immediately wrapped her arms around me, and hugged me tight. "I know how angry and hurt you were. I'm just so grateful that you allowed me to explain myself. I know it doesn't take back any of the horrors you had to go through, and I'm so sorry for that. I wish I could do it all over again."

"I just wish you didn't leave. Everything might not have gotten so messed up."

"I know. I know." She rocked me in her arms as I cried.

"I don't know what to do. I don't know what's right anymore. I just feel so lost."

"What do you want? What is it that makes you truly happy?"

I pulled away from her, wiping my nose on the back of my hand. "It's him. He makes me happy."

"Then be with him. You can get through anything, and you can do it together. Everything is so much harder when you're alone." She looked down as a tear fell onto her lap. "I left instead of giving your father the chance to help me through my issues. I regret it every second of every day."

"You do?"

"I thought I was doing the right thing by leaving you. I thought I was protecting you from my mess. You and your father deserved better than an alcoholic mother and wife. I told myself that I wasn't capable of giving you what you deserved. I left in the hopes that your lives would be better because of it; but, leaving the two of you was the biggest mistake I have ever made, and I will never get to undo it."

I reached out and took her hand in mine. "I'm sorry."

She kissed the top of my hand. "I'm sorry, too."

I looked into her eyes – the same eyes as mine – and I took a breath to steady my voice. "I forgive you."

She looked back at me in disbelief. Then, she hugged me again, and we cried in each other's arms. Years of heartache and resentment poured out of our eyes, and washed away the pain. I did not know where we would go from here, but I knew that was not the point. All that mattered was what had happened in this moment. I had allowed myself to begin to forgive her, and I would learn to forgive myself.

Eventually, I walked Claire to the door.

"Think about what you want to do," she said. "Let me know when you decide."

"I will." I gave her one last hug before she stepped out onto the landing.

She hesitated when she looked down at the cement stairs, causing me to stick my head out from behind the doorway.

T.J. was sitting on the stairs, and quickly rose to his feet when he saw us. He moved out of the way so Claire could pass.

"What are you doing here?" I asked. "Is everything okay?"

"I'm fine. I came to make sure everything was okay with you."

"How long have you been sitting out here?"

He shoved his hands into his pockets. "It's a nice night. I wasn't keeping track of the time."

I stepped down two steps and sat on the top landing. "It is a nice night." I patted the empty space beside me.

T.J. sat in between me and the railing. "How did it go?"

I exhaled for what felt like the first time all day. "It went really well, actually. I opened up to her and told her about my drinking – why I started, how I couldn't stop, and how I've been working with you to make sure it never happens again." I looked at him out of the corner of my eye. "She said a lot of things that sounded like you."

He smiled. "Like what?"

"Like how I need to trust myself, and stop beating myself up about the mistakes that I've made. She said that mistakes are necessary for us to learn from. She also said that I need to let people love me, and to love myself."

"That's all true. She's been through a lot. She's an addict in recovery, so she's learning from all of her mistakes. She's trying to make sure that you don't go down the same path she took."

"She said she regrets her decision to leave every single day. It's the one mistake she will never be able to fix. That's a lot of guilt to live with."

"It is. We have to live with the choices we make, and they're not always good."

I rested my elbows on my knees, and propped my head up with my hand. "She made me think twice about breaking up with Chase. I'm left with this feeling like I don't know if I made the right choice or not."

"To me, the choice is crystal clear."

"What do you mean?"

"You have to ask yourself one question: do you love him?"

"Of course I do."

"Then you need to fight for what you love. You're a warrior, remember?"

A slow smile began to creep onto my face. "Thanks for coming to check on me."

"Any time, doll face."

"You wouldn't be here if you had a life, you know." I leaned in and nudged him with my shoulder.

"If it weren't for Chase, you would be my life."

I caught my mouth before it dropped completely open. I looked into his eyes. "Tanner was right." It came out as more of a statement than a question.

T.J. averted his eyes. "The only time you can't fight for what you love is when she's in love with someone else."

"I didn't know."

"I didn't want you to know."

"I'm so sorry. I can't–"

"I know," he interrupted. "I know."

I covered his hand with mine. "You have done so much for me, T.J. I don't know how I can ever repay you."

He stood and stretched his arms up over his head. "You can repay me by staying sober. Stop running away from your feelings. Your avoidance is your downfall."

I stood. "So, I'll see you tomorrow?"

"You will." He winked, and trotted down the stairs.

I walked inside my apartment, and grabbed only my keys. I locked the door after stepping back outside, and jogged down to my car – the only thing I had left of my father. I started the engine, and rolled the windows down.

The further I got from the city streets, the faster I went. I was not focused on where I was headed, as a million thoughts raced through my mind. For the first time, instead of craving a bitter liquid to dull my senses, I wanted to feel everything; I needed to feel every emotion that I had inside me – I needed my mind clear and sharp.

I had forgiven my mother. Moreover, I allowed myself to. Had I not started drinking in California, I don't know that I would have been able to forgive her. I would not have been able to truly understand what she went through; but I walked in her shoes, and I searched for solace in exactly the same places. Though forgiveness was not a quick wave of a wand, magically making everything better, I felt a heaviness lifted off of my shoulders. I still felt grief over the death of my father; I still felt heartache remembering my teenage years that were taken from me; I still felt hurt over the loss of my mother for eight important years of my life. Some feelings would never change. The one thing that was different, though, was the absence of hate. It was blatantly apparent. I no longer felt angry.

Driving down the quiet road, the wind whipped through my hair. I recalled Chase sitting in the passenger seat after he had restored my Chevelle as a surprise for Christmas. He watched me whenever I drove it, his eyes always looking into my soul. He saw me for who I was during that time, and he accepted me for the shell of a person I had become. I was broken, cynical, and closed off. He fell in love with me in spite of it all. He brought the light back into the darkest places of my heart, and he showed me how good it could feel to be loved.

I had pushed him away so many times before in the beginning, but this time felt different. I had cut off all communication with him, forcing a choice upon him that he did not ask for – much like my mother had done to me many years ago. It was a decision she regretted in hindsight – a decision that changed our lives forever. Why had I pushed Chase away? What was I scared of? T.J. had taught me to face everything, and deal with it. It was okay to be scared, but it was not okay to back down. I had to face my emotions. I had to face my fears.

I slowed my car down, and came to a stop in front of a tree. Bark was missing from part of the trunk, while the remaining pieces were blackened and damaged. It took me a few seconds to realize where I was, where I had subconsciously driven to. Nine months ago, I had wrapped my car around this tree. I was trapped inside of the mangled metal, half-conscious, and was about to be burned alive. Chase had followed me there, and risked his life trying to pull me out of the wreckage.

I stepped out of the car, and walked towards the tree. The grass was still missing from where my tires had skidded off the road. I touched the tree as the fragments of that night flashed through my mind. If it weren't for Chase and his father, I would have died. Now, I was here and Tim was not. I was given a second chance that he was not so fortunate to receive. Life was short, and it would be a waste to spend it on the run from my feelings. Living in the past did not allow me to appreciate what I had in the present – and what I had was irreplaceable.

I jumped back in my car, and sped off en route to my apartment. Thundering down the roads, I could not get home fast enough. The sense of urgency I felt only grew with each turn I made. Throwing the shifter into park, I sprinted to my stairs, and climbed them by twos. I didn't waste time to catch my breath once I was inside my apartment. I had wasted too much time already.

Chapter Seventeen

GUARDIAN ANGELS

"Would you stop bouncing your leg? You're making me nervous!"

"I'm sorry. I can't help it," I whined. "What's taking so long?"

Shelly slammed on her horn for the third time. "People drive like morons! Relax. It's not like Chase is going anywhere." Shelly did her best to calm my nerves as we sat in traffic just outside of the airport.

Last night, I booked the first flight to California that was available. I didn't call Chase to tell him I was coming. I didn't want to explain everything on the phone, and I was afraid he would try to talk me out of it. I needed to see him in person, and it had to be soon. Every second that passed felt like another second too late to fix the mess I had created.

"Finally!" Shelly shouted as the cars began to move. "I wish you would let me come with you."

"I need to do this on my own."

"Do you think T.J. is going to be pissed that you're missing the last few training sessions?"

"I'm hoping he understands." I had texted him last night, explaining that I would be away for a few days. He did not respond.

Shelly pulled up to the curb at the drop-off area. She popped her trunk, and leaned over the center console to give me a hug. "Text me when you land. Call me after you talk to him."

I hugged her tightly. "Thanks for driving."

"Thanks for finally coming to your senses."

I laughed. "Hopefully, it goes well."

"It will. I know it will."

I hoisted my luggage out of the trunk, and waved goodbye to Shelly one last time before entering the busy airport. Being here for the third time this year, I had memorized all the steps. I waited as patiently as I could until it was time to board. A Mothra-sized butterfly flapped her giant wings inside of my stomach when my flight number was called.

I tried to sleep on the plane, but my nerves were on high alert. I recited all of the things I wanted to say to Chase in my head over and over again until we landed. Waiting for everyone to exit the plane felt like water torture, and waiting for my luggage was even worse. All I wanted to do was take off running until I arrived at Chase's apartment.

I checked the time while I waited for a cab outside. Chase would be just about to go on stage when I arrived – wherever he was playing. I knew that I would probably have to wait in his empty apartment until he returned after two o'clock in the morning. I tried to prepare myself for the fact that he might not be coming home alone; I had not thought of a plan for that scenario yet, and hoped I wouldn't have to worry about it.

I paid the cabbie when he parked in front of Clutch. Taking an enormous deep breath, I rolled my luggage through the familiar front door. The bar was exactly how I had left it – jam packed with people. I could see that a band was setting up on stage, and I stretched up onto my toes to catch a glimpse of any familiar faces. I made my way towards the bar, pulling my luggage through the crowd, still trying to see who was performing tonight. My luggage tilted sideways and rolled over someone's foot.

"Sorry!" I shouted back over my shoulder. I bent down to pick it up by the handle, and smacked right into someone's back. I cringed, and looked up apologetically. When I saw who it was in a plain black t-shirt, and perfectly fitting jeans, my stomach did a backflip. It was Chase.

At least a dozen emotions flashed across his face all at once. His lips parted as his mouth hung open, and his expression finally settled on utter shock.

I tried to breathe, but it felt as if I had stepped out onto the moon without an oxygen tank. The words I had rehearsed were suddenly wiped from my memory. The noisy room sounded muffled. It was hard to hear anything over the pounding of my pulse in my ears.

"Holy fuck!" Dave shouted from a few feet away. "Look what the cat dragged in!"

I looked at Dave and offered a half-smile before returning my eyes to Chase, whose eyes had not left me.

"What are you doing here?" Chase finally spoke.

"I needed to talk to you. It's important."

He crossed his arms over his chest as his eyebrows pushed together. "You could have picked up the phone. I only called you a billion times."

I became nervous, sensing his anger. All I could do was shrug my shoulders at him. No words could express the urgency of my visit. "I needed to see you."

"Well, you saw me. I have to go now." With that, he turned and pushed his way through the crowd towards the stage.

Dave stepped out from behind the bar and gave me a playful shove. "Did the hot mess express just let out?"

I stifled a laugh. "Yeah, pretty much."

He leaned in close. "Don't let his tough guy act fool you. He's been a wreck without you."

"He has?"

Dave winked. "Did you really think he wouldn't be?"

I threw my arms around him. "I missed you."

"I missed you, too. Thanks for leaving me, you bitch."

I grimaced. "I'm sorry. I... I really don't know what to say."

"I get it. I'm just giving you a hard time." He gestured to my suitcase. "Do you need help getting that upstairs?"

I shook my head. "I can manage. Thanks." I glanced up at the stage, but Chase's back was turned as he fiddled with a microphone stand.

"Go up and get settled," Dave suggested. "We can catch up another time."

I nodded, and lugged my suitcase to the door. I was halfway up the stairs when Chase appeared. He jogged past me, and unlocked the apartment door at the top, holding it open for me.

"Thanks," I puffed as I dragged the luggage the rest of the way up, and into the apartment.

"I should be in around two," he replied before disappearing down the stairs, closing the door behind him.

I paced in the living room for the first twenty minutes. Everything was in the same spot as it was before I left. It had only been a couple of months, so I don't know what I expected to change. So much had happened with me that it felt like I had been gone much longer.

I didn't know what to do with myself. I couldn't unpack, for fear that Chase would not want me to stay. I couldn't eat, due to the knots that twisted in my stomach. I eyed the pool table, but playing by myself wouldn't exactly be entertaining. I decided to shower the stale smell of the airplane off of me, in the hopes that it would help me relax.

Afterwards, I sat on the bed wrapped in a towel. I called Shelly, praying that she would answer and help kill some time.

"Hey, how's it going?" she answered.

"I don't know. He seemed mad when he saw me, but he let me into his apartment to wait for him. The time is passing so slowly!"

"Just get comfortable and watch a movie or something."

"What if he hates me? What if he doesn't want to be with me anymore?"

"He doesn't hate you. You bruised his ego a little. He'll get over it."

"I hope so."

"I know so."

"Love you, Toad."

"Love you, Frog."

I changed into yoga pants and a tank top, and fussed with my hair in the mirror. I wanted to look good enough when he arrived, yet casual enough for two in the morning. I settled myself on the bed, and turned on the TV. My eyelids grew heavy as I flipped back and forth between two movies I had no interest in watching. I continuously glanced at the clock throughout the night. Midnight meant it was three o'clock back in New York. I fought the sleepiness for as long as I could, but eventually I passed out.

A little while later, I opened my eyes feeling as if Chase was shaking me awake. I remembered falling asleep with the lights and TV on, but everything was now off. Only the light of the moon was shining through the window. I sat up in bed, disoriented. I still felt like I was moving. A rattling sound crept into my ears, as if a train was passing through the apartment, causing all of the dishes and glasses to shake in the kitchen. That is when I realized what was happening.

I grabbed my phone off of the nightstand, and clicked on the flashlight app. The floor jerked and swayed underneath my bare feet as I tried to navigate out of the bedroom. I held onto the doorframe, watching the cabinets in the kitchen swing open, spilling their contents out onto the floor. Ceramic and glass crashed and exploded everywhere. I looked down at my bare feet, trying to remember where I had left my sneakers. I spotted them across the room, next to the front door. That was my way out.

On a silent three-count, I let go of the doorframe and attempted to steady my legs, as if I was surfing through choppy waters. I stumbled only a few feet before I fell. I began crawling instead, shards of glass cracking under my hands and knees. My skin was being sliced, but I knew I had to keep moving. Solid and striped balls were knocked off of the pool table and rolled across the floor in all different directions; the pool sticks followed. A loud crash froze me in my tracks, and I looked behind me to see the flat screen television face down in the middle of the living room. I focused my attention forward, and fixed my watery eyes on the door ahead. Mere seconds felt like hours as I made it through the trembling apartment.

At the door, I scrambled to get my shoes on. Glass had slashed through parts of my pants, and I could see red smears of blood on the wooden floor in the light from my phone. I grabbed onto the doorknob and pulled myself to my feet. Without stopping to think, I began my descent down the stairs. Thrashing from side to side in the narrow stairwell, I dodged pieces of the ceiling that were falling from above.

When I reached the bottom, the rumbling and shaking stopped. I stood still, holding my breath and refusing to believe that it was really over.

A loud sound split through the air. I quickly ducked down, covering my head with both arms. A large wooden beam dropped from the ceiling near the top of the staircase, crashing through several of the steps. I looked up when the dust had settled, worried that the rest of the ceiling would cave in next. Spinning around, I turned the door-knob and pushed against the door, but it did not budge. A sinking feeling washed over me as I tried to open the door again: I had dreamt of this moment – I was now trapped in the stairwell.

I pressed my ear against the door, and listened for any sounds on the other side. Chase, Dave, and over a hundred people were inside the bar when the earthquake struck. At the moment, all I could hear was the sound of my own breathing. I tucked my phone into the strap of my tank top, and pounded on the door as hard as I could.

"Help!" I shouted. "Can anybody hear me?" I slammed my fists against the door, and then listened again. Nothing.

"Chase!" I screamed. I smashed my shoulder into the door, pushing against it with all of my body weight. Something must be blocking it from the other side. I stepped back and tried kicking it until my legs tired out. I looked up at the fallen beam at the top of the stairs, and back at the unopened door in front of me. I couldn't go backward, and I couldn't go forward. I was stuck. Sweat began beading on my fore-head, trickling down my face and neck. I could feel the panic setting in.

I covered my face with my hands and began to cry. Chase was on the other side of this door, and if he was not banging it down to come get me – something was very wrong. I squeezed my eyes shut, trying to ignore all of the horrific things that flashed through my mind; I had to stick with the facts, for now. Breathing deeply, I positioned myself as if I was standing in front of T.J. I could hear his voice telling me to punch harder, and to throw my back into it. "You are a warrior," he would say. "Get back up and keep fighting!"

I began throwing punches against the wooden door, one harder than the next. The sound of my fists making contact with the door

sounded so loud in the silence. Once my knuckles were sore and bleeding, I used my foot instead. I kicked the same spot in the door over
and over. Finally, I saw it crack. My kicks became faster, and I didn't
stop until the door had split open from the middle. I rammed my
shoulder into it, and crashed through to the other side. Several bar
stools, and a beam from the ceiling were piled in pieces in front of the
door that had blocked me in. I climbed over them and scanned the
room with my phone, shining the light above my head to reach as far
as I could.

People were lying on the floor, with wood and glass scattered everywhere around them. Part of the ceiling had collapsed in the far corner,
and many of the windows had shattered. To my left, I could see people
huddled behind the bar. Some of them began to stand, shaking the
glass and dust out of their hair.

"Are you okay?" I asked. My voice echoed in the still room.

"I think so," one man answered.

"Dave, are you back there?" I called. He had to be. I waited,
praying to hear his voice in return. My throat felt dry as I tried to swallow. No response.

Several women that had taken cover under one of the pinball
machines stood up, brushing themselves off. I shined my phone in
their direction, crunching on broken glass as I stepped over the stools
that had been knocked over.

"Are you girls okay? Is anybody hurt?"

"We're okay, but one of our friends was in the bathroom," a blonde
sniffled. Her knee was bleeding, but she didn't seem to notice.

"Use the flashlights on your phones. Stay together, and be careful
where you step."

They nodded in unison and began shuffling past me.

My heart was racing as I continued to look for Chase. The stage
was covered in debris, and the lights above it had fallen. Chunks of the
ceiling covered the surrounding area. I saw a brass cymbal and a guitar
sticking out from underneath one of the wooden beams that had
crashed on top of the stage. My hands trembled, as it looked like the
worst of the damage was in this area.

"Chase?" I called. "Chase, where are you?" I choked back a sob when I did not hear a response from him. Reminding myself to breathe, I did my best to remain calm. Panicking would get me nowhere. Chase was here, somewhere. I had to keep searching.

I picked up hunks of sheetrock, moving them aside to uncover anything or anyone that might be underneath. A white sneaker caught my eye, and I quickly pushed the wood and broken bass drum off of the body that the sneaker was connected to. It was the drummer of Chase's band. I struggled to recall his name – was it Chad? I crouched down and gently shook his arm, shaking it harder when he did not wake up. Philip should be here, and I wondered if Brooke was, too. I covered my mouth with my hand as I started to cry again.

Several people walked by me on their way to the door. I watched them exit the bar, stepping over the people that were unconscious, or worse, lying on the floor. I couldn't blame them for wanting to get out. The air inside the bar was musty and thick, making it hard to breathe.

I cleared everything off of the drummer's body and left him there until I could get help. I was afraid to move him and cause more harm.

"Chase!" I yelled. "Chase!" I continued picking up fragments of the building and band equipment. I tried to move a large part of the ceiling from my path, but it was heavy. I was going to leave it, until I spotted a large hand sticking out from under it. A familiar leather cuff was attached to its wrist. Frantically, I bent down to find Chase lying on the ground sporting a decent-sized gash on his forehead. A thick stream of blood had seeped into his hairline, staining his golden hair red. I breathed a small sigh of relief – finding him was only half the battle.

I touched his face with my shaking hand. "Chase," I croaked. "Chase, please wake up." I thought to check for a pulse, but hesitated as two very different scenarios played out in my mind. I pressed two of my fingers against his neck, and held my breath. He had a pulse!

I shoved my phone back into my shirt and tried to lift the wood that was crushing his torso. Pulling with all of my might, the piece barely budged. "Come on," I grunted. Then, I was reminded of tire flipping, and T.J.'s voice sounded in my head again: "Press up with your legs." Squatting down, I positioned myself appropriately and pressed upward through the heels of my feet. My whole body shook as the wood lifted until I was able to free Chase's body. Once it was up, I tossed it over and kneeled down next to his lifeless body.

I was not sure if giving CPR was the right thing to do in this situation, but it was the only other thing I could think of. Mimicking what I had only seen in movies, I pumped my hands against his chest, and held his nose while I puffed air into his mouth. I did it again, and again, pressing harder each time out of desperation. I had lost track of how many times I repeated the routine. More survivors watched me in silence as they passed by. I averted my eyes from their somber expressions and concentrated on Chase's face instead.

"Come on, Chase," I sobbed. "Just wake up already." Tears spilled down my cheeks as I attempted to breathe the life back into him. As I pressed against his chest, his eyelids fluttered. Unsure if I should stop, I continued pumping my arms. Then, his eyes opened.

"Merritt?" he whispered.

"I'm here. You're alive."

"Everything hurts."

"Can you move your arms and your legs?"

His legs slowly moved, and his hands found their way into mine. "Are you okay?"

I nodded, my face soaked from the tears. "I'm okay as long as you're okay." I buried my face in his chest. "I couldn't find you."

Chase shifted, attempting to sit up. I pointed the light from my phone onto the floor so he could see. He took the phone and faced the light towards me. My knuckles were swollen and purple, with blood streaks running down my fingers. "You're hurt. What happened?"

"We'll talk about it later. We need to get you to a hospital. Let's get you up." I wrapped my arm around his back. "Lean on me."

He growled from the pain as he got to his feet.

I steadied him, holding onto his midsection. "Can you stand?"

He propped himself up against the nearby wall. "I'm good."

I looked over at the bar. "I'm going to find Dave. He has to be back there somewhere."

"I'll come help you."

"No. You stay here. You're hurt. I'll be right back."

"Please be careful. Nothing in here is stable right now."

I walked as quickly as I could; pain shot through my ankle, undoubtedly from kicking through the door earlier. I swung myself under the bar, shining my light in front of me. There was broken glass and liquid everywhere from fallen liquor bottles. I spotted Dave's black rimmed glasses next to my foot, and then saw him lying underneath the shelves that had detached from the wall.

"Dave!" I cried. "Chase, I found him!"

"Is he conscious?" Chase called back to me.

"No." I crouched down, and checked for his pulse. It was so faint, I barely felt it. "His pulse is weak! I have to get him out of here." I placed his glasses back on his face, though the lenses were badly cracked. Then, I hooked my arms under his armpits, and began dragging him backwards. I could hear sirens outside. I needed to get Chase and Dave out there as quickly as possible.

"Let me help." Chase tried to bend over, but winced and clutched his ribs.

"I've got Dave. Just focus on walking out that door." Breathing hard, I kept a steady pace pulling Dave's body to the exit. "You are heavier than you look, buddy."

"He's going to be okay. Don't worry, baby."

My heart skipped a beat at Chase's word choice.

Outside, the lights atop the emergency vehicles were blinding in the darkness. A paramedic saw me dragging Dave into the street, and ran over to help.

"His name is Dave. He has a pulse," I offered as the man called for a stretcher. "I found him underneath some shelves. He needs medical attention, too," I said touching Chase's arm. "He was unconscious when I found him, and I think his ribs are broken."

"That's a pretty nasty gash on your forehead," he said. "Let's get you into the ambulance." He pointed to the truck.

I looked up at Chase. "I'm going back in. Your bandmates are still in there."

"The rescue teams are here, miss. They'll get them." The paramedic pointed to the trucks of men and women that were preparing to go inside. "The hospital is quickly filling up. You've already saved two lives tonight. You should get checked out, too," he said, pointing to my hands.

I looked back at the bar one more time, reluctant to leave those people behind. I still had not found Philip, or Brooke, if she was in there. Chase tugged on my elbow, and I followed them into the back of the ambulance.

The ride to the nearest hospital was quick, but the wait in the Emergency Room was not. We waited almost an hour and a half before Chase could be seen. I was worried about internal bleeding in his head, or that a lung had been punctured by his rib. The minutes ticked by slowly.

I checked my phone for the time, but it was dead. "I must have used all the battery up with the flashlight. You should call your mom. I need to call Shelly. I don't want them to see the news and freak out."

"Good idea." Chase slipped his phone out of his pocket. The screen was cracked in several spots, but it still worked.

I rested my head on Chase's shoulder, listening to Beverly's voice on the other side of his phone.

"What do you mean there was an earthquake? This damn thing never works," she muttered. I pictured her smacking the remote on her palm.

"Give me it before you break it," I heard Tanner say.

"Oh my God, Chase," Beverly gasped. She was probably seeing the same footage that we were watching in the hospital. "Are you alright? Where are you?"

"I'm in the hospital with Merritt. Everything is okay," he reassured.

"Merritt's with you?" She and Tanner said in unison.

Chase laughed as he turned his head to look at me. "She arrived last night. She was just in time to get me and a friend out of the bar after the earthquake hit. I was knocked out, and she saved me."

"Jesus Christ! I want you both to come home!" she cried.

"We will," he said. "I will call you after the doctor checks me out."

"I love the both of you so much."

"We love you, too," I called.

Chase handed me the phone so that I could call Shelly. I lowered the volume a few notches while it rang, so her shrieking wouldn't deafen me.

"Chase? Why are you calling me? Why hasn't Merritt texted me back? Is everything okay?"

"I could answer all of those questions if you'd let me get a word in."

"Merritt? What's going on?"

"There was an earthquake. I'm in the hospital with Chase now. We're okay."

"An earthquake? Holy shit, Merritt! How bad was it? Are you hurt? Is Chase hurt?"

"I'm fine. Just some cuts and bruises. Chase is waiting to be seen. This place is packed right now."

"When are you coming home? There are aftershocks, you know. You guys need to get the hell out of there!"

"I know. I just wanted to let you know what happened, in case you saw the news. Can you do me a favor?"

"Anything."

"Can you swing by the gym at some point today and just let T.J. know that I'm alright? My phone died."

"Of course. Does Chase's family know?"

"Yes, he just spoke to them."

She blew out a breath of air. "God, Merritt. Why are you always in harm's way?"

"I don't know," I replied.

"I love you, Frog."

"Love you, Toad."

Several minutes later, the doctors called Chase in to do a CAT scan of his skull, and an X-ray of his ribs. He had a concussion, which was expected, but no broken ribs. The cut on his forehead was stitched up, and he was instructed to ice his injuries to help with the swelling.

We remained in the waiting room, periodically asking for updates on Dave. I lied to the receptionist, telling her that I was his sister. She told me she would let me know when I could see him. I was happy to stay; I felt safe in the hospital, and we didn't exactly have a place to go back to. Chase nodded off, but I could not fall asleep. My pants were shredded from crawling over broken glass, and blood covered my exposed knees. The nurse was kind enough to give me a bag of ice for my knuckles while I waited. Every body part ached, but I welcomed the pain. It meant I was alive – I had survived, and so had Chase.

After the sun came up, Chase opened his eyes and smiled sleepily at me. "Have you been watching me sleep this whole time?"

"I was so worried that you were..." I could not say the word. "I thought I was too late for my second chance."

He tucked a curl behind my ear, and stroked my cheek with his thumb. "I would give you a hundred chances."

I leaned over in my seat and pressed my lips against his. It had been so long since I felt them. They were even better than I had remembered.

"Miss Adams?" a nurse called. She smiled when I stood. "He's awake now. He'll have some nasty bruising on his head, but he'll be fine. His shoulder was dislocated, so he's in a sling. He can go home in a couple of hours."

"Oh, thank God," I breathed.

"Would you like to see him?"

"Yes, please." I held my hand out for Chase to take as he hobbled over to me.

"I'm so glad you guys are alright," I murmured as we followed the nurse down the hallway.

"Our fathers were with us tonight for sure," he replied.

I smiled at the thought. "We have two incredible guardian angels watching over us."

The nurse led us behind a curtain. Dave was sitting up in bed; his right arm was in a sling and he sported cuts all over the left side of his face. He managed a smile when he saw us.

"Hey there, sis."

"I am so glad you're okay." I hugged him gently.

"You look like shit, Abercrombie."

Chase chuckled. "You don't look too hot, yourself." He gestured for me to sit in the chair next to Dave's bed, but I shook my head. He needed to sit more than I did.

"Thanks to this one, we're both okay," Chase said.

Dave's face twisted in confusion. "What do you mean?"

"Merritt was able to get downstairs, break down the door, rescue me, and then drag you out to the ambulance." He was looking at me with pride in his eyes.

Dave's hand reached out for mine. "You came back just in time to save us."

I squeezed his hand, tearing up again as I thought about what could have happened had I not flown to California when I did.

"Your hands!" Dave gasped, turning them over to look at my bloodied knuckles.

"It's nothing," I reassured him. "Do you remember what happened to you?"

"When the quake happened, the shelves of liquor collapsed. All I remember is trying to dodge the flying bottles. Something knocked me out, and I went down. The doctor said I dislocated my shoulder."

I cringed, remembering what it was like to be in a sling similar to his.

"How bad was the damage?" Dave asked.

"It was so hard to see in the dark, but beams in the ceiling were falling. That can't be good structurally."

"Did you see Donnie there last night?" Chase asked.

Dave shook his head.

My eyes widened, remembering Donnie's pregnant wife. I thought about Chad, lying there in the midst of the debris; then I thought about Philip, and Brooke. I looked at Chase. "Can you text Philip?"

"I texted all of the guys while I was waiting to be brought into the examination room." He shook his head. "No responses yet, but that doesn't mean anything."

"Is there anyone you need us to call?" I asked Dave.

"I texted my mom when I woke up. She already booked me a flight back home. She's freaking out. You guys need a ride anywhere?"

Chase ran his fingers through his hair. "When are you heading to the airport?"

"As soon as they let me out of here. My flight leaves at noon."

Immediately, Chase took out his phone. "I'll get us the earliest flight I can."

My eyebrows shot up. "Back to New York?"

He was quiet while he tapped on his screen. When he had finished, he looked up at me and smiled. "Done. We leave at two."

"You can drive my car," Dave offered, patting his sling.

"We'll have to go back to the apartment to get our things." A lump formed in my throat as I thought about having to go back there.

Chase's fingers intertwined with mine, and he carefully kissed my swollen hand. "We'll be quick."

I bit my bottom lip to keep it from trembling. I didn't want the boys to see how terrified I was after what had happened. Though their injuries could have been much worse, they were fortunate enough to be knocked unconscious for the duration of the earthquake. I remembered every detail as it ran through my mind on a constant loop. I couldn't wait to be flying hundreds of miles away from this place.

Chapter Eighteen

IT HURTS BUT I'LL LIVE

In the daylight, we were able to see the full magnitude of the damage that had been done. The street we rode on had cracks running throughout it; one road we passed was soaked with water from the shift in the underground pipes; firefighters attempted to put out a fire in one of the buildings we drove by. People walked the streets to capture pictures of what they saw, stepping over the fallen bricks and chunks of cement that lined the sidewalk. If you looked quickly, most of the stores and buildings looked intact. Looking more closely inside, however, looked like a tornado had ripped through each building. The palm trees stood tall and brave amidst the broken city.

Chase, Dave, and I were quiet as we rolled to a stop. My hands were throbbing, and I was still wearing torn yoga pants. All three of us were filthy, bruised, and cut up. We looked exactly like the natural disaster victims I had always seen on the news; with the exception of a hurricane here and there, New York was a safe place to live. I couldn't imagine living in a place like this, where something so scary was considered normal. I stared at the bar, my stomach twisting violently. I took a breath before stepping out of Dave's car.

We saw Donnie as soon as we walked inside. He looked unscathed, and I hoped his wife looked the same. "It's good to see you guys," he said, hugging each of us. He paused after he let me go. "Wait. What are you doing here?"

"She came back in the nick of time," Dave said. "She pulled me and Chase out of this mess last night."

"How's Rachel?" I asked.

"She's fine. She's at her mother's house." He looked around the bar, heaving a sigh. "This place is a wreck."

"How long do you think it will take you to get it up and running again?" Dave asked.

"It has never been this badly damaged before." Donnie looked at me. "What does it look like upstairs?"

"It... it was dark. Everything happened so fast."

"I looked up into the stairwell. Shit's a mess in there. Good thing you got out of there."

Chase hugged me to his side. "She was trapped in there for a while."

Donnie's eyes surveyed my appearance. "The door was broken off the hinges."

"Yeah. Sorry about that."

His eyebrows lifted. "You did that?"

"She's one badass bitch." Dave gave me a wink.

"We're going back to New York today," Chase informed him. "We need to grab our things upstairs."

Donnie nodded. "Be careful. I don't know what's stable in this place."

"Stay down here," I told Dave. "You don't need to be climbing the stairs with one arm."

Donnie uprighted a nearby stool. "Take a seat, Dee."

Chase shook his head as he stared at the mangled door leading to our apartment. "I'm so sorry I couldn't get to you."

"All I care about is that you're alive." I stepped over the pile of wood, and entered the stairwell. The beam that blocked the entrance at the top of the stairs had tumbled to the bottom. I climbed over it, and held out my hand for Chase. Slowly and carefully, we ascended up to the apartment.

"Oh, God," Chase murmured once inside. His eyes became watery, and I knew he was imagining me being alone in the midst of this destruction.

I touched his arm. "Don't think about it. Let's just get our things and get out of here."

He wiped his eyes quickly.

The bedroom was as big of a mess as the rest of the apartment. The television had fallen off of the wall, and the curtain rod had fallen off the window; the lamp on each nightstand had broken on the floor, and glass was everywhere. I gathered my things, shoving them into my suitcase, and helped Chase pack up his clothes from the dresser and closet. I tossed everything from the bathroom into my luggage, and zippered it shut. Chase and I changed into clean clothes, and then rolled our suitcases to the door.

Chase stopped to look around one last time. "I'm going to miss this place," he said aloud.

"Donnie will fix everything up. I'm sure it will be ready sooner than you think."

The wheels were turning in his head, and he did not respond.

———

CHASE SLEPT MOST OF THE PLANE RIDE HOME. I, ON THE OTHER hand, remained awake. I had struggled to sleep after my accident last year, and was used to getting only a couple of broken hours of shut eye. Now having been through yet another traumatic experience, I was prepared for the long, sleepless nights I had ahead of me. Towards the end of the flight I had finally drifted off, but awoke in a panic when we hit the landing strip. I gasped, gripping the armrest between me and Chase.

"It's okay, baby," Chase whispered. "We just landed."

I nodded as I steadied my breath. The shaking was something I never wanted to feel again. Seeing Chase on the ground clinging to life was another. I looked into his tired green eyes, and felt so grateful that he had made it out of the earthquake in one piece.

"What's going on in that head of yours?" he asked, one corner of his mouth slightly turned up.

"There's so much I need to say to you. We never got the chance to talk."

He kissed my forehead. "We'll have plenty of time to talk once we are settled at home."

Home. I had a newfound appreciation for Staten Island. I resisted the urge to kiss the ground when we stepped off the plane.

Shelly and Brody were waiting outside to take us back to Chase's house. She burst into tears as soon as she saw me.

"Be gentle," I warned, holding my arms out to embrace her.

"It's all over the news," she sobbed as she hugged me. "I can't believe you were in that!"

"I can't either," I said, reaching out for Brody.

"You're like a cat," he said with a grin. "What's left, seven lives now?"

"That is so not funny," Shelly scolded.

I watched Chase try not to wince as Shelly squeezed his midsection.

"She's stronger than she looks," I said, taking his suitcase from him.

"Give me that." Brody took it from my hands. "Get in the car, you two."

When we pulled up to the house, Beverly, Tanner, and Khloe were waiting out on the front steps. Beverly held onto Khloe's arm when she attempted to run to us. She whispered into her ear, most likely reminding her not to jump on us.

I knelt down and opened my arms wide, signaling to Khloe that it was okay to come to me. She leapt down the stairs, and charged into my arms.

"Merry!" she screamed.

"I am so happy to see you, my angel girl!"

"Me too!" She clung to me like a tiny koala.

"Hey, save some for me," Chase called. He sat down on the top step, and I placed her gently into his lap. She did her best not to squeeze him too hard, and kissed his forehead next to his stitches with her tiny lips.

Tanner bear hugged me. "I'm glad you're okay, big sis."

"So am I," Beverly said. She took my face into her hands. "Thank you for bringing him home. It's a miracle that you went there when you did."

I wrapped my arms around her, fighting back the tears.

"You smell, Chasey," Khloe said pinching her nose in between her fingers. "You need to take a bath."

Chase chuckled. "You didn't say that to Merry. She smells, too."

"You tell him I smell like roses."

Khloe grinned, showing all of her tiny Tic-Tac teeth. "Merry smells like roses."

"Why don't you two go take a shower, and relax?" Beverly said. "I'm making dinner for us tonight, if you're up for it."

Chase looked at me, and I smiled. "Of course we'll be up for it."

The second we walked inside my apartment, I inhaled the familiar smell of home. "Why don't you shower first?"

"Are you sure?" Chase asked. "You can go first if you want."

I shook my head. "I'll get our things settled in here. You go ahead."

In my bedroom, I began putting my clothes away. I opened the small box with the necklace Chase had given me for Valentine's Day inside. Running my finger over it, I silently thanked my father and Tim for watching over us in California. I wondered how many people were not as lucky. I plugged my phone in to charge. When it turned on, a series of texts popped up on the screen. Brooke and Philip were alright, as were the rest of Chase's bandmates. I felt a wave of relief wash over me, and texted her back.

When Chase reappeared in the room, I held my phone up. "Brooke texted. Everyone's fine."

His smile spread across his face. "That's great news."

I stood, holding out my knuckles in front of me. "How badly do you think these are going to hurt in the shower on a scale of one to ten?"

He made a face. "Probably an eight."

I walked into the bathroom. "I can take an eight."

Though my cuts stung, it felt good to wash the remnants of the earthquake off of my body. I tried to push the scary memory of the actual quake out of my mind, and focus on the important things: everyone we knew had survived, and Chase was home.

When I returned to the bedroom, Chase was lying on the bed in his boxers with a frozen bag of peas on his ribcage. Purple bruises were sprawled underneath his chest, and down the side of his body. I sat on the edge of the bed beside him in my towel, stroking his arm.

"How do you feel?"

"It hurts, but I'll live."

"Thank God for that," I murmured.

"Ready for that talk now?" He interlaced his fingers with mine.

"I have been working through a lot of things over the past two months. I learned a lot working with T.J. He helped me to see that I wasn't taking responsibility for my actions. I was making choices, and then blaming it on my mother as if she was responsible for all of things that were wrong in my life. Then she told me that she was an alcoholic, and I wasn't mad at her — I was mad at myself. Without even knowing it, I had done the very same thing that she did. I felt like the world's biggest piece of shit, and I convinced myself that I wasn't good enough for you. I was ashamed of the person I had become, and I didn't understand how you could love me.

When I saw you with your arm around that girl, and how happy you looked performing, I told myself that you would be better off without me. I had issues; I came with baggage, and I thought I didn't deserve someone like you. I was spiraling out of control, and I didn't want to bring you down with me."

Chase looked at me with pain in his eyes. "That is not how I saw you. Not once."

"It's how I saw myself. I was my own worst enemy for a while."

"So, what changed?"

"I met with my mother again, the night I booked my flight to come see you. I hugged her, and I told her that I forgave her for everything. She admitted to me that she regrets her decision to leave every single day. Knowing that my father is gone, knowing she lost all those years with me — she made a mistake that can never be undone. I felt so sad for her. That has to be the worst pain in the world, to know that you will never be able to have a second chance.

I don't want to spend the rest of my life knowing that you're the one wrong I can't make right. If I love you, then I have to stop being the person that doesn't deserve you, and start being the kind of person you deserve – the person I deserve to be for myself. I was so stupid to think that letting you go was the right thing to do. You're supposed to fight for what you love, and I will fight for you every single day." Tears spilled out of my eyes as I envisioned Chase, unconscious on the floor just hours before. "I thought you were gone when I found you last night. I thought I had lost you forever."

"You didn't lose me. You will never lose me. I will always be right here with you. I told you – you are the only one for me. I don't ever want to be with anyone else." He stroked my cheek tenderly. "When you left to come back home, I was angry at first. I was so frustrated with myself that I didn't know how to fix your problems, and I was even more frustrated that you didn't want my help. In a way, it hurt to hear how great you were doing with T.J.'s help. It felt like he had something that I didn't. You trusted him to help you; you trusted him enough to let him in. Yet, you always pushed me away. It was really difficult for me; but, the more I thought about it, the more I realized that it wasn't about me. It was about you. The most important thing to me was you – your health, your happiness. I wasn't alright knowing that you weren't alright. So, I told myself that if you needed to do this, I was going to stand by you, no matter what the consequences were for me.

You can give me your worst; you can push me away, and tell me that I deserve better, but you will never be able to convince me of the lies your fear tells you. I know you. I know who you truly are inside, and I know that we are exactly the kind of people we deserve to be with. You are so strong, you are capable of anything. I just want to show you that I could be strong enough for you – that I could be good enough for you." He stroked my cheek. "I'm in awe of you, Merritt. I always have been. When you came back to California, I wanted to pack my things and leave with you instantly."

"You did?"

"You came back for me, and I knew that was all I needed. I spent the past few months chasing after my dream, but without you in my life – it just didn't seem worth it. For a moment, I had the woman of my dreams and the career of my dreams, and I felt like I was on top of the world. When you left, the world came crashing down. My heart wasn't in it anymore. Nothing means anything if I don't have you."

"But you were so happy performing."

"I was happy, but I wasn't as happy as I was with you. I had fun, but it wasn't as much fun as it was when you were there. What is the point of building the life you've always wanted if the girl you love isn't there to share it with?"

"We can go back together. Once Donnie fixes up the bar—"

"No," Chase interrupted. "I don't want to go back. All I want is my old life back. I want to see you every day, to help my family out with the shop, and live a normal life. Between being in the bar all hours of the night, and almost losing you in that earthquake," he shook his head. "I don't want to put our relationship in danger ever again. If I lost you, I would never have been able to forgive myself."

"You'll never lose me. Besides, I think we've hit our quota on life-threatening situations, at least for a while. Look at all we have been through: you saved me from a burning car crash, and I saved you from an earthquake. I think our relationship can survive anything now."

He flashed his brilliant smile, and I felt an aching in my heart. How I had missed that face staring back at me, showing me what forever could look like in his sparkling eyes. Life was about making choices, and as long as we chose to be with each other, nothing else mattered. I pressed my lips against his, running my fingers through his hair as if I had never felt its softness before. His tongue parted my lips, and I welcomed it home. He removed the towel from around my body and let it fall to the floor, letting me know what he wanted. Sitting up, he leaned his back against the headboard while I straddled my legs on either side of him. I set the bag of peas on the nightstand, reminding myself that he was an injured man as I pulled open the drawer for a condom. The months without him had felt like years, and after everything we had been through, I needed to feel as close to him as possible.

I drew him into me, and our hips rocked back and forth in a slow and steady rhythm. My arms and legs were wrapped so tightly around him that there wasn't an inch of space between us. Both of his hands were entangled in my hair, his kiss becoming more intense with each passing second. Soon I heard his familiar groans.

I leaned back to plant my hands behind me on the mattress, deliberately slowing my hips down so that the moment would last as long as possible. He watched me, his eyes filled with desire.

"We should take it slow," I breathed. "You're hurt."

He smirked, and with that, he flipped me over onto my stomach. I propped myself up on my hands and knees as he pushed himself inside me again. I gripped the sheets when I heard his moan echo in the room; I shivered when I felt his hand slide down in between my thighs; and I cried out as I felt his fingers glide against me. The way he touched me made me feel such intense pleasure, every nerve ending in my body was tingling from head to toe. He met my mouth with his and took my bottom lip in between his teeth as he drove himself deeper into me with long, slow strokes. His left hand cradled my jaw as he kissed me with more passion than I had ever felt before. The way he made love to me, Chase made sure that I understood exactly how he felt: I was his, and he was mine, and we would never be apart again. All of my fears and insecurities melted away. I knew it was true.

I moaned and hummed and called his name, unable to contain what I was feeling. Without letting me catch my breath, Chase flipped me onto my back.

I giggled, looking up at him. "I guess you're feeling better."

He hiked my knees up to my chest and plunged inside me. "It feels like it has been so long," he said, half-groaning and half-whispering.

I took two handfuls of his ass and squeezed as I lifted my pelvis up to meet his. Sweat was dripping from the small of his back and I knew he was fighting his mounting urge. I spread my legs as far as I could so I could feel every inch of him inside me. He growled louder and his thrusts only lasted a few more seconds until his fingers dug into my skin. His entire body tensed, and he exhaled as he collapsed next to me on the bed.

"God, I missed you," he panted.

I curled my body around him, resting my head in the crook of his neck. "You don't ever have to miss me again."

"I don't plan on it. You're stuck with me forever."

I smiled. "Promise?"

He held up his pinky, awaiting mine. "I promise."

Chapter Nineteen

ENDINGS ARE JUST NEW BEGINNINGS

*W*alking through the gym doors, I felt anxious. I had not spoken to T.J. since the night before I left for California. I also had not fully finished my last week of training, and was hoping we could pick up where we had left off, despite his revealing confession. When I told him that I was coming in today, he replied with everyone's favorite text: "K." I didn't know what kind of mood he would be in, but I still breathed a bit easier when I saw him waiting for me in the ring.

He gave me a slight smile when we made eye contact. As I got into the ring, his eyes tightened when he saw the scabs and bruises on the tops of my hands.

I stuck my hands into my pockets, thankful that my shorts were loose enough.

T.J. held out his hands. "Show me."

Reluctantly, I removed my hands from my pockets, and held them out in front of me.

"I saw what happened on the news. When Shelly showed up at the gym, I thought... I thought the worst." He stepped back to look at the cuts on my knees. "What happened?"

"I was asleep when the earthquake started. The shaking kept

knocking me onto the floor, so I had to crawl over all the broken glass. That's why my knees are cut up."

"And your knuckles?"

I exhaled, not wanting to revisit the terrifying experience. "I couldn't open the door to get out of my apartment. Something was blocking it from the other side. I had to break the door down so that I could get to Chase. He was crushed by a big piece of wood." I laughed nervously. "I heard your voice in my head the entire time."

One of his eyebrows arched. "What was I saying?"

"You told me to get up and keep fighting. Every time I would start to panic, every time I felt helpless, you came into my mind. I survived because of you."

He shook his head. "You survived because of you."

"You taught me how."

We stood there in front of each other, unsure of what to say or do next. I wanted to hug him, but I didn't know if it would be crossing the line. Before I knew how he truly felt, I wouldn't have thought twice about it. I didn't want things to be different between us, though I was not foolish enough to believe that they wouldn't be.

"T.J.," I started.

He held up his hand. "Please don't. It will only make it worse if you say it out loud."

"I won't say anything ever again. I just need to say this. I need you to hear it."

He pulled the brim of his hat lower, almost covering his eyes. "Fine."

"You have become such an important part in my life in such a short amount of time. You were able to cut through all of my bullshit, and you helped teach me things about myself that nobody else could. I know I can't be what you want me to be, and I'm so sorry for that, because you deserve to have everything you want... but I hope that we can still be friends. I hope that I don't have to say goodbye to you. That would be a huge loss. Your friendship means the world to me."

After thinking for a moment, he folded his arms across his chest. "What are your plans once you finish training?"

"I've thought about it, and I would like to continue coming here. I know I won't be training every day with you, but I like it here. I think it's good for me to be here."

"So, you're not going to back to California?"

"No. I'm here to stay."

"Well," he sighed, pausing dramatically. "I can't have you warm up with punches if your hands are injured. I guess it's time I showed you how to do that Ninja Turtle spinny thing."

My eyes widened. "Really?"

"It's only fitting on your last week of training."

"Right now?"

"Right now."

I threw my hands around his midsection and hugged him tightly. "Thank you!"

"For what?" he chuckled.

"For everything."

"Alright, alright." He stepped back, pulling me off of him. "You ready, Curly Sue?"

I squared my feet, taking my stance in front of him. "Ready."

———

WITH MY DRINKING AND THE EARTHQUAKE NOW A COUPLE OF months behind me, and Chase by my side, everything was better than it had ever been. Some would say my life was back to normal, but normal for me was loss, death, and pain – that was the average standard that I was used to. My life now was not normal – it was fantastic. Though I was still learning and healing, I was stronger than I had ever felt before, and I had a newfound sense of confidence to go with it. Clawing my way out of the trenches of my former life was the most difficult thing I had ever done; yet I was finally able to appreciate everything I had been through. It had all lead me to where I was today.

Today, our family and friends were coming together to celebrate Chase's birthday. After surviving a natural disaster, it was truly a celebration of his life – and our lives together. When I asked him what he wanted for his birthday, his response was: "To relax with my family and friends in the pool."

I surveyed the Brooks' backyard. Shelly had helped me decorate with balloons and streamers along the fence. Tanner was standing in front of the barbecue in his swim trunks and his aviator sunglasses, with Charlotte at his side in her striped bikini. Khloe was taking her job with the veggie platter very seriously, making sure all of the vegetables were lined up perfectly.

My eyes settled on Chase, who was floating in the pool as the strong August sun reflected off the water. His arms and legs were spread wide, dangling off the float and into the water; his blonde locks shimmered in the sunlight; his bronzed skin accentuated the cuts in his muscular stomach. He lifted his head when he noticed me watching him, and grinned from ear to ear. I felt my cheeks pushing up as I smiled back.

I had almost lost him. I was reminded of that every time I looked at him – not because I was wallowing in sad, old memories; but because I wanted to always be aware of how precious our lives were. I had spent so much time holding on to anger, so much time worrying about the what-ifs. Tim had given me a second chance at life by saving me, and now I had returned the favor by saving his son. We were going to live out our second chances together, and I was determined to be the person he deserved to be with – the person I deserved to be.

"Brody is on his way with more ice," Shelly called from the far side of the yard.

I held up my thumb, and jogged to open the sliding glass door for Beverly.

"This place looks amazing," Beverly said as she set two bowls of chips on the patio table.

"It's easy when you've got a yard like this. Thanks for letting us have the party here."

She waved her hand. "Of course. I'm just thankful that everyone is here. Together."

"You and me both." I checked the time on my phone. "Is there anything else I'm forgetting?"

Shelly walked up beside me, draping her arm around my shoulders. "You've taken care of everything. Go get changed so we can jump into that pool!"

"I second that!" Chase called.

"Okay, okay! I'm going."

Tina and Kenzie were coming through the front door as I walked inside.

"Hey, guys! Everyone's in the back. I'm going to run up and get my suit on."

"Holy balls!" Tina exclaimed. "You finally got the tattoo!"

Kenzie's eyes were wide as she reached out and ran her fingers over my arm. "It's beautiful."

I smiled proudly. "Thanks."

"Didn't it hurt?"

"I've been through worse."

"You liked the pain, didn't you?" Tina asked, jabbing me in my stomach.

I smirked, taking the bowl of fruit from Kenzie. "Thanks for bringing this."

"Well, I wanted to bring jello shots, but Kenzie decided fruit would be better," Tina said flatly.

I laughed. "You always were the smarter sister, Kenz."

Tina shoved me playfully. "I can still kick your ass, you know."

"Very doubtful!" I called as I began trotting up the stairs.

I quickly tied the strings of my bikini around my neck, and shimmied into the bottoms. I grabbed a towel from the linen closet, and made my way out to the backyard again.

Chase whistled when I stepped onto the patio. "That's my girl!"

Shelly was in the pool, her arms and legs wrapped around Brody as they floated together.

"Hey, Brody. Thanks for bringing the ice." I sat at the edge of the pool and dipped my legs into the cool water.

"No problem. I told the guys to text me when they were on their way in case we needed more, but we should be good."

"Should I start throwing the burgers on now?" Tanner asked.

"Are you guys hungry?"

"Starved," Shelly shouted. "Fire it up!"

"Yes, ma'am," Tanner replied.

Chase slid off the float and swam over to me. "Aren't you coming in?" He ran his fingers up my legs, raising goosebumps all over my skin.

"I will once everyone gets here."

"You don't have to feel anxious." He sat his sunglasses atop his head. "You made this party amazing. All that's left to do is enjoy it."

I leaned down to kiss his soft lips. "I just want you to have the best birthday."

"I'm so proud of you." His eyes sparkled as they looked up at me.

"We all are," Shelly agreed as she and Brody floated past us. "I never thought I'd see you get to the point that you're at now. I should send T.J. a fruit basket to thank him for fixing you with his voodoo fighter magic."

I kicked water at her with my foot. "You're an idiot."

She giggled as she hid behind Brody to avoid the splash.

"Speaking of T.J.," Tina interjected. "Will he be gracing us with his shirtless presence today?"

"He couldn't make it," I lied. I never invited him. I wasn't sure how Chase would feel about T.J. if he knew he had developed feelings for me while Chase was on the other side of the country. I didn't want any drama, especially not on his birthday.

Khloe came running out of the house in her pink and white polka dot two-piece. Her belly stuck out like a miniature Buddha, and she was wearing pink heart-shaped sunglasses.

"Where are your swimmies?" Tanner called as she ran past him.

"I don't need swimmies anymore!" she yelled over her shoulder. She stopped next to me at the edge of the pool. "Can you catch me, Chasey?"

Chase backed up into the middle of the pool, and held his arms up. "One... two..."

"Three!" she squealed as she leapt into the water.

"How are those ribs feeling now?" Brody joked.

"They're not so sore anymore," Chase said, spinning around with Khloe in his arms.

"He's Superman," I said, standing. I walked into the house to look for Beverly. She should be outside enjoying the party with us. I poked my head into the kitchen to find her squeezing lemons into a pitcher of water. "Whatcha doing?"

"I figured I would wait inside until everyone has arrived. I want to be able to hear the doorbell."

"I can wait in here," I said. "Go in the pool."

"How does the water look?" she asked. Tim had always been the pool expert. This was the first summer without him, and Beverly had to hire someone to open the pool unbeknownst to the boys. As usual, she did not want them to know she was struggling with something without their dad.

"It's amazing." I stood beside her and gave her a hug. "*You* are amazing."

"Right back at ya, kid." She squeezed me tightly.

"Now, go out there and enjoy that pool."

She reluctantly picked up the pitcher and left the kitchen.

I cleaned up the lemon remnants, and wiped down the island. I watched everyone outside through the window by the sink. Everyone was smiling. Everyone was here. Everyone was okay.

The doorbell rang, jolting me out of my thoughts. I walked to the foyer and opened the Brooks' front door. "Hi."

Claire's smile mirrored my own. "Hi. I, uh, brought watermelon."

I took the container from her. "I told you, you didn't have to bring anything. Thanks for coming."

"Thanks for inviting me."

I gestured for her to come inside. "I wasn't sure if you would want to come." I shrugged. "It is a little awkward, I guess."

Claire nodded in agreement. "My daughter invited me to a party. I wouldn't miss that for the world." She pointed to my inked up arm. "That looks great."

I looked down at the beautiful warrior princess permanently drawn on my skin. "I know you never liked tattoos."

"This one suits you."

I smiled. "Come on. Everyone's out back. I'll introduce you."

THE END

Want More Tanner Brooks?
Read Book 3: The Other Brother

Obsessed with TJ?
Read Book 4: Fighting the Odds

MORE FROM KRISTEN

The Collision Series Box Set with Bonus Epilogue
Collision: Book 1
Avoidance: Book 2, Sequel
The Other Brother: Book 3, Standalone
Fighting the Odds: Book 4, Standalone
Hating the Boss: Book 1, Standalone
Inevitable: Contemporary standalone
What's Left of Me: Contemporary standalone
Dear Santa: Holiday novella
Someone You Love: Contemporary standalone

Want to gain access to exclusive news & giveaways?
Sign up for my monthly newsletter!

Visit my website: https://kristengranata.com/
Instagram: https://www.instagram.com/kristen_granata/
Facebook: https://www.facebook.com/kristen.granata.16
Twitter: https://twitter.com/kristen_granata

Want to be part of my KREW?
Join Kristen's Reading Emotional Warriors
A Facebook group where we can discuss my books, books you're
reading, and where friends will remind you what a badass warrior
you are.

Love bookish shirts, mugs, & accessories?
Shop my book merch shop!

ACKNOWLEDGMENTS

Thank you to all the readers out there, especially my friends and co-workers who have encouraged me along my journey. Thank you for the reviews, and thank you for spreading the word about my books. I feel so lucky to have such an amazing support system.

I would like to thank my cover designer, for both *Collision* and *Avoidance*. Miro was excellent to work with, quick, and always managed to take my visions to the next level. If you're looking for a designer check out his work: https://qtbdesign.wixsite.com/qtbdesign

I would also like to thank my headshot photographer and friend, Val. I am super awkward when standing alone in a photo, but she made me feel completely at ease. Her work is flawless. See for yourself: https://www.facebook.com/BluFoxPhoto/

I need to say a huge thank you to one of my very best friends, Dorthy. For 180 days of our school year, we have carpooled together – one hour there, and one hour back – in constant traffic. For countless hours, she listened to me talk about my books, let me bounce ideas off of her, and she even shared some of her very awesome ideas with me (Those cracks on the title of *Avoidance?* Yep, that was her idea!)

Last, but never least, I am beyond grateful for my wife, Stacy. She has spent many nights staring at the back of a laptop as I typed; she has listened to me obsess over the reviews I received; she has read and re-read each chapter I wrote; she took the kids out of the house so I could have some peace and quiet to work in; and she has always pushed me to keep going, no matter how discouraged I felt at times. I could not have gotten as far as I have in this process without her support and love.